there

was

an

old

woman

Also by Hallie Ephron

Fiction

Never Tell a Lie

Come and Find Me

Nonfiction

The Bibliophile's Devotional

1001 Books for Every Mood

Writing and Selling Your Mystery Novel

there
was
an
old
woman

HALLIE EPHRON

WILLIAM MORROW
An Imprint of HarperCollins*Publishers*

THERE WAS AN OLD WOMAN. Copyright © 2013 by Hallie Ephron. All rights reserved. Printed in the United States of America. No part of this book may be used or reproduced in any manner whatsoever without written permission except in the case of brief quotations embodied in critical articles and reviews. For information address HarperCollins Publishers, 10 East 53rd Street, New York, NY 10022.

HarperCollins books may be purchased for educational, business, or sales promotional use. For information please write: Special Markets Department, HarperCollins Publishers, 10 East 53rd Street, New York, NY 10022.

FIRST EDITION

Designed by Diahann Sturge

Library of Congress Cataloging-in-Publication Data

Ephron, Hallie.
    There was an old woman : a novel of suspense / Hallie Ephron. — 1st ed.
        p.   cm.
    ISBN 978-0-06-211760-1 (hardcover)—ISBN 978-0-06-211761-8 (pbk.)—
ISBN 978-0-06-211762-5 (ebook)   1. Psychological fiction.   2. Suspense fiction.   I. Title.
    PS3605.P49T47 2013
    813'.6—dc23

                                                                    2012027410

---

13 14 15 16 17   OV/RRD   10 9 8 7 6 5 4 3 2 1

For Jerry, whose love of old things inspires me

Acknowledgments

Stories come in fits and starts, and this one took its good sweet time to build, untangle, smooth, and interconnect. I have many people to thank for help along the way.

For technical detail and background, thanks to Kathleen Hulser, senior curator at the New York Historical Society; Clarissa Johnston, MD; Michele Dorsey, Esq.; and Shilo Hebert, RN. For inspiration, thanks to Jane Zevy, who survived her own fire in the Bronx, and Harlene Caroline, who let me visit her when she was cleaning up her mother's house. Thanks to David Fitzgerald and Naomi Rand for helping me find the perfect geographic location to set the fictional neighborhood of Higgs Point—a real salt marsh with a view of the Manhattan skyline. The amazing history of the neighborhood was worth bonus points.

Thank you so much, Roberta Isleib and Hank Phillippi Ryan, my writing pals. Thanks, Anne LeClaire, for helping me decide where to begin.

Special thanks to my agent, Gail Hochman, and my editor, Katherine Nintzel. I could not be in better hands. Thanks to Danielle Bartlett, Shawn Nicholls, Seale Ballenger, and so many others at HarperCollins for the support, hard work, and good wishes that helped launch this book.

And thank you, Jerry Touger, for having my back and making it possible for me to have this life.

there

was

an

old

woman

Chapter
One

Mina Yetner sat in her living room, inspecting the death notices in the *Daily News*. She got through two full columns before she found someone older than herself. Mina blew on her tea, took a sip, and settled into her comfortable wing chair. In the next column, nestled among dearly departed strangers, she found Angela Quintanilla, a neighbor who lived a few blocks away.

Angela had apparently died two days ago at just seventy-three. After a "courageous battle." Probably lung cancer. When Mina had last run into Angela in the church parking lot, she'd been puffing away on a cigarette, so bone thin and jittery that it was a miracle she hadn't shaken right out of her own skin.

Mina leaned forward and pulled from the drawer in her coffee table a pen and the spiral notebook that she'd bought years ago up the street at Sparkles Variety. A week after her Henry died, she'd started recording the names of the people she knew who'd taken their leave, beginning with her grandmother, who was the first dead person she'd known. Now four pages of the notebook were filled. Most of the names conjured a memory. A face. Sometimes a voice. Sometimes nothing—those especially upset her. Forgetting and being forgotten terrified Mina almost more than death.

Mina found lists calming, even this one. These days she couldn't live without them. Some mornings she'd pick up her toothbrush to brush her teeth and realize it was already wet. She kept her Lipitor in a little plastic pillbox with compartments for each day of the week, though sometimes she had to check the newspaper to be sure what day it was.

Now she started a new page in the notebook. At the top she wrote the number 151, Angela's name, and the date, then she opened the drawer to tuck the notebook back in. There, in the bottom of the drawer, were her sister Annabelle's glasses. Mina picked them up. The narrow white plastic frames had seemed so avant-garde back in the 1960s when Annabelle had decided she needed a new look. She'd worn them every day since. It was probably time—good heavens, past time—to throw them away, along with Annabelle's long nightgowns, flowered cotton with lovely lace collars that she used to order from the Nordstrom catalog. Mina preferred short gowns that didn't get all twisted around her legs when she turned in her sleep.

It was odd, the things one could and couldn't throw away. She'd kept Henry's New York Yankees cap, the one he'd worn to Game 5 of the 1956 World Series when Don Larsen pitched a perfect game in Yankee Stadium, and she wasn't even a baseball fan.

And then there were the things you had no choice but to carry with you. She touched the side of her face, feeling the scar, raised numb flesh that started at her cheekbone and ran down the side of her neck, across her shoulder blade, and down into the small of her back.

Mina tucked Annabelle's glasses back into the drawer along with her catalog of the dead. She picked up her cane and stood carefully.

What she really didn't need was to fall again. She already had one titanium hip, and she had no intention of going for a pair. She knew too many people who went into a hospital for a so-called routine procedure and came out dead.

She carried her tea outside to the narrow covered porch that stretched across the back of the house. After an icy, miserable winter and a soggy spring, it was finally warm and dry enough to sit outside. Her unreplaced hip ached, and the old porch glider screeched an appropriate accompaniment as Mina settled into the flowered cotton cushions she'd sewn herself. She took off her glasses to rub the bridge of her nose, and the world around her turned to a blur. She was legally blind without her glasses, but she'd been secretly relieved when the doctor told her she was far too myopic for that laser surgery everyone talked about.

"Oh, shush up," she said when Ivory gave a plaintive mew from inside the storm door. "You know you're not allowed out here."

She put her glasses back on, and the porch and the marsh beyond snapped into focus. Mina rocked gently, taking in the view from Higgs Point, across the East River and Long Island Sound, and on to the Manhattan skyline. As a little girl, she'd watched from this same spot behind the house where she'd lived all her life as, one after the other, Manhattan's skyscrapers had gone up. When the Chrysler Building poked its needle nose into the sky, she'd imagined that her bedroom was in the topmost floor of its glittering tiara. Then up went the Empire State, taller and without all that frippery at the top. It had been a dream come true when Mina, single "still" (as her mother so often reminded her) and just out of school, got her first job there.

Mina remembered wearing a straight skirt with a kick pleat, a peplum jacket, a crisp white collared shirt, and a broad-brimmed lady's fedora that dipped down in the front and back, thinking that was all it took to make her look exactly like Ingrid Bergman. Movies, the war, and where you could find cheap booze were all anyone talked about in those days.

Two years later, the dream turned into a nightmare. For years after, the roar of an airplane engine brought the memory back, full force, and yet there she had been living and there she remained, right in the flight path of LaGuardia Airport. It was only after the long days of even more terrifying silence after 9/11 that the waves of sound as airplanes took off, one after the other, had become reassuring. *All is well, all is well, all is well.*

Right now, what she heard was a buzz that turned into a whine, too high pitched to be an airplane. Probably Frank Cutler, her across-the-street neighbor. Installing marble countertops or a hot tub. Making a silk purse or . . . what was it they called it these days? Putting lipstick on a pig.

At least he wasn't rooting around in her trash or practicing his golf swing again. The last time she'd asked him to please, please stop using her marsh as his own personal driving range, he'd grinned at her like she'd cracked a particularly funny joke.

"Your marsh?" he'd said. Then added something under his breath. And when she politely asked him to repeat what he'd said, he told her to turn up her hearing aid. *Ha, ha, ha.* Mina's eyesight might be fading, but her hearing was as sharp as it had ever been.

The buzz grew louder. Perhaps he was using a band saw. When he got around to adding dormers to the second floor, maybe he'd find the front tooth she'd lost playing under the eaves with Linda McGilvery when they were five years old. Linda, who'd been fat and not all that bright but awfully sweet, and who'd died of leukemia, what, at least forty years ago, though it still seemed impossible to Mina that she could remember so clearly something that happened so long ago. Insidious disease. Mina had been a bridesmaid at Linda's wedding. Awful dress—

The sound morphed into a whinny, and then into *whap-whap-whap,* yanking Mina from a billow of pink organza. It was a siren, not a saw. And it was growing louder until she knew it had to be right there in her neighborhood. On her street.

As Mina hurried off the porch and up the driveway, the sound cut off. An ambulance was stopped in front of the house next door, its lights flashing a mute beacon. Sandra Ferrante lived in that house, alone for the past ten years since her daughters moved out. Two dark-suited EMTs jumped out of the ambulance and hurried across grass that hadn't been mowed in months, pushing their way past front bushes that reached the decaying gutters and nearly met across the front door.

A third EMT—a man in a dark uniform who nodded her way—opened the back doors of the ambulance, unloaded a stretcher, and wheeled it up to the house. Had the poor woman finally managed to kill herself? Because as sure as eggs is eggs, drinking like that was slow suicide.

Mina stood there, hand to her throat, waiting. Remembering the ambulance that had arrived too late for her Henry. It didn't seem possible that that had been thirty years ago. He'd died in his sleep. By the time she'd realized anything was wrong, he was stone cold. Still, she'd called frantically for help, as if the medics who arrived could re-start him like a car battery. A massive pulmonary embolism, the doctors later told her. Even if he'd suffered it at the hospital, they said, he wouldn't have survived. That was supposed to make her feel better.

Finally Sandra Ferrante was wheeled out. A yellow blanket was mounded over her. Mina found herself drifting closer, trying to overhear. Was she alive? Coherent?

Sandra lifted her head and looked right at Mina. She raised her hand and signaled to her. Asked the EMT to wait while Mina made her way over.

Up close now, Mina could see that the whites of her neighbor's watery eyes were tinged yellow, and she could smell the sour tang of sweat and urine mixed with cigarette smoke.

"Please, call Ginger," Sandra said.

Ginger? Then Mina remembered. Ginger was one of the daughters.

Sandra grasped Mina's hand. Mina gasped. Arthritis made her fingers tender.

"Six four six, one . . ."

Too late, Mina realized Sandra was whispering a phone number. Mina tried to repeat the numbers back, but they wouldn't stick. The EMT pulled out a notebook, wrote the numbers down, tore out the page, and handed it to Mina. She'd also written *Bx Met Hosp* and underlined it. Bronx Metropolitan Hospital.

"Please, tell Ginger," Sandra said, pulling Mina close. "Don't let him in until I'm gone."

Chapter
Two

The freight elevator of the Empire State Building descended slowly, bouncing a little as it landed. A maintenance worker pulled open the scissor gate and Evie Ferrante, her colleague Nick Barlow, and the team of four movers they'd brought with them emerged from the car—like clowns, Evie thought, spewing out of one of those tiny circus cars— along with a rolling platform loaded with tools and packing equipment. An officer from building security had escorted them down, presumably to make sure they took only the old jet engine that the Five-Boroughs Historical Society had been authorized to remove.

In this cavernous sub-subbasement, the ceilings were low and the lighting meager. Here none of the art deco architectural detailing of the building was present, just the structural bones. Evie had to watch out to keep from tripping over coal cart rails embedded in the floor or banging her head on the yellow pipes that snaked along overhead. A roach the size of a silver dollar skittered past her feet and into the shadows.

They followed the security officer into the core of the building, past massive support columns of bare concrete with veins where moisture had hardened into lime deposits. If she closed her eyes, the cool dampness and the smell could have convinced her that she was walking through ancient catacombs.

Evie's heart quickened. There, sitting on the floor among some cardboard boxes, was a battered Wright Whirlwind engine, or what was left of the one from the B-25 bomber that had lost its way on a foggy Saturday morning in 1945 and slammed into the north side of the building. The wings and propeller had sheared off on impact. The plane itself had turned into a fireball, feeding on its own fuel and taking out offices on four floors.

Evie crouched beside the engine, savoring the moment. She was about to bring to light an artifact that no one had thought to look for. She hadn't made history—that wasn't her job—but she was about to preserve an important piece of it.

"Holy shit," said Evie's onetime mentor, Nick. "That's it, isn't it?" The expression on his face was of unabashed delight. "You did it. Congratulations."

"Thanks." Nick had been so incredibly generous to her. He'd been stoic if not supportive when she'd gotten promoted over him to senior curator, her academic degree trumping his many years of experience. "That means a lot to me, coming from you."

The engine was round, about five hundred pounds of metal, five feet in diameter and caked with dust. With its center crank and rusting cylinders that radiated out, the thing resembled a miniature space station that had been through an intergalactic war. Upon impact with the building, the engine had been pulled right out of its cowling, and it had shot partway across the seventy-ninth floor before plunging to the bottom of an elevator shaft. It was miraculously still intact, not twenty feet away from where workers had hauled it from the elevator pit days after the accident.

It surprised Evie that so few people knew about the spectacular crash. Maybe it was because a few days later the United States had dropped an atomic bomb on Hiroshima.

"This is so cool," Nick said. He crouched beside her. "They're just going to let us take it?"

Evie waved the release and letter of agreement she'd worked so hard to get. Finding the engine had been a reward for persistence. She'd been looking for artifacts to feature in the upcoming *Seared in Memory* exhibit, the first she'd curated solo, and it had occurred to her to wonder what had happened to the plane engines after the fire. From Alice Chen, a friend from college and now director of community relations for the Empire State Building, Evie had learned that not only did one of the engines still exist, it hadn't been moved. Getting the building owners to agree to let the Historical Society feature the engine in the exhibit had taken months of diplomacy. It helped that one of the Historical Society board members was the wife of a senior partner in the property management company that ran the building.

While the movers got started assembling the polyurethane-sheathed cage that Evie had designed to protect the engine during transport, Nick set up lights and Evie started to take pictures. Of the engine. Of Nick standing over the engine, his arms spread to give a sense of scale. Of the closed door just beyond with white stenciled letters that read AUTHORIZED PERSONNEL ONLY. Of that door open, shooting down into the pit where the engine had landed. It must have sounded like a bomb exploding, a quarter of a ton of burning metal plummeting from more than a thousand feet overhead.

It took the rest of the morning to get the engine wrapped and hoisted onto a platform. By the time they were ready to leave, Evie's arms and legs were coated with dirt and rust—and those were just the parts of her that she could see. She was glad she'd worn jeans and steel-toed work boots.

As they were bringing the engine up in the service elevator at the Historical Society, her cell phone vibrated. Maybe it was Seth. He'd promised her dinner at her favorite soup dumpling restaurant in Chinatown for a change. Handsome in a Colin Farrell kind of way, without the mustache, he and Evie had met at an auction. He'd outbid her for a gold-and-pearl tie tack that had belonged to Stephanus Van Cortlandt, New York's first American-born mayor. It was a refreshing change to date someone who'd actually heard of Stephanus Van Cortlandt or knew that the pattern tooled on those gold cuff links was acanthus leaf. It wasn't the worst reason she'd had to go to bed with a man.

The doors opened on the second floor, where the main exhibit hall was located. A minute later there was a chime. A text message. Evie fished out the phone.

The message was short and sweet. It was not from Seth; it was from her sister, Ginger, and it was so not what she wanted to see.

Chapter
Three

It's mom. Call me. xx Ginger

Why now? Not again. Evie knew she should return the call right away, and as she and Nick entered the Great Hall of Five-Boroughs His-torical Society, pushing ahead of them a platform truck with the B-25 Wright Whirlwind engine wrapped up on it like a gigantic pastrami sandwich, that's what she was intending to do. But her boss's reaction to their arrival sidetracked her.

"Wow. Is that what I think it is?" Connor Kennedy's familiar voice boomed behind her. A moment later, he was in her space and she could smell his cologne and cigarette breath. He stood absolutely still and silent, staring at the engine. Moving the thing had eaten up a good chunk of Evie's budget, but judging from Connor's reaction, it had been worth it.

"So this is going to be sensational," he said, doing a 360 and sur-veying the disarray in the exhibit hall with apprehension. "We are going to make it, aren't we?"

"Of course we'll make it. We always do," Evie said, sounding more confident than she felt.

The parquet floor of the Great Hall was awash in packing crates. The other two members of Evie's small staff were assembling bases and plexi mounts for the installation. The museum's resident electrician was drilling into the wall and wiring one of six massive flat-screen monitors. One of the janitors was sweeping up wood and plaster dust with a wide push broom.

Outside, beyond a row of narrow two-story arched windows, bright yellow banners for the upcoming exhibit snapped in the breeze. Dramatic red-orange letters on them read: SEARED IN MEMORY. Below that and smaller: *June 10–November 17.* Just three weeks until it opened.

Evie could envision the room, silent and cleared of debris. Each of four historic fires would have its own timeline and photographs, audio and video. Artifacts she'd culled from their own collection and borrowed from others would be mounted, lit, and documented. Together, each grouping would tell its own story.

She walked Connor through the half-finished installations. Greeting visitors and already in place was a magnificent red-and-black steam-powered pumper like the one used to fight the Great Fire of 1776 that destroyed the Stock Exchange and much of lower Manhattan. The next section, commemorating the fire during the ugly 1853 Civil War Draft Riots, would feature blowups of inflammatory broadsides ("We are sold for $300 whilst they pay $1000 for negroes") that stoked passions so much that anyone with dark skin risked being chased through the streets, beaten, and even killed. One of her favorite pieces in that section was a long speaking trumpet, the kind that would have been used to shout orders to firefighters over those five hellish summer days when the city burned.

Another section remembered the 1911 Triangle Shirtwaist Factory fire, arguably the saddest of all time. In the center was a raised platform where they'd set a battered fireman's net that couldn't save the young, mostly immigrant women who'd thrown themselves from the windows of the upper floors of the Asch Building. Foam-core mounted photographs, showing views of the devastated factory interior filled with charred sewing machines and coffins lined up tidily on the floor like fallen soldiers, were already on the wall. Something about the photographs from that one always did her in, filling her head with the gut-wrenching smell of smoke, a smell seared in her own memory.

The list of the 146 who died in that fire was particularly heart-breaking. Mary Goldstein had been only eleven; Kate Leone, fourteen; most of the rest were in their teens and early twenties. A few of the bodies remained unidentified a hundred years later.

Journalists back in those days were allowed, encouraged even, to write unabashedly emotional prose, and Evie had selected a quote from a reporter's viscerally melodramatic eyewitness account:

> I learned a new sound—a more horrible sound than description can picture. It was the thud of a speeding, living body on a stone sidewalk. . . . Thud-dead, thud-dead—together they went into eternity.

Thud-dead, thud-dead, together they went into eternity. The elegiac passage, more poetry than prose, moved Evie profoundly. She couldn't imagine today's *Daily News* or *New York Times* printing anything like that.

As she finished showing Connor around, taking notes on his suggestions for ways to tweak the displays and adding to her to-do list, she was reminded what being senior curator meant. Much as she might delegate, she was the one responsible for seeing that every little detail, down to the spelling on the signage and the training of security guards, was done properly and completed in time for the opening gala.

When Connor stopped to chat with Nick, who was carefully cutting away the protective covering they'd built around the airplane engine, her phone chimed again. Evie reached into her pocket and turned it off.

Evie meant to call Ginger back. Really, she did. But she got pulled into one meeting and then another. Two hours later, eating a midafternoon granola bar instead of lunch, she was back in her office, the door closed, trying to finish editing transcripts of eyewitness accounts of the fires before the voice-over actors arrived to record them. When her cell phone rang, she recognized the number with its Connecticut area code and for only an instant considered not answering it.

"Didn't you get my message?" Ginger started right in.

"I'm sorry. I was tied up. I was going to call back but . . ." Evie bit her lip and took a breath. She didn't want to make it sound as if her time was more important than Ginger's. "Listen, I am sorry. I should have called you right back. How's Ben? The kids?"

"You know that's not what I called about. It's Mom."

"Again," Evie said, at the same time as Ginger.

Even though there was nothing even remotely funny about that, and even though she knew that laughing was wildly inappropriate, Evie couldn't stop herself. A moment later, Ginger was laughing, too, and that made Evie laugh even harder until she nearly dropped the phone and had to sit down to keep from peeing in her pants.

At last, laughed out and gasping for breath, she wiped tears from her eyes. "So how bad is it?"

"She fell and dislocated her shoulder this time. And I guess it was a while before she managed to call for help. Mrs. Yetner left me a message. She's at Bronx Metropolitan. The shoulder's not all that serious. It's everything else that's the problem."

Evie thought she had a pretty good idea what that meant. "You saw her?"

"Just for a few minutes. She was barely conscious. Stabilized is what the doctor called it."

"Stabilized," Evie said. Did that mean she was going to get better? Or was she going to stay as sick as she was?

"On top of everything else, the EMTs who pulled her out alerted the health department. They sent an investigator over to the house. They say the place is a health risk. If it gets condemned—"

"Condemned? You've got to be kidding."

"I guess it's gotten that bad. If Mom can't go back, she won't have anywhere to go and, well . . ."

Evie finished the thought: *then she'll have to move in with one of us.* Ginger couldn't be thinking that Mom could move into Evie's one-bedroom apartment. Ginger was the one with a house. A guest room.

"Evie, I can't always be the one," Ginger said.

"Why does it have to be either of us? She's a grown-up."

"She's never been a grown-up, and you know it. And now she's in the hospital. All alone."

Right. Alone because one after the other she'd pissed off the friends she and their father had once had. Alone because she hadn't been able to hold a job for years. Thinking about her mother made Evie furious and unbearably sad at the same time. Talking to her was even worse. And seeing her?

"No way." Evie looked down at the pile of audio scripts, sitting on her desk, deadline looming. At her to-do list that only seemed to grow longer, no matter how much got checked off. "Come on, Ginger, I can't take time off right now. This exhibit is my first. It has to be great. It's opening in three weeks, and there is still so much to do. I promise as soon as I'm done, the very minute it opens, I will pitch in."

"Pitch in?" There was a long silence. Then Ginger sniffed, and Evie realized she was crying.

"Ginger?"

"I don't want you to *pitch in*," Ginger said, her voice a harsh rasp. "I want you to take charge."

"I will. I will."

"And not in three weeks. Now."

"But—"

"Surely you're not the only person who works over there. No one is irreplaceable."

"I . . . I just can't. I'm sorry."

"Sorry? *Sorry?* Sorry doesn't cut it. I have a life, too. In case you've forgotten"—Ginger's voice spiraled up—"I'm taking classes. The paralegal certification exam is in four weeks. Ben is working two jobs. Lisa's got dance classes and soccer practice. And . . . and . . ." Ginger blew her nose. "And why is it that every time, every fucking time she crashes, I'm the one who has to drop everything?"

There was a knock at Evie's door, and Nick stuck his head in. He pointed to his watch. The voice-over actors must have arrived, which meant the meter was ticking—they charged for their time whether the script was ready or not.

Evie put up her hand, fingers splayed. *Five minutes.* Nick nodded and disappeared.

Ginger was saying, "—can't do it, Evie. Not this time. I'm tapped out. Completely tapped out. It's your turn. I'm sorry, but this time you don't have the luxury of cutting her off unless you're planning to cut me off, too."

In the silence that followed, Evie could hear the massive schoolhouse clock behind her desk *tick-tick-ticking.* The last time she'd seen her mother, they'd arranged to meet for brunch at Sarabeth's in Manhattan, halfway between Evie's Brooklyn apartment and her mother's house at the edge of the Bronx. They were supposed to meet at noon. When Mom hadn't shown up, and hadn't shown up, Evie had tried calling her. No answer at home. No answer on her mother's cell.

As minutes ticked by, Evie had gone from being furious with her mother, late as usual, to being hysterical and in tears, imagining the worst as she tried to flag a taxi to take her to Higgs Point. Good luck with that. Three cabs refused before she snagged one that would.

When she got to the house, her mother was passed out in front of the TV. "I must have lost track of time," she said when Evie finally managed to rouse her. Later, as Evie made an omelet, she caught her mother sneaking some vodka into her orange juice. She'd tried to talk to her mother about her drinking, but her mother flat-out denied it, like she always had. Evie was the delusional one, she'd insisted, then screamed at Evie for butting in and trying to run her life.

On the bus and subway ride home, Evie had seethed with anger. That was it, she promised herself. Never again. If her mother couldn't stop drinking long enough to get herself to Manhattan for a lunch date with her daughter, wouldn't even admit that she drank, then to hell with her. Evie was finished. Finished taking care of her. Finished talking to her even.

After that, Evie stopped returning her mother's calls. Screened out her e-mails. Maybe if she cut her off completely, she told herself, her mother would get serious about drying out. But the truth was, it was a huge relief to sever the cord, to allow herself to give up responsibility for caring.

That had been months ago. And now Ginger was finally fed up, too, but she couldn't walk away. She wasn't wired that way.

"Okay, okay." Evie couldn't believe she heard herself saying it. "I'll take care of it. I'll go up to the house tomorrow and start getting things cleaned up. I'll go over to the hospital in the afternoon. Stay—"

"And stay? Oh, would you?"

"Just for the weekend."

"But—"

"Then we'll see." Evie swallowed. "And you're right. It is my turn."

Chapter
Four

Before she left work, Evie told everyone that she might have to take some time off. Ginger was right, of course. The exhibit would launch just fine without her. Nick could manage the final details as well if not better than she. Besides, even though it looked like an unfinished mess, the exhibit installation was nearly complete.

She left Seth a message, too. Told him she had a "family emergency." Her mother. That she had to spend a few days sorting things out.

Early the next morning, she took the subway and then the bus from her tiny apartment near Sunset Park deep in Brooklyn to Higgs Point at the southern tip of the Bronx. She tried not to think about what she'd find when she got there.

She took her time walking to the house. The bright blue sky was streaked with mare's-tail clouds. Leaves on the trees and bushes were still that electric green of early spring. Of course it would be the same in every neighborhood throughout the city, even Manhattan, but she rarely slowed down enough to notice.

In return for Evie's agreeing to deal with the house and watch over their mother in the hospital, Ginger said she'd sort out the health insurance. Fortunately their mother was still covered as a firefighter's widow. Fortunately, too, their father had had the prescience—though it was no secret that firefighters died young—to purchase mortgage life insurance. When he died, their mother owned the house outright.

Evie shifted her backpack to her other shoulder. She'd brought a few changes of clothes and her toothbrush. The closer she got to her mother's house, the slower she walked. It was its own world, this spit of land in a corner of the South Bronx with the East River on one side and the Long Island Sound on the other. Lanes that ran higgledy-piggledy were lined with long, narrow, shotgun houses built close together. Off any official planning grid, these lots for summer cottages had been divided early in the twentieth century, long before the Whitestone Bridge made it easy to get there. The most fortunate houses, like her mother's, were lined up along Neck Road at the edge of one of the city's only surviving marshes. Evie had no idea why Soundview Lagoons had been spared the indignity of landfill.

She passed the house where her friend Alicia had lived. She'd smoked her first cigarette behind its garage and almost started a fire in the dry grass. Made out with Joey Mendez on the glider on the back porch. Now the house was badly in need of a coat of paint; instead of curtains in the window of what had been her friend's slope-ceilinged bedroom, there were torn shades. The house next to Alicia's looked oddly palomino, white paint peeling off to reveal great patches of dark brown.

A little farther on, three blocks from her mother's house, stood Sparkles Variety. Evie smiled to see it still there. The granite-block building was decades older than anything else nearby. Its sign had a few residual metallic spangles that caught the light. The store was open and apparently busy—half the angled parking spaces in front were filled. Around the side, where customers must have pulled up their cars to fill up even before Evie's family had moved there, stood an old gas pump. Once painted bright red and yellow, it was now mostly rust. With its big round disk on top, it had always reminded Evie of an overgrown chess pawn, AWOL from its regiment.

The grouch who pretty much lived behind the cash register at Sparkles used to scold Evie and Ginger if they so much as breathed on a piece of candy they weren't prepared to buy. He kept *Seventeen* and *YM* magazines in plastic pouches so they couldn't be browsed, and *Penthouse* behind the counter wrapped in brown paper with only the title showing. Inside the pay phone he'd posted a time limit, and a sign on the front door warned customers against bringing any food or beverage into the store. He wouldn't have stood for anything taped to the front window, never mind the welter of flyers plastered across it now. Evie stopped to scan them, resting her backpack at her feet.

Some of the notices were in English, others in Spanish. Yard sales. English lessons. A used book sale at the library. A "Preserve the Marsh" meeting at a nearby community center. A potluck supper at St. Andrews.

She peered into the store. She knew she was postponing the inevitable, but what the heck. Her mother's house wasn't going anywhere.

A bell—the same one from her youth?—tinkled overhead when Evie pushed through the doorway. The interior smelled the same, too. Sawdust and dried sweat. And there was still an actual pay phone just inside the front door. She scooped her finger into the change return slot and came back with a dime.

The enormous ice cream freezer where she and Ginger had discovered root-beer-flavored Popsicles was still there near the front. As Evie peered through the sliding glass top, she realized that she was starving. She'd left her apartment having had only coffee. Sitting right on top was a Ben & Jerry's Peace Pop. Cherry Garcia. Her favorite. She carried the ice cream to the cash register. The rod over the counter was festooned with rolls of bright shiny lottery tickets. Her mother had long been a steady scratch ticket customer.

The clerk, a tall young man with sharp eyes and a beaky nose, pressed some keys on the familiar-looking massive silver-painted cash register and the cash drawer flew open with a *ka-ching* that took her right back. On a shelf behind the counter was a display of flashlights and batteries. Every house out here had a good supply—all it used to take was a stiff breeze for the power to go out, and then hours for it to get fixed. She remembered her mother had a bowl full of spent batteries, back in the day when it was illegal to throw them in the trash.

"You think rechargeable batteries save energy?" she asked the clerk.

He blinked at her, as if seeing her for the first time. "Only if you remember to unplug the charger when they're cooked."

She'd read that somewhere. "Stupid design. You'd think gadgets would come with a truly-off switch. Instead they sit around doing nothing but suck energy."

"Wouldn't you think rechargeables would be recyclable?" he said. "They're not. So we carry regular batteries, the ones without mercury, made in the good old U.S. of A. All they do is leak potassium hydroxide into landfills." The logo silkscreened on his sweatshirt over his heart, Evie noticed, showed a crab and a fish above wavy water lines. A slogan underneath read: ASK ME ABOUT SOUNDVIEW WATERSHED PRESERVATION.

"Soundview Watershed Preservation?" she said.

"Huh?"

"Your shirt. It says to ask."

When he smiled, he was almost handsome. There was a cleft in his chin and at least two days' worth of stubble on his face. From under the counter he pulled a brochure and offered it to her.

"Come to a meeting," he said. "At the community center. Monday night."

Evie reached for the brochure. On the front was a color photograph of the marsh. She turned it over. One of the photographs on the back was of a small group of people standing at the water's edge. They all had binoculars around their necks. There, beside a tripod-mounted spotting scope, was the store clerk, the tallest person in the group.

"Sure," Evie said. But she hoped she wouldn't be here long enough to get involved in some local crusade.

The man leaned back and folded his arms. She felt her face flush as he took in her zippered fleece vest, Dolce & Gabbana jeans she'd picked up at Century 21, and Frye boots that she'd had for the last ten years, ever since her last semester at NYU.

"I know you," he said. "Don't I?"

Evie knew that was the oldest line in the book. Still, she squirmed under his gaze. *Was* there was something familiar about him?

"I got it," he said. "You're one of the Ferrante girls. I remember you from P.S. Sixty-eight. You"—he narrowed his eyes—"don't you have a sister, too?"

"Ginger," she said. Of course he'd remember Ginger. She was the pretty one.

"Right. You two used to come in here for ice cream and—"

"Candy." Evie laughed. She and Ginger had regularly surrendered their allowances and paper-delivery money in exchange for, in Evie's case, Pop Rocks, SweeTarts, and cherry-flavored Lik-m-aid. Ginger went for the M&Ms and peanut butter cups.

"Finn Ryan," he said, offering her his hand.

She shook it. His fingertips felt calloused. Evie recalled that the curmudgeon who'd presided over the candy and magazines had been named Mr. Ryan. "Didn't your dad own this store?"

"He did. Died a few years back and I inherited all this." He gave a grand gesture and a sardonic smile. "It was perfect timing. I had nothing better to do so I came home."

Now she remembered the tall, gawky, older kid she'd sometimes notice sweeping the floor or stocking shelves. More often he'd be sprawled on an old couch in the back of the store, all knees and elbows and sneakers already the size of bread loaves, reading comic books or playing Nintendo to the telltale *boop-beep-boop* of *Super Mario*. She wanted to ask where he'd returned home from. What had he been doing with himself since P.S. 68? Why hadn't he sold the store?

"You still into video games?" she asked instead.

"You still living in Brooklyn?"

Ouch. His look said he'd pegged her as one more privileged, over-educated hipster refugee from Park Slope. If only she could afford an apartment in Park Slope.

"Don't worry. I'm not moving in. I'm just here . . ." Her phone vibrated. She slipped it out of her pocket far enough to see who was calling. Seth. She'd call him back later. "I'm just here for a few days to help my mother out."

"How's your mother doing?" Finn asked. She could tell from the uneasiness of his look that he knew about her mother's problems. Though if he lived here, how could he not?

"She's in the hospital."

"I'm sorry." He paused. "You're staying in the house?"

"I think so. Though I haven't been over to see how bad it is."

He nodded. Good poker face.

Evie took the paper off the ice cream bar, wrapped it around the stick, and took a bite. Her favorite flavor, but she could barely taste it. Then she realized she hadn't paid.

Her cell phone played a broken chord. Seth had left her a message. She dug around in her backpack and came up with her wallet.

"My treat," Finn said. "Consider it a little gift to welcome you home."

This wasn't home, but Evie didn't say so. She thanked him and headed out the door. Just before it banged shut behind her, she shot a look over her shoulder.

He was leaning back, his arms folded, watching her and smiling. One of his front teeth was chipped. She absolutely did remember him.

She was glad she'd worn those jeans.

It was a few blocks from Sparkles Variety to her mother's house. Evie was licking the last vanilla ice cream off the stick when the rich, sulfurous odor of low tide enveloped her. Many of the houses near the water had been spiffed up. One had been painted a surprisingly pleasant shade of pink and had barrels of purple and white pansies in front. Another had a brand-new front porch and incongruous double doors with fancy etched glass.

Her mother's street, Neck Road, ran parallel to the water. Evie turned onto it, pausing to take in the first slice of water view between close-set houses. A little farther on, she gasped when she saw the house that she no longer thought of as her home.

Chapter
Five

Her mother's bungalow had looked run-down, sure, last time Evie was there, four months ago. But nothing like what she saw now. The cream-colored siding was tagged with bright blue graffiti, MKT75 in six-foot letters. Weeds in the front yard and driveway were knee-high. The only actual grass was sprouting from the roof gutter. The little garage, where Evie assumed her mother's twelve-year-old silver Subaru was parked, listed away from the house.

The first wooden front step creaked as she stepped on it. The third felt dangerously punky with rot. The screens in the metal storm door were torn. Evie pulled the storm door open, found the right key on her key ring, unlocked the front door, and pushed inside.

A musty, sharp odor oozed out. Mold. Cigarettes. Sour milk? Eyes tearing, Evie dropped her backpack off the side of the steps and into the weeds. She took a gulp of air and held her breath, then covered her nose and mouth with the bottom of her fleece vest and ventured into the house.

The narrow entry hall was dark. She found the light switch and flipped it. Nothing. No wonder, she realized as she shaded her eyes from the outside light. No bulb.

Straight ahead she could make out the stairs up to the second-floor bedroom she and Ginger had shared. A narrow hallway led to a bathroom tucked under the stairs and beyond that, her parents' bedroom.

Evie turned instead and entered the kitchen. She threaded her way around piles of newspapers and loaded paper bags and plastic garbage bags. The sink was overflowing with dishes, and the faucet was dripping. Evie reached over and turned it off. Pushed open the red-and-white gingham curtains that were gray and crusty with dust, and opened the windows. On the sill, a row of African violets were brown and withered.

She looked around in dismay. The little kitchen table where she and Ginger used to do their homework was adrift in papers and mail. The counters were stacked with boxes and cans. Cat food? Her mother didn't even like cats, and yet there were dozens of empty cans of it.

A trio of small black moths fluttered in front of her. She clapped her hands and got one of them. At least a dozen more were resting on the ceiling, and when Evie opened the cabinet where her mother had always kept cereal and crackers, more flew out.

She poked a toe at one of the garbage bags on the floor. Glass clinked, and roaches skittered between the piles across the redbrick vinyl flooring.

Evie made her way through the rest of the house, trying not to feel overwhelmed. The living room was full of broken lawn furniture, orphaned lampshades, and ashtrays overflowing with cigarette butts. The brown vinyl-covered sectional sofa was buried under loads of rumpled clothing and bedding and newspapers. More books and magazines and newspapers were piled on the coffee table.

In the midst of the disarray was a large packing box with the SONY logo. That's when Evie noticed a fancy new flat-screen TV hung on the wall where there'd always been a string sculpture of an owl mounted on mustard-colored burlap.

The only part of the living room that felt familiar was the fireplace and the mantel over it. Sitting there were framed photographs: Ginger and Ben at their wedding, Evie's high school graduation picture, her dad. Evie picked that one up and wiped away a layer of dust. It was one of the few photographs that had survived the fire that nearly destroyed this house when she was six years old.

For an instant, Evie smelled smoke, even though she knew nothing was burning, and for a moment she saw herself standing across the street with Mom and Ginger, watching flames shoot from the roof of their house, knowing that Blackie and her litter of puppies were trapped in her parents' bedroom closet.

She shook off the memory. Until yesterday, her mother had been living in this . . . squalor was the only word for it. She swallowed a lump in her throat. What on earth had happened? Her mother had never been a hoarder. Even at her worst, she'd cared about appearances. She'd always kept a neat house, and never went out without lipstick. Her grammar and table manners were impeccable. Something must have come unscrewed.

Returning to the kitchen, Evie opened the refrigerator, expecting the worst. But there turned out to be very little inside. On the top shelf sat a baking dish. She lifted the foil. Whatever was in it had shriveled and desiccated. She peered into a pink bakery box and poked at the remains of a mummified cake, its pink-and-white frosting hard to the touch. A half gallon of milk was dated four weeks ago. The veggie bin contained a plastic bag with a slimy head of lettuce in it and a bag of something that looked like prunes and smelled of rotten egg.

All of it had to go out. Now. Evie undid the twist on a half-full garbage bag already on the floor. A sharp medicinal smell rose from the open bag and she peered inside. Empty liquor bottles. She pulled one out. Vodka. Grey Goose. Her mother had moved up to an expensive brand.

Evie pushed a pile of papers off the kitchen chair and sat. As far as she knew, her mother's only sources of income were what she got as the widow of a firefighter—a pension and Social Security. So how could she afford expensive vodka and a brand-new high-def TV?

But before Evie could follow that thought, she heard a scrabbling overhead. Instinctively she ducked. Then she looked up at the stained, cracked ceiling. Above her was the slope-ceilinged bedroom she and Ginger had shared. As she stared she heard more sounds, like something hard rolling across a wood floor. More scrabbling.

Vermin—Evie shuddered—had to have gotten in upstairs. What she wanted to do was run out of the house screaming. Instead, she waded through the kitchen, pushed aside the bags stacked in front of the broom closet, and opened the door. Its orderly interior seemed to belong to a different house. Standing on the floor beside a bucket filled with cleaning supplies were a broom and a carpet sweeper. On the shelf over them, clean rags were folded beside a pocketed canvas bag filled with garden tools. In that bag Evie found a pair of leather work gloves.

Armed with the broom and the gloves, Evie returned to the front hall. She looked up into the dark stairwell. If only she could pawn this problem off on someone else.

Slowly, she climbed the stairs. In the near pitch-black of the upstairs landing, she stopped and pressed her ear to the closed bedroom door. She could hear movement on the other side. Rustling. A squeak. A rolling marble sound, again followed by the scrabbling. Then a thump.

Evie stomped hard on the floor. Silence followed. She imagined raccoons or squirrels or, God forbid, skunks on the other side of the door, frozen and waiting for her next move.

She groped for the doorknob, twisted it, and with a bravado she wasn't sure she had, threw open the door. It slammed against the inside wall. She caught a flurry of movement in the sunny, slope-ceilinged room. A whirl of gray disappeared through the back window facing the water. Then another.

Evie stood in the middle of the room, her heart pounding, and took in the damage. All in all, it was not nearly as bad as she'd feared. The seat of the skirted chair at the dressing table was torn open, some of its stuffing mounded like massive dustballs on the floor. There were acorns and sticks on the floor. But the beds she and Ginger slept in, tucked under the eaves, were unmussed, still covered with the familiar pink-and-white chenille bedspreads.

It took her a moment to realize that the window wasn't open. It was broken. The bottom pane was completely gone. But there seemed to be no glass on the floor of the room. She looked out through the broken window. Shards of glass glittered just outside on the porch's sloping roof. Didn't that mean that the window had been broken from the inside?

Chapter
Six

Before Evie left the upstairs bedroom, she took down from the wall the framed Georgia O'Keeffe poster—a white camellia blooming out of a field of pale blue and turquoise—that she and Ginger had picked up at an after-Christmas sale at the Met. She found some duct tape in the kitchen and used it to secure the picture over the broken window. At least that would keep squirrels and wet weather out until she could get the window properly replaced.

Downstairs, she put away the broom and gloves. Her parents' bedroom and bath were the only rooms left to assess.

She felt her way through the dark downstairs hallway to the tiny room tucked under the stairs, opened the door, and peered in. The familiar room, barely big enough for her parents' double bed and two bureaus, smelled like a rank subway tunnel. Wrinkled clothing covered the bed. Evie recognized the pink terry-cloth robe she and Ginger had given their mother for a Mother's Day years ago. More ashtrays on the bureaus overflowed with cigarette butts. Evie raised the window shades and tried to open the windows, but they wouldn't budge.

Her mother's bottle of Jean Naté sat on the bureau, as always. Evie unscrewed the top and poured a little into her hands. The scent reminded her of fresh laundry and lemon meringue pie. It was what her mother smelled like after a shower. And sometimes, her father had smelled of it, too.

Evie closed the bottle and put it back.

When she shifted the clothing on the bed, she realized that the bedding beneath was damp and smelled sour. She stripped the sheets. The mattress was wet, too.

Working quickly and trying not to gag, she balled the sheets up with the dirty clothes, hauled the bundle out through the front door, and dumped it by the side of the house. As she stood there, hands on her hips, taking great gulps of fresh air and girding herself for hauling out the mattress, a red sports car rolled up and pulled into the driveway across the street. That house was spruced up and freshly painted in shades of tan, maroon, and a deep green, the bushes in front sculpted into perfect spheres—all that tidiness a tacit rebuke to her mother's house. A man Evie didn't recognize got out and looked across the street. He gave her a puzzled look and raised his hand.

Evie turned away and went inside. She didn't know him and had no desire to explain the mess her mother had made. By the time she'd wrestled the mattress off her mother's bed, set it on end, and shoved it out the front door, the man had disappeared. She pushed, pulled, and dragged the mattress up the side of the house where she propped it under the bathroom window, leaning the nasty side, soiled and pitted with cigarette burns, against the house.

That's when she heard a steady *drip, drip, drip* coming from beneath the house. Under the bathroom. She stooped and looked through a hole in the wood lattice paneling that covered the gap between the house and ground. She couldn't see anything, but she could certainly smell it. Raw sewage.

Frustration welled up inside her. What next? Evie reached out and yanked on a nearby oak sapling that had already grown a foot tall. But it was too deeply rooted to budge, and all Evie had to show for her effort were fingers scraped raw. The rot in the house was deep rooted, too, nurtured by decades of unhappiness, fertilized with denial.

Evie heard a tentative throat clearing. She pivoted away from the house and the sapling, a little embarrassed to have been caught taking her frustrations out on a weed. Standing on neatly mowed grass beyond her mother's scraggly yard was a diminutive elderly woman, leaning on a cane. She had on a pink cardigan and a collared blouse with a double strand of fat white pearls around her neck.

Evie brushed away tears she hadn't even realized she'd shed. "Mrs. Yetner?" Amazing. The old woman was not only still alive but remarkably little changed aside from the cane and the back that was stooped rather than ramrod straight. Evie and Ginger had considered Mrs. Yetner ancient even when they were growing up.

"Ginger?" the woman said. She pulled a tissue from the wrist of her sweater sleeve and dabbed at her nose as she pinned Evie under her sharp, speculative gaze, magnified through thick glasses. "No, of course not. You're the other one, aren't you?"

Chapter
Seven

"Right, I'm the other one." The girl stood and collected herself.

She seemed to Mina to be so . . . vexed wasn't quite the right word. More like at wit's end. Well, who wouldn't be, given the ungodly mess her mother's house had turned into? And so fast.

When Mina first spotted the girl—or woman, as they liked to be called these days, though the reasoning escaped her—maneuvering a mattress up against the side of Sandra Ferrante's house, she assumed it had to be Ginger. But the minute the girl looked up, Mina realized this was the younger sister. The taller, ganglier one. Not the one who sold Girl Scout cookies but the one who kicked around a soccer ball and skinned her knees.

"I'm Evie," the girl told her.

Eve. Now there was a name that didn't go out of fashion. Not like Harriet. Or Freda. Mina had always been the only Mina anyone had heard of, except for every once in a while when vampires came back into fashion and people remembered the Mina who, despite Count

Dracula's attentions, had been saved and gotten married, as if that were preferable to an eternity of pure passion, forever and ever with no "death do us part." Mina wondered where she'd put her copy of that book. She wouldn't mind reading it again.

"I had an older sister, too," Mina said, and wondered why on God's green earth she'd offered that up.

"I didn't know that."

Well, of course she didn't. Annabelle had moved in with Mina a few years after the girls next door went off to college. Then—for what? Six years? No, eight—Mina and Annabelle been widowed sisters living in the house in which they'd grown up. And even with Annabelle gradually fading, like those early colored photographs in the album that lost their vividness even though they were rarely exposed to light, life was quite lovely really. So much simpler and less fractious without men around to make a mess and have opinions.

Annabelle had been growing increasingly forgetful, even difficult at times, when the doctors confirmed their worst fear. Dementia. Progressive and unstoppable. Mina had been so determined to take care of her at home. All that changed a few years later when Mina was woken up in the middle of the night by a knock at the door. The nice young fellow who'd taken over running the store was standing on the step with his arm hooked in Annabelle's, like he was escorting her home from a dance. Only instead of a prom gown, Annabelle was wearing her thin nightgown with a white lace collar. She was also barefoot, her toes blue with cold.

Finn said he found Annabelle shivering on the store's front steps. It was a miracle she hadn't gotten lost, or worse.

The next day, Mina had started looking into nursing homes. She found one that was just a twenty-minute drive away. Annabelle lasted there for two years more, finally succumbing to pneumonia. Mina was so grateful she'd been there when Annabelle passed, holding her hand.

"Did you call my sister?" the girl asked, bringing Mina back to the present.

"Yes. Your mother asked me to. She said to call Ginger and tell her . . . tell her . . ." Mina frowned. She had repeated the words Sandra Ferrante asked her to convey, over and over to herself. Written them down, even, on the same slip of paper where the EMT wrote Ginger's phone number.

But when she made the call, Ginger hadn't been there. She'd called again and still no one answered. Mina usually refused to talk to machines—it made her feel ridiculous and unseemly—but she'd swallowed her distaste and left a message, telling Ginger that her mother had been taken off in an ambulance. She took so long explaining what happened that before she could repeat Sandra Ferrante's message the phone gave a long, insulting bleat. Even Mina knew what that meant. Time had run out.

Now she had no idea where she'd put that little piece of paper, and just as she'd known they would, Sandra's words had slipped from her grasp.

"Well, I'm sure your mother will tell you herself, won't she? God bless her. How is she doing?"

"I'm going over to the hospital later today." The girl gave her a twisted, shaky smile. "I'm so sorry. Must be difficult living next door to all this." She gave a helpless wave toward her mother's house.

"I try not to notice," Mina said. The Ferrantes' had never been *House Beautiful,* but lately it had become especially run-down. Though Mina often lost track of time, it seemed to her that it hadn't been in nearly this appalling of a state even two or three months ago. No wonder the girl was chagrined.

To make her feel better, Mina added, "Fortunately, if I take off my glasses, everything looks lovely. When you can't see dirt, it makes cleaning so much simpler. Just like when you can't see your own wrinkles."

The girl gave her a thin smile. In return, Mina offered a sympathetic cluck and added, "It must be overwhelming coming home to this."

"Completely. Honestly, I don't know where to begin. I've been here all morning, and I've barely made a dent. I never thought it would be this bad."

The poor thing in her tight jeans and leather boots did seem spectacularly out of her element, like a prairie chicken washed up on Coney Island. Clearly she was overmatched to the task at hand. Well, who wouldn't be?

"I know you're not asking for advice," Mina said, "but that's never stopped me from offering it. Take one thing at a time." She poked her cane into the tall weeds that began just past her property line, pushing aside a tangle of knotweed and a burgeoning tree of heaven, then waded over to the girl. Reaching up and putting her hand on the girl's shoulder, she said, "You know, anything looks less daunting after a sit-down and a nice cup of tea."

Chapter
Eight

Are you a good witch or a bad witch? Evie had been tempted to ask as she let herself be shepherded into Mrs. Yetner's house. She and Ginger had always called Mrs. Yetner the white witch because of her white-white hair and skin the color of parchment. She still wore the same cat's-eye glasses she had when Evie was younger, satiny-white plastic frames with a sprinkle of rhinestones at the corners. Now that vintage look had come back in style.

Mrs. Yetner had been a severe presence who sucked in her cheeks and stared down her nose at any neighborhood kid who dared to mouth off to her. But she'd also been kind, in an unobtrusive way, except when Evie trampled her hydrangea and Shasta daisies en route to rescuing a soccer ball.

But for all the years Mrs. Yetner had been their neighbor, Evie had never actually been inside her house. Now Evie looked around in awe at the spotless kitchen with its black-and-white checkerboard tiled floor, two-basin porcelain-over-cast-iron sink standing on legs, and pair of pale-green metal base cabinets with a matching rolltop bread box sitting on a white enamel countertop. Spatulas and spoons hung from hooks on the wall, all with wooden handles painted that same green. The utensils had the patina of old tools, used for so long that they bore the imprint of their owner's hand. Evie felt as if she'd stepped into a 1920s time warp. These days people replaced their belongings long before any of them acquired the dignity of age.

One of the few newish items in the room was a recycle bin, shoved against the wall and filled to the brim with neatly folded newspapers, cat food cans, and glass. Even Mrs. Yetner's garbage was clean, Evie thought, recalling the abysmal mess at her mother's house.

Mrs. Yetner left her cane resting in a corner and picked up a kettle. Bright, mirror polished with a pair of brass cylinders over the spout, like mini organ pipes, it at least was not old. She tipped back the cylinders and filled the kettle with water, then set it on the front burner of a green-enamel stove. The stove's white-and-chrome dials were spotless, as were the porthole windows in the oven's two doors.

A fluffy white cat brushed against Evie's leg as Mrs. Yetner struck a match and lit a burner. There was no *tick-tick-ticking* like a modern gas stove, just a *whoosh* as the flame caught. Evie lifted the cat and buried her face in its warm back. The cat draped itself, languid and boneless in her arms, and purred like a wheezy truck engine.

"Ivory doesn't take to most folks," Mrs. Yetner said. "Cats know their people."

"I never knew I was a cat person," Evie said, setting the cat down. "How can I help?"

Mrs. Yetner pointed to a wooden corner cabinet with glass doors. "There's tea and china in there." Her arm trembled and she glared at it, balling her hand into a fist and lowering it to her side. Evie noticed that she was wearing two wristwatches on her arm, and her fingers were gnarled like tree roots. "And there's milk in the icebox."

Evie opened the cabinet. The shelves were lined with green-and-white shelf paper patterned like gingham, the edges cut with pinking shears. No pantry moth would dare take up residence in there.

Tea bags were in a mason jar on the bottom shelf. Evie unhinged the clamped lid and fished out two. From the shelf above, she took down a pair of delicate teacups and matching saucers, decorated with pink roses and blue forget-me-nots. So *not* dishwasher-safe. But then, as she realized when she looked around, there was no dishwasher.

She set the cups and saucers carefully on the table and placed a tea bag in each cup. Inside the refrigerator, on a shelf lined with plastic wrap over paper towels, she found the milk and set it on the table, too.

The teakettle went off, a strident three-tone cadence. Mrs. Yetner pulled it off the burner. She poured hot water in the cups and settled in a chair at the table.

"This kitchen is amazing," Evie said. "That wonderful old stove. The floor. Do you know how special it is to find a period kitchen so intact? In fact, this whole house . . ." Evie's gaze traveled past the kitchen's arched doorway, through to the narrow dining room, and on to the living room with windows looking out over the water. The footprint and floor plan of the house were identical to her mother's, and yet it felt utterly different with its mahogany paneling and thick cove moldings that belonged more in a manor house than in what had started out as a beach cottage.

"Go ahead," Mrs. Yetner said. "Have a look around. The tea needs to steep, anyway."

Evie got up and walked through, pausing to touch one of the fluted columns mounted on a half wall separating the dining room from the living room. A memory flickered. Before the fire, her parents' house had had columns separating the rooms, too, only theirs had been plainer, not topped with these Doric scrolls—volutes, to use the technical term.

Mrs. Yetner followed as Evie walked to the fireplace in the living room and ran her hand across the cool, voluptuously carved marble mantel. "This is so lovely," she said. Her parents' fireplace surround was plain brick that someone, in a misguided effort at redecorating, had painted fire-engine red.

"My father salvaged that from a mansion in Manhattan," Mrs. Yetner said. "But it's far too grand for this house, don't you think?"

"Your father was a builder?" Evie asked.

"He was. And a businessman. And an attorney. That's him," Mrs. Yetner said, indicating a framed sepia family portrait on the mantel. "Thomas Higgs."

"Higgs?" Evie asked. "As in Higgs Point?"

Mrs. Yetner smiled and nodded.

Evie examined the photograph. A man in a suit and tie was seated before the same marble mantel, his slim, severe wife standing behind him. Two children, little girls maybe six and eight, stood rigid and unsmiling beside him. Only the baby sitting in the father's lap, wearing a long white dress and holding an old-fashioned carpenter's plane, seemed at all happy to be there.

"That's me." Mrs. Yetner pointed to the smaller of the two girls. "And that's my sister, Annabelle. The little one in my father's lap, that's my brother."

Alongside other pictures on the mantel were an oyster shell and the dark, leathery, helmetlike shell of a horseshoe crab. Propped up at the other end was a small white plate with a decal of the Coney Island Parachute Jump. Beside it was a metal paperweight of the Trylon and Perisphere from the 1939 World's Fair.

But the keepsake that caught Evie's eye was a metal miniature of the Empire State Building. Evie picked it up. From its silhouette, Evie realized it had to be old. Its top was stubby, the way the building had looked in the 1930s before its owners abandoned the fantasy that gigantic, cigar-shaped dirigibles could come nose to nose with its mooring mast and disembark passengers onto a gangplank more than a thousand feet in the air.

"You must have gotten this a very long time ago," Evie said.

Mrs. Yetner blinked, and for a few seconds she seemed at a loss for words. She picked up another framed photograph from the mantel. "This is me and Annabelle again. A little bit older."

Evie looked closely. Two young girls stood barefoot on a beach. Their long skirts and the scarves on their heads were being whipped around by the wind. Each had her arm around the other's waist.

"Which beach is this?" Evie asked.

"Right down the street, if you can believe it. There used to be a beach there. Saltwater meets freshwater. It was lovely for swimming."

Mrs. Yetner put the photograph back. Evie was still holding the little replica of the Empire State Building. Cast out of pot metal, what must once have been crisp details now blurred and melted, almost like candle wax. When she looked up, Mrs. Yetner was staring at it, too.

"I used to work there," Mrs. Yetner said.

"Really?"

"I bought that the day I interviewed for the job. Kept it because I thought it brought me good luck." There was something in Mrs. Yetner's expression that Evie couldn't read.

"When was that?"

"Oh, my, who remembers?" She gave a vague wave. "End of the war."

"I ask because I work at the Historical Society, and we're mounting an exhibit about some of New York's great fires. And one of them was when a World War II bomber crashed into the building. That was back when the building looked like this." Evie held out the souvenir. She went on, trying not to sound too excited. "So of course I'm wondering if it's at all possible that you were working there when . . ."

She was interrupted by the doorbell. Mrs. Yetner turned sharply, her eyes wide. There was a sharp *rat-tat-tat,* then a man's voice. "Aunt Mina?"

Mrs. Yetner turned back to Evie. She plucked the little statue from Evie's palm and dropped it into her own pocket. "Would you mind getting that?" she said, adjusting her pearls and smoothing her sweater. "Sounds like my nephew has arrived."

Chapter
Nine

Mina didn't like where the girl's questions were going, not one bit. So for a change she was happy to hear Brian's voice. He'd told her he was coming by Saturday. That was today. But, as usual, he hadn't bothered to say when exactly he was going to show up. He never stayed for tea unless he was trying to pitch one of his can't-miss schemes.

Once he'd tried to get her to invest in vitamins. Another deal had involved leasing oil rights in Namibia. Namibia, for goodness' sake! When she'd questioned him about it, he didn't seem to know where the country was, aside from "somewhere in Africa." Now he was on and on about some real estate scheme. She usually tossed Brian some sort of bone to get him out of her hair.

As the girl went to get the door, Mina scuttled into the living room. Where had he left those papers he'd wanted her to look at? Sure enough, there they were, under today's newspaper on the lamp table.

She heard the front door open. A pause. Then, "Well, hello there." Brian's deep sonorous voice. "And who are you?"

"Just a neighbor. My mother lives next door."

Brian was always at her about how forgetful she was becoming, so the last thing she wanted was for him to come through and find the papers she'd promised to read sitting exactly where he'd left them. Mina tried to stuff the papers into the drawer of the mahogany coffee table, but they wouldn't fit.

"Really?" Brian said. A long pause. "Your mother lives in that house?"

Longer pause before the girl said, "Your aunt is in the living room, waiting for you."

Mina was glad that the poor girl didn't think she needed to apologize for the state of her mother's house. Certainly not to Brian. She shoved the papers under a sofa cushion, then she sat on it and pulled the crocheted afghan over her. Ivory jumped into her lap and started to purr.

Seconds later, Brian stomped in from the kitchen. "Hello, Aunt Mina."

As he started toward her, Ivory gave a yowl and disappeared under the couch.

Brian had always been on the scrawny side, but in his forties he'd turned portly and thickened in the jowls. Nearly sixty now, he still had that shock of wavy hair, only instead of auburn it was nearly black. When men colored their hair, they always made it too dark. Like shoe polish.

At least he was predictable, you could say that for him. Always favored double-breasted jackets with brass buttons and cordovan leather loafers, like what he had on now. But fine feathers didn't make fine birds.

"Did you at least look at the agreement?" he said, not bothering with *Hello* or *How are you today?*

"Shouldn't you be at work?" Mina said, giving him a bland look and adjusting the afghan around her.

He looked back at her with that lethal combination of exasperation and bemused contempt. "It's Saturday. I don't work weekends, remember? And I told you I was coming over." He shot his cuffs before folding his arms and narrowing his eyes at her. "You do remember, I told you I was coming back?"

Of course she remembered. But she'd long ago learned that with Brian, evasion worked out better than engagement. "I must have forgotten to write it on my calendar."

Mina heard water running in the kitchen and the *tink* of bone china. The girl was washing up. She seemed awfully sweet, but Mina hoped she'd be careful. That gold-rimmed service that once belonged to her mother had only a few cracks and a single chip.

"So *did* you look at the papers I left?" Brian asked.

"Button your shirt, Brian," Mina said. "And don't you think you should be wearing socks?"

"Do you even still have them?" Brian asked.

"I'm sure they're here." Mina waved a vague hand, a gesture her mother had perfected to avoid answering inconvenient questions. "Somewhere."

The water stopped running, and the old pipes thunked. A moment later the girl peered into the room from behind Brian. She was holding a dish towel. "I'd better be going," she said. She snapped the towel and folded it smartly.

Mina pushed the afghan off her lap and started to get up.

"Don't bother. I can let myself out," the girl said.

"It's no bother," Mina said, following the girl out and pointedly ignoring Brian.

At the door, the girl turned to face her. "Would you mind if I came back another time? You see, I was starting to tell you about my work for the Historical Society. We're mounting a new exhibit, and I'd love to talk to you some more about what it was like, working in the Empire State Building back then. That's when the plane hit the building. We have surprisingly few first-person accounts."

Mina forced a smile and said, "Of course. Come back any time. Though I hope you won't be disappointed. My memory is not as reliable as it once was."

"Who knows, maybe talking will bring back what it was like to work in that building."

As if that were something Mina could forget. As the girl trotted down the steps, Mina could almost feel the Empire State souvenir that she'd slipped into her pocket growing hot.

Chapter Ten

"What building?" Brian asked, his voice startling Mina. She was still standing at the open door, watching as the girl made her way back to her mother's house.

"I have no idea what you're talking about."

"So what *was* she asking about?" Brian reached around her and pushed the door shut.

Mina went into the kitchen. The girl had left the dishes neatly stacked on the counter. "Just this and that."

Brian was right behind her. "This and . . . ?" He shook his head. "So it's her crazy mother who lives next door?"

Mina didn't answer.

"That heap is an accident waiting to happen, if you ask me. If the inside is anything like the outside—"

She turned to face him. "Good thing it's not your problem."

He rolled his eyes. "So what did she *want*?"

Mina sighed. "Not everyone wants something, Brian."

"Did you look at the papers I left?"

She wondered if he grasped the irony of this exchange. Annabelle had had such high hopes for her little boy. Instead, they'd gotten this.

"What papers?" she said.

"The papers I brought over last week."

"Did you?"

"Don't you remember? We talked. You promised you'd read them."

Mina didn't say anything.

Brian narrowed his eyes. "You forgot all about it, didn't you? Or maybe you lost them? It's okay if you did. I can print another copy. Or maybe the typeface was too small? Was that the problem?"

"There's no problem."

"Aunt Mina, I know we've had our differences over the years, and when Mom got sick, I was pretty useless."

That took her aback. She hadn't credited him with that much self-awareness. What was he up to?

"But this isn't for me," he went on. "It's for you. Your money won't last forever, and this would offer you financial security. You'd be set for life. Think of it as your silver safety net."

Snake oil was more like it. And what business did he have sniffing around in her finances?

"Thank you very much, but I'm already set for life, or at least for what life I've got left. And if not, well, that's not your problem, is it? Don't worry, you'll own the house when I die."

"I don't want this goddamned house!" Brian slammed his hand down so hard on the kitchen table that the salt and pepper shakers jumped.

Mina took a step back, her hand at her throat. Suddenly she felt very alone.

"Sorry, sorry!" Brian put up his hands. "I didn't mean to yell. It's just that talking to you . . . sometimes talking to you is like talking to a brick wall. Please try to think about it, Aunt Mina. You'd have security. A regular income."

Mina sucked in her cheeks and stared at him. He shook his head and looked up at the ceiling, as if the good Lord Himself was up there, commiserating. She followed his lingering gaze to the scorch mark on the ceiling. That was from a few weeks ago when she'd ruined her mother's teakettle and, in the process, set fire to the kitchen curtains.

Mina turned and opened the corner cabinet. One at a time, she hung each teacup on its hook and set each saucer on the stack. She closed the cabinet and turned back to him. "I'm sure I put those papers somewhere. We can talk about it next time you come for a visit."

"If you can't find them, I'll bring another copy. We can sit down and read it together." Brian was like a dog worrying a bone long after there wasn't a shred of meat left on it.

Pivoting away from him again, Mina walked to the sink and turned on the tap. She ran the water hard, shook some Ajax onto the porcelain, and began to scrub it down. As she worked at a stubborn stain, her hand spasmed. She dropped the sponge, frozen by the painful cramp that contracted her hand into a claw. Damned arthritis. She flattened her hand on the counter, spread her fingers, and waited for the muscles to relax. She snuck a look over her shoulder to see if Brian had noticed. But he was already moving toward the door.

As she rinsed away the suds, she heard the front door open and close. At last he was gone. She turned off the water and stood there, holding on to the thick cool edge of the sink. Didn't want the house? *Pfff.* She knew full well this house was the only reason he kept showing up and sniffing about. She and Annabelle had owned the house outright for years, ever since their mother died. *Unencumbered.* That single word had given Mina peace of mind, knowing all she had to do was pay the taxes and keep up with repairs.

Brian knew exactly how she felt. He couldn't even look her in the eye when he'd spouted all that mumbo jumbo about a security net and regular income. She should have destroyed those papers instead of hiding them and feigning ignorance. She should have burned them. That's what she'd do now.

She remembered exactly where she'd put them. She went into the living room and lifted the sofa cushion she'd been sitting on.

The papers were gone.

Chapter
Eleven

Evie could hear Mrs. Yetner and her nephew arguing even before the door closed behind her. Tolstoy's famous quote came to mind: Every unhappy family was unhappy in its own way.

The way Mrs. Yetner talked down to him, Evie couldn't help but feel sorry for the poor guy. He was no match for his aunt. Evie had to laugh, remembering the innocent shrug she'd given him when asked about a document he'd left for her to read. Evie had seen Mrs. Yetner stuff a sheaf of papers under the sofa cushion before she settled herself on it.

That must have been Brian's dark gray Mercedes parked at the curb. Mrs. Yetner's vintage Ford Mustang was parked in her drive-way. Evie remembered that car with its silvery-blue body, white vinyl top, and distinctive Mustang snout. A period piece from the '70s, it was still pristine, shiny clean outside. She walked over to it. Neat as a pin inside, too. Just like the house.

Mrs. Yetner's was an orderly existence, buttressed by selective amnesia. If only life were that simple, Evie thought as she crossed back over Mrs. Yetner's lawn and waded through the knee-deep weeds in front of her mother's house. Then she could pretend not to notice that the ground was littered with roof shingles. She could turn a deaf ear to the creaking front steps. Pretend that she had taped the Georgia O'Keeffe print over the broken window as a decorative touch.

She went inside, stepping past one of the two garbage bags full of empty liquor bottles. How long had it taken for her mother to drink her way through all that? She dragged the bags outside.

She wanted to at least get the kitchen sorted before she left for the hospital. She unplugged the refrigerator and washed out the inside with cleaning solution. When she was done, she left the door open to air out as she started stuffing garbage into a new bag, setting aside any mail that she found layered through the trash. There were so many cat food cans. Her mother must have started feeding stray cats around the same time she'd given up emptying ashtrays—plates and bowls and coffee cups everywhere were filled with cigarette ash. It was a miracle she hadn't set fire to the house. Again.

Under a mound of ash in a pie tin, Evie found the keys to her mother's Subaru. Attached to the key ring was a piece of leather. Embossed into it was:

I ♥ MOM

Evie rubbed the tooled surface between her thumb and forefinger. She remembered the summer when she'd made that at Y camp, and the pleasure on her mother's face when she'd given it to her.

Her breath caught in her throat. Evie did love her mother. But even then she'd been terrified that one day she'd turn into her. It had been a relief to discover that though she liked the buzz of a glass of wine, more than two made her queasy. When she was overwhelmed or sad, she never turned to drinking. Instead, she made lists. Or cleaned closets. Straightened drawers. Alphabetized spices.

Evie tied off another full garbage bag and dragged it to the front door. The therapist she'd seen for a few sessions had pronounced her "well defended." Evie had wondered if that was a good thing or a bad thing, and then she decided it didn't matter.

Opening the front door, she heaved the bag out onto the lawn, taking care not to stand on the weakened steps. She'd stepped back inside when she heard a door slam. Through the murky kitchen window, she saw Mrs. Yetner's nephew out on the street, unlocking the door of that Mercedes. Then he paused and nodded across the street to a man—the one who'd been driving a red car and whose wave Evie had ignored.

Evie pulled away from the glass. Waited until she heard a car engine rev. She was about to look out again to see if the Mercedes was gone when her doorbell rang. She thought for sure it was the nephew, come to ask her something about Mrs. Yetner. But when she looked out through the peephole, it was that across-the-street neighbor looking back at her.

When she pulled open the door, he smiled up at her from below the broken step. "Hi. I live across the street." He offered her a fleshy hand, and Evie pushed open the storm door and shook it. The punky top step creaked when he stepped on it and peered inside. His breath smelled of cigarettes and mouthwash.

"You must be Evie. Your mom talks about you all the time. I'm a good friend of Sandy's."

Sandy? That had been her mother's nickname growing up, but she'd hated it ever since the movie *Grease.*

"Heard she took ill," he said. His smile was sad and he had rosy cheeks, spidered with veins. A drinker, of course. *After a few martinis, Mom probably stopped caring what he called her.* The thought was so cold and mean, Evie stopped herself. At least her mother still had a friend who obviously cared.

"I'll let her know you were asking after her, Mr.—"

"Cutler. But please, call me Frank."

"Frank. I'll let her know."

"Well. I . . ." He paused. Like he hadn't thought ahead to what he was going to say. "Just wanted to know how she's doing. And of course when she's coming home."

"I'm sorry, I don't really know myself. I'm going over to the hospital later today. I'll let her know you came by." She started to shut the door.

"If I can help in any way?" His gaze shifted overhead. "Because I fix things for her all the time. I've been trying to get her to let me go up and fix that window for the longest time. Maybe I can take care of it before she gets back?"

"No." Evie felt an embarrassed heat rise into her cheeks. Her mother probably didn't want Frank to see what a mess the house had turned into. "No thanks."

He stepped back. "Sorry. I . . ." He blinked three times. "I was just trying to help."

"I know. I appreciate it. And once I figure out what's what, I'll get back to you. I'm sure you understand."

"Of course." He stood there like he wanted to say something more but couldn't manage to get it out. "So, if there's anything I can do, you know where to find me." He jerked his thumb in the direction of the house across the street. "Whistle. Or better yet, call." He offered her a business card.

Evie took it and promised she would.

Chapter Twelve

Back in the kitchen, Evie considered the man's card with his name, address, and phone number. How nice that her mother had found companionship right across the street, someone who shared her twin passions: smoking and drinking. He'd probably upgraded her to Grey Goose.

Which reminded Evie of Seth, who was so particular about his martinis, sensitive to the nuances of vodka that completely escaped Evie. She slid her phone out of her pocket. One message. She played it.

"Hi, babe. Sorry to hear about your mom. Sounds like you've got your hands full." There was a pause, and music and laughter in the background. "Listen, I scored a pair of Knicks tickets for tonight. Courtside seats. Meet you in the bar at the Club at six? We can get Chinese another time, right?"

Wrong. And what didn't he understand about *family emergency*?

"Sounds like a narcissist," had been Ginger's take on Seth. Evie hated it when her sister turned out to be right. Her suggestion that perhaps he wasn't the most generous of lovers had been uncomfortably on the mark, too.

Evie texted him back a terse *Sorry, can't make it,* shoved the phone back in her pocket, and got back to work.

It was four by the time Evie left for the hospital. Even after a hot shower, she felt a miasma of stale alcohol and cigarettes clinging to her. The towels in the linen closet had been infused with that stench. She'd splashed herself with her mother's Jean Naté and made a mental note to add laundry detergent and dryer sheets to her shopping list. With her mother's car, she'd have the luxury of loading up at the Path-Mark a mile away.

She unlocked the little one-car garage and raised the overhead door. There was her mother's Subaru. A taillight was broken. She walked along the driver side. The left front fender was scraped, too. Evie sniffed. Did she smell gasoline over Jean Naté?

Boxes were clustered near some old car batteries on the floor by the car door. One box contained cigarette cartons. Another was nearly full of liquor bottles. Evie pulled one out from between the cardboard inserts. More Grey Goose. Apparently vodka and cigarettes were being delivered by the caseload.

Evie pushed the boxes away from the car door and got in. The interior smelled sweet, like fermented apples. She looked around and found the source: a rotting apple had sunk into the drink holder. She gouged it out with a tissue and tossed it into one of the nearby boxes. Then she buckled the seat belt, slipped the key into the ignition, and turned it halfway.

The lights on the dash came on. She rolled down the window to let out the cloying smell. Adjusted the mirror. And then turned the key farther to start the engine.

It caught, gave a sputter and a wheeze, then died.

Evie sighed. She turned the key again. *Wha-wha-wha.* The engine cranked. And cranked. But no matter how much she pumped the gas, it wouldn't catch. When she tried turning the key again, the engine barely roused itself and the engine light dimmed.

That's when she realized that the needle on the gas gauge was pointing to empty.

She slammed her hand against the steering wheel. The horn gave a feeble bleat. She wanted to scream. It probably wasn't the first time that her mother had parked the car and left it running until it ran out of gas.

Evie sat for a moment, pulling herself together, then popped open the glove box. She looked in vain for an AAA card. She was pulling out the owner's manual when her cell phone rang. She almost didn't bother to look, thinking it would be Seth, his feelings hurt by her brusque response.

But it was Ginger.

"Are you at the hospital yet?" Ginger asked.

"I was about to leave."

"How bad is it?"

"Disgusting. Stinky. Garbage everywhere. Cockroaches. Pantry moths. Squirrels. I'd give it a twelve on a scale of one to ten."

Ginger groaned.

"I started cleaning out the kitchen. Tossed out a mattress. Covered a broken window." She gave the car key one more futile turn. "And now the damned car won't start. So I'm going to have to take the bus to the hospital."

Evie leaned forward and picked up a white paper bag from the floor of the passenger seat. It was printed with the black-and-red logo for Ruth's Chris Steak House. Inside was a leftovers container that she didn't dare open. Beneath it was an empty champagne bottle. Veuve Clicquot.

"It wasn't bad when I was there last," Ginger said.

"When *were* you here last?"

"Mom's birthday."

Two months ago. Evie had sent a card, but for the first time she hadn't called. Now that felt mean. How big a deal would it have been to pick up the phone?

"I brought her a cake," Ginger said, rubbing it in.

That explained the cake in the refrigerator. "Did you take her out for a steak dinner, too?"

"You're kidding, right? I don't even take myself out for steak dinners. I brought her a lasagna."

And there was the baking dish with blue moldy stuff in the fridge. Maybe Frank had been the source of the steak dinner. How many bottles of champagne had they gone through before this now empty one for the road?

"The house was just the usual messy," Ginger said. "And Mom was pretty upbeat. She was excited about how she'd be getting money each month, I guess because her Social Security kicked in."

"So you haven't seen her since her birthday?" Evie asked. That was surprising. Ginger had always been the "dutiful" daughter.

"We were supposed to get together, but she kept canceling. You know, that's nothing new."

Evie did know. "Guess what she's drinking these days."

"Vodka."

"What brand?"

"I don't know. Smirnoff?"

"Grey Goose."

"So?"

"It's expensive. There's the better part of a case of the stuff in the garage. And a big flat-screen TV in the living room."

"Really?"

"She didn't have the TV when you were there?"

"Uh, no. I would have noticed."

"So how come she's got a brand-new TV but the place is falling apart? I mean really, literally falling apart. She didn't say anything when you saw her at the hospital?"

"They had her so blitzed out on pain medication and tranquilizers and anticonvulsants, she barely even opened her eyes."

Anticonvulsants would be for delirium tremens. Her mother had had those before, after she "fell down the stairs" and fifteen-year-old Evie found her unconscious.

"Ask her yourself," Ginger said. "You are going over, aren't you?"

"Right now," Evie said, getting out of the car. She walked out of the garage and pulled the garage door down with a *whump*. "But I bet this will be just like the last time she crashed. And—"

"Yeah, right," Ginger cut her off. "As if you even know what it was like the last time. Or the time before that. You'd cut and run."

Evie didn't say anything. Her fingers cramped around the phone as she walked toward the bus stop.

"You think she's jerking us around again, don't you?" Ginger said. "That this is one more fire drill designed to get our attention? Well, it's not. So brace yourself."

Chapter
Thirteen

A little while later, Mina looked out her kitchen window and saw Sandra Ferrante's daughter walking up the street as she talked on her cell phone. She wondered why she'd decided not to drive her mother's car. Family could be so complicated.

Cats, on the other hand, made lovely, undemanding companions who required nothing more than food, water, and a little bit of attention. Ivory had emerged from under the couch and threaded her way back and forth across Mina's legs.

Mina put a package of frozen chicken on a plate to thaw, high on a shelf out of the cat's reach. She'd make a pot of her mother's chicken cacciatore. Neither Mina nor Annabelle had been particularly close to their mother, who had been, for the most part, as perfunctory a cook as she was a parent. She'd lavished attention on their brother, and later on his grave after he died at twenty-one in Iwo Jima.

Mina would have liked to have had a child. A daughter, she thought. But she'd been far too old to start a family by the time she and Henry married, though for the first few years they'd tried. So now Brian was the closest thing she had. And she was the closest thing to a parent he had left.

Mina fished the replica of the Empire State Building from her pocket and set it back on the mantel in the living room. It was uncanny how the girl zeroed in on it. She looked out the living room window, across the driveway to Sandra Ferrante's. The girl had left her mother's windows wide open. The house must have been in desperate need of a thorough airing out.

At least Sandra Ferrante's house looked lived-in. The house on the other side had been dark and unoccupied all winter. Why someone hadn't broken in, she couldn't fathom. The Jamesons hadn't even left timers on the lights. Whoever was supposed to be taking care of the property was doing so haphazardly, and Mina had to keep clearing away flyers that accumulated in the storm door.

Now Angela Quintanilla had gone and died, and her house would be empty, too—which reminded Mina. She should write a condolence card and drop it at Angela's house. If the family was there, she'd stop in and pay her respects.

From a drawer, Mina pulled out the pile of sympathy cards she'd purchased over the years. She hated ones that were religiously preachy, or sappily poetic, or so euphemistic that you couldn't even tell someone had died. She picked out one with a spray of lily of the valley against a pale blue background. Inside was the message *Sorry for your loss.*

She settled in her chair and began to write in a careful hand: "Angela was a lovely person, and I was so sad to hear of her—" Mina stopped. *Passing?* She hated the euphemism. But *death* felt cruel somehow, though it was perfectly accurate. Not that it mattered. She remembered she'd barely read the condolence cards that she'd received after her Henry and later Annabelle died. Just receiving them had been a comfort.

She finished writing the note, then licked and sealed the flap.

Mina had been to Angela Quintanilla's home a few times over the years. As she recalled, it was a few blocks up along the water. She could drive, but it would do her good to walk. She tried to take a brisk walk every day, even if it was only to the store and back.

She changed into comfortable shoes and put on her car coat. As she started up the street, on past Sandra Ferrante's forlorn-looking house, she remembered from the obituary that Angela's funeral was at St. Andrews. Annabelle's little memorial service had been held there, too. The turnout had been respectable but sparse. When you died old, not many people who really knew you were left. Mina had been surprised when her new neighbor, that Frank Cutler, had shown up. Though he'd been nice enough, she doubted if he could have picked Annabelle out of an old lady lineup.

After two blocks, Mina paused to rest for a few moments and button her coat. With the sun low it had turned chilly. She'd forgotten how far up Angela's house was. As she continued walking, she wondered whether the house would go on the market. It was a sweet bungalow with white shingles and candy-apple trim, though it probably needed work. She hoped it would be bought by someone who appreciated its quirky charm. Who'd love the view and want to protect the marsh.

She paused to catch her breath again a half block farther along in front of an empty lot that she didn't remember being there. She turned up her collar. It didn't seem possible that Angela's house was this far away. Was it?

Sure enough, when she turned to look behind her, there was Angela's house. No wonder she'd missed it. One of the front windows was cracked. Another had a hole in it. Battered asphalt roof shingles littered the ground, and what might once have been chrysanthemums in window boxes were nothing but dried twigs.

A bright yellow sign stuck to the front door read WARNING. Sagging yellow tape strung between sawhorses across the start of a cracked concrete front walkway told passersby to KEEP OUT.

Mina took a quick look around her, raised the tape with her cane, and stepped under it. She marched up to the front door. Where there had once been a doorbell, two wires stuck out of the door frame. She pulled the storm door open and rapped on the front door with her cane. She didn't expect anyone to answer, but she did want to get a better look.

Wedged inside the storm door, partially hidden by the yellow warning sign taped to the outside, was a smaller official-looking notice, also on bright yellow paper. Across the top it said WORK PERMIT, and below that DEPARTMENT OF BUILDINGS.

Mina plucked it from the door frame and held it close so she could read the fine print. It had been issued a few days ago, Thursday, May 16. That had been the day after Angela died.

Mina felt a chill when she read what was checked off under DESCRIPTION OF WORK.

Demolition and removal.

Chapter
Fourteen

It was past five when Evie stepped off the bus in front of Bronx Metropolitan Hospital. The building was covered in white brick and, typical of so many big buildings that had gone up in the 1960s, tiered like a wedding cake. A broad cantilevered canopy covered the entrance. A siren flared as an ambulance drove off, then fell silent when the glass door slid shut behind Evie.

She made her way through the crowded lobby to the information desk, where she got her mother's room number. As she walked to the elevators a pale woman with reddened eyes stumbled past with her cell phone to her ear. Another woman rushed across the lobby, carrying an enormous gift bag and a bunch of pink helium balloons.

Hospitals ushered people in and out, and hosted all manner of crises in between, she thought as she rode a crowded elevator to the eighth floor. But no amount of intellectualizing could ease the anxiety that built in the pit of her stomach the closer she got to her mother's room.

She exited the elevator onto a hushed floor, the only sound the

metal clatter of a hospital cart and the *shush* of elevator doors closing. Room 8231. Evie stood for a few moments outside the door to her
mother's room.

Brace yourself. Ginger's words came back to her.

Taking a deep breath, she pushed open the door and stepped
inside.

Evie barely recognized her mother. Thin and haggard, she was
propped up in the hospital bed nearest to the door. Her once lustrous
auburn curls had turned a flat slate gray and stood out from her skull
like the puff of a ripe dandelion.

Another patient was sleeping in the bed by the window. Evie drew
the curtain between the beds and pulled over a chair.

Her mother seemed to be asleep, too. Her cheeks, flushed with
broken blood vessels, gave the illusion of robust health. Her eyes
were closed, but the lids trembled as if she were dreaming. One arm
was taped to her chest. Her other hand rested on the bedcovers, the
nails stained yellow with nicotine. Evie winced at the dark bruising
on the back of her hand where an IV line fed into a purple vein.

It's just a movie. That was what Evie used to tell herself whenever things got ugly, when her mother woke her and Ginger in the
middle of the night, transformed into the banshee that she became
when she and her father were fighting drunk. On nights like that,
Evie and Ginger hid under their beds and tried to sleep. When it was
warm enough, they crept outside with their blankets and pillows and
slept in the backyard. Or in the car. They'd occasionally take refuge
in Mrs. Yetner's garage.

Evie's mother had never, ever copped to having a drinking problem. Maybe she didn't remember her bouts of drunkenness; maybe
she simply chose not to. Perhaps pride kept her from admitting, even
to herself, that she could behave so monstrously.

What Evie felt now, looking at the much diminished figure in the bed, wasn't pity, and it certainly wasn't rage. How could it be? After all, her mother had so utterly defeated herself.

Evie leaned forward, resting her head in her arms on the side of the bed. She felt sad and completely exhausted, and she let those feelings wash over her, barely aware of voices and footsteps from the hall, the snoring of the woman in the other bed, announcements that came over the loudspeakers.

The next thing she felt was a light touch on the side of her head. Her mother was stroking her hair, the same way she did when Evie was a little girl. For a few moments, Evie surrendered to it. Then she raised her head.

Her mother was looking across at her, smiling. "You came." Those once clear dark brown eyes seemed cloudy. Without another word, her mother pushed herself to a seated position with her good arm and swung her thin legs off the bed. Evie took her mother's arm and steadied her as she got to her feet and slid her feet into slippers that were sitting by the bed. Evie rolled the IV rack along after as her mother took one shuffling step after another to the bathroom. The thin hospital gown hung loose. Her silhouette was like those starving children she'd seen in photographs, belly distended and arms and legs stick thin. Through the open back of the hospital gown, Evie could see that her mother's back was mottled with bruises.

Her mother waved off Evie's offer to come into the bathroom with her. Evie waited outside the door. And waited. And then helped her mother back into bed.

"Water?" Evie asked. Her mother nodded. Evie poured water from the plastic pitcher on the bedside table into a glass with a straw in it. Her mother sipped. The water level had barely receded before her mother made a face and pulled away.

Evie put the water back on the table.

Her mother held her gaze for a moment.

"How are you feeling?" Evie said, because she didn't know what else to say.

Her mother shook her head and closed her eyes.

Evie said, "Your neighbor, the man from across the street? He stopped by the house."

Her mother gave her a startled look.

"I didn't know you were friendly with him. He offered to repair—"

"Did you let him in?" her mother asked, anxiety flaring in her eyes.

"No," Evie said, glad that she hadn't. "I told him thanks but no thanks."

Her mother started to say something more, but a nurse came into the room. As the nurse wrapped a blood-pressure cuff around her arm, her mother said under her breath, "So he knows I'm here?"

"Mom, everyone in the neighborhood knows you're here. The ambulance—remember?"

Her mother winced and let her head drop back on the pillow, her lips a thin tight line as the nurse pumped air into the cuff. The nurse released it slowly, gave the cuff a puzzled look, and pumped it a second time. This time she seemed satisfied. She checked the IV, wrote something in the chart hanging on the end of the bed, and left.

"God, what I wouldn't give for a smoke," her mother said.

Evie realized that the nurse had left a wake of cigarette-scented air in the small room.

"Mom, the health department is threatening to condemn the house."

"The house?" Her mother blinked several times, like she was absorbing this information.

"It's an awful mess. I'm going to need money to get the house cleaned up and repaired."

"I can take care of it. There's money," her mother said with a vague wave. "Plenty of money. When I get home."

"When you—?" Evie wondered if Ginger could have been wrong about how sick her mother was. "The doctor told you when you can go home?"

"Soon. When I'm ready." With her good arm, her mother pushed herself up straighter. Her face turned pink. "I'm not a child, you know. So don't think you can just move in and take over."

Evie wasn't sure she'd heard right. "What?" she asked. "Mom, I—"

"That's what you do, isn't it?" Her mother's face reddened some more. "Boss everyone around. Take charge. Oh yes, Evie knows what's best for everyone. Everyone except herself. As if you care a twig about what happens to me."

Whiplash. That's what she and Ginger had called it when the switch flipped. Only she couldn't be drinking. Not here in the hospital.

Her mother grabbed Evie's wrist and squeezed so hard that it hurt. "Stop looking at me like that. I can't stand it when you talk down to me. "

Her mother's breath was sour, but there was no alcohol on it, Evie thought in a disconnected corner of her brain as she tried to yank her arm free. But her mother's grip had frozen like a vise. "I was only asking so—"

"*I was only asking,*" her mother mimicked.

Evie was speechless with fury and bottled-up hurt.

"I . . . don't . . . need . . . you or anyone else," her mother said through gritted teeth. "Don't you even think—" The final word died on her lips as she shuddered. Her eyes rolled back in her head, and her body went rigid with spasms.

"Mom?" Evie jumped up. "Mom? Mom! Help!"

She groped for the emergency call button. Over and over she pressed it. Her mother lay there quaking. Was anyone coming to help?

Evie ran out in the hall and headed for the nurses' station. A nurse met her halfway. By the time they got back to the room, her mother had gone slack. Heart pounding, Evie watched the nurse take her mother's pulse.

A moment later, her mother's eyes blinked open. A sheen of sweat coated her forehead and her gaze wandered about the room, across the nurse, until it fastened on Evie.

"You came!" she said.

Chapter

Fifteen

Going home from the hospital, Evie rode by herself in the back of the bus. She rubbed her wrist, trying to erase the sensation that she was still in her mother's grip. She pushed up her sleeve, sure there'd be a mark, but there wasn't. In the end, the damage her mother wrought was invisible.

She took out her phone. She'd promised to call Ginger.

"Evie?" Ginger said, picking up on the first ring.

"You were right. This time it's different."

"I know. So?"

"So." Evie could see her mother's face, all hope and innocence when she'd woken up after her seizure. "One minute she's talking to me, normal, you know? The next minute she's bat-shit crazy. Saying the meanest things."

"Oh, Evie. Surely you know by now that you shouldn't get upset by anything that she says. The doctors have her all doped up on loads of medication."

"It was more than being doped up. She's screaming at me. Telling

me to stop trying to tell her what to do with her life. Then she shud-
ders and goes blank. She's not there. And she's not there. And I'm
starting to panic because she's still not there. And then, just like that,
she's awake again. And she recognizes me. But"—Evie swallowed
the lump in her throat—"she thinks I just showed up. It was like something out of *Groundhog Day*."

"Oh, Evie," Ginger said.

"Did you notice her belly?" Evie asked.

"I know, it's awful. The nurse calls it ascites. It's a symptom of
late-stage liver disease."

"Late stage? What does that mean?"

"Didn't you talk to Dr. Foran?"

"Didn't I—?" Evie stopped herself from biting back. Ginger
never meant her *Didn't-you*s to come out in the know-it-all, passive-
aggressive way that they did. "There were no doctors around, and
until this minute I didn't even know her doctor's name."

"I'll text you the phone number."

"Thank you."

"So what's your plan?" Ginger asked.

"*My* plan?"

"Tonight? Tomorrow?"

Evie had assumed she'd sleep at the house, but she hadn't bar-
gained for the mess, not to mention the smell. But what was the alter-
native? It would take an hour and a half to get home to Brooklyn and
another hour and a half back tomorrow morning.

"I'll probably stay there tonight," Evie said.

"You'll be okay?"

"I'll be fine. If not, I'll go home."

"See what you can figure out about her finances," Ginger said.
"If there are unpaid bills lying around. Maybe you can find a current
bank statement?"

Evie yawned. The day was catching up with her. "I asked her about money."

"And?"

"She says there's plenty."

"Really? Well, la-di-da."

"It's a good thing, too, because between fixing the house so she can live in it and getting her some help when they send her back home, it's going to be expensive." The bus was getting near her stop. Evie stood and walked to the front.

"Hey, I thought you had a date with Seth tonight," Ginger said.

Evie held on to the grab bar overhead as the bus slowed and pulled to the curb. "I told him I couldn't make it. Family emergency. He's going to the basketball game."

A pause. Then, "Oh." Ginger's *oh* was filled with understanding and tinged with regret, and Evie hated that one stinking syllable. Ginger was like a heat-seeking missile when it came to piercing Evie's confidence and poking at her vulnerabilities.

Ginger quickly filled the silence with "Don't worry. You'll—"

"Worry?" Evie got off the bus. "I'm not worried." She took a breath and coughed bus exhaust. "It's really no big deal, and he's not the one. He was never the one. Got to go." She disconnected the call before Ginger could start in with her favorite platitudes.

Chapter
Sixteen

"So what do you make of this?" Mina said. She was standing at the checkout counter at Sparkles showing Finn the work permit she'd snitched.

He examined it. "I . . ." His gaze traveled from the front of the store to the back, and he lowered his voice. "Where'd you get this?"

"From Angela Quintanilla's house. Have you seen what a mess it is? I went to pay a condolence call and found the house roped off and this stuck to the front door."

"And you helped yourself?"

Mina fiddled with the top button of her sweater and smiled. "It blew off the door, and I picked it up."

"So that's your story and you're sticking to it? You know, one day they're going to arrest you for—"

"For what? I was picking up litter. *Pfff*. Besides, they wouldn't want to draw attention, would they? And there's another house not two doors away from this one that's already been demolished. Did you know that?"

"I heard, but—"

"So who's responsible? I'd like to know that, and I'm sure I'm not the only one."

"I don't know anything more than you do."

"But you talk to everyone. Surely—"

"Haven't heard a thing."

"So I think you should find out."

"But—"

"You're an attorney, aren't you?"

"Was."

The bell over the front door tinkled. Mina looked over. It was Sandra Ferrante's daughter. She dropped a slip of paper as she entered the store. Stooped and picked it up.

When Mina turned back, Finn had slid the permit under the mat on the counter.

"Hi," the girl said as she picked up a shopping basket from the stack nested by the register. She looked tired and frazzled.

"Hey," Finn said. "Need help finding anything?"

The girl consulted her crumpled scrap of paper. "Roach bomb?"

"Over there, against the wall," Finn said, pointing to the far side of the store.

"Lightbulbs?"

"They're over there, too."

Mina followed Finn's gaze as he watched the girl walk off. When he turned back, Mina winked at him.

He chuckled. "You're entirely too observant for your own good."

"Have to be blind as a bat not to see," she said. "So that permit. You'll look into it?"

Finn took the permit out again and read it, front and back. "SV Construction Management. Soundview?"

"Do you know them, or are you guessing? Because guesswork I can do myself. You have a computer, don't you? Isn't that what they're for?"

"Mrs. Yetner." He shook his head.

"Do you need a retainer?" Mina found her change purse in her bag, opened it, and pulled out a neat roll of bills—about a hundred dollars. She thrust it at him. "Here."

"You are relentless," Finn said, taking the money from her. He opened the roll, peeled off a single, and tucked it into his shirt pocket. "There. That's plenty," he said, giving her back the rest.

"That's ridiculous," Mina said. But she put the money away before he could change his mind.

The girl brought her basket to the register, and Mina watched as Finn began ringing up the items. When he got to the third frozen chicken potpie, he said, "Gourmet dinner?"

"Easy dinner," the girl said.

Finn bagged the groceries in two bags. Mina picked up one of them. "I can take this for you," she said heading for the door.

"You really don't have to," the girl said, following her outside.

"I don't mind," Mina said, and she didn't. The bag was light, and it was always more pleasant walking with a companion. Besides, the girl looked dead on her feet and Mina wanted to be sure she got back in one piece.

"See you later?" Finn called after them.

The girl gave an absentminded wave.

Mina and Sandra Ferrante's daughter walked in companionable silence until they were a half block from home.

"Why did you take the bus?" Mina asked.

"My mother's car won't start."

That explained it. "If it's not one thing, it's another."

"You can say that again."

They were in front of Mina's house. "Thanks," the girl said, taking the grocery bag.

"So how's your mother doing?"

"Fine. Good, actually."

Mina gave her a long look. The poor thing couldn't even meet her gaze.

Chapter
Seventeen

Evie realized that Mrs. Yetner was only trying to be kind, asking about her mother, but Evie was finding it overwhelming enough without having to deal with the concern of others. Peace, quiet, and some time alone were what she craved.

She closed some of the windows and plugged the refrigerator back in. Started a potpie in the oven and put the rest in the freezer. Pure comfort food was exactly what she needed, never mind that it was mostly cornstarch and salt.

She put away the rest of her purchases. In the bottom of one bag, along with her receipt, she found another copy of the Soundview Watershed Preservation brochure. The photographs of the marsh on the back cover could have been taken from her mother's back porch. She set the brochure on the mantel.

Other than pretending that stems of feathery marsh grass were their magic wands, Evie and Ginger had always been oblivious to the marsh and its wildlife. Mostly Evie had been embarrassed by its farty smell.

Now she didn't mind that smell so much. It was preferable by far, she thought as she took in the remaining mess, to sewage and rotting food. At least the smell in the house was better than when she'd first gotten there. Sleeping there wouldn't be as miserable as she'd feared.

While she waited for the pie to heat up, Evie went methodically from room to room, looking on every surface, in every drawer and box and closet, grabbing any mail or official-looking papers that might help her assess her mother's finances. She piled everything she found on the kitchen table.

It was only when the smell of baking chicken pie filled the kitchen that she remembered how often her mother had made them for dinner. How their freezer had been packed with Stouffer's potpies and Swanson TV dinners and Van de Kamp's fish sticks.

Evie pulled the pie from the oven, let it cool a bit, and then devoured it directly from the baking tin. After that, she began to sort the papers she'd accumulated. Piece by piece, she fell quickly into a rhythm, separating bills and statements into categories, setting aside the occasional personally addressed envelope, and discarding junk mail and advertising circulars. She'd done this kind of thing countless times when the Historical Society acquired paper archives, separating the wheat from the chaff.

When she had everything categorized and sorted by date, she stopped to assess. REMINDER. PAST DUE. OVERDUE. The words were in bold on envelope after envelope. Water, gas, electricity, heating oil bills: all were at least two months overdue.

And yet there were also envelopes with checks. Social Security. Fireman's pension. In all, the uncashed checks added up to about fifteen thousand dollars, plenty to pay off unpaid bills.

Evie opened her mother's latest bank statements. There was only five hundred in checking; a little over four thousand in savings.

There'd been no activity in either account since mid-March. No deposits. No withdrawals. No nothing.

She was afraid to open the latest credit card bill. But when she did, she found a zero balance due. Zero! She opened the three earlier statements. Her mother hadn't even used the credit card in March, when the overdue balance had been more than eight thousand dollars with finance charges accruing to the tune of hundreds of dollars a month. In April that balance had been paid off in full.

How had her mother paid the bill? Evie went back to the bank statements but found no checks corresponding to the payment. And how on earth was her mother managing to keep herself stocked with vodka and cigarettes, never mind cat food for strays, if she wasn't withdrawing money or using her credit card?

The only mail left to be sorted was about a dozen pieces that looked personal. There was the birthday card Evie had sent, unopened. Two more of the envelopes also looked like greeting cards. One turned out to be happy birthday from her mother's dentist; another birthday card was from "Frank." Of course, the neighbor who'd come over and introduced himself that morning. She put all three cards on the mantel.

Finally, there were five identical brown envelopes, each with her mother's name and address handwritten on the front. She picked up one of them. It was thick, as if a sheaf of papers was folded inside. The flap wasn't sealed. Evie lifted it and looked inside. She pulled out a bundle wrapped in a sheet of white paper. She opened it up to find a stack of hundred-dollar bills.

What on earth? Evie started to count them. When she got to twelve, the doorbell rang.

Chapter
Eighteen

Startled, Evie dropped the envelope. Cash scattered across the linoleum floor. As she scrambled to pick up the hundred-dollar bills and stuff them back into the envelope, there was a rap at the door and a voice. "Hey, Evie. It's Finn."

"Hang on. I'm coming," she called as she cast about for somewhere to stash the cash-filled envelopes. She stuck them in the refrigerator's veggie bin. Then she went to answer the door.

Finn stood at the foot of the front steps. "Hope it's okay I came by this late. I saw you were up."

He *saw* she was up? Then she realized that anyone on the street side could have seen in. She'd left the kitchen curtains open.

"It's supposed to rain tomorrow," Finn said, apparently unruffled by Evie's silence. "So I brought you this." He pushed forward a panel of plywood. "For the window. And you left this in the store." He held out a six-pack of beer, raised his eyebrows, and gave her a tentative smile.

Nice gambit. Evie hadn't seen this guy in, what, decades? She *felt* safe with him, but she knew better than to go on instinct alone.

He must have sensed her reticence, because he set the beer on a step. "Listen, never mind. I'll just . . ." He propped the plywood panel against the front of the house, held up his hands, and backed away.

How dangerous could a mudflat-hugging birdwatcher be? Besides, she needed to take a break. Her shoulders ached and she was bleary-eyed. A cold beer was exactly what she needed, almost as much as she needed someone to talk to.

"Come on," she said, stepping aside so he could come in.

He cantered up the steps, scooping up the beer, then stopped just shy of the threshold. "You're sure?"

Evie felt herself drawn into his smile. She took the six-pack from him. He had strong-looking hands. No ring. A thick braid made of black silk or maybe hair was tied around his wrist. As she looked down at the bottles, slippery with condensation, she could feel him watching her.

"Okay, so you didn't leave the beer at the store." He poked a sneakered toe against her foot. "I wouldn't want to start with a lie."

Start?

"You know, I used to have the worst crush on you."

Even though she knew she was being played, Evie felt herself blush. She turned and walked through to the kitchen and set the beer on the counter.

"Listen," he said, following her, "I thought—" He stopped, staring at the piles of papers on the kitchen table. "Whoa." Then he took in the disarray of the two rooms beyond. "I had no idea it had gotten this bad. No idea at all. "

"Believe it or not, it's a lot better than it was. And I'm done for now. I need to take a break."

"How's your mom?" He gave her a searching look.

Evie started to say *fine,* but all that came out was a hoarse croak. She turned away, tears pricking at her eyes. "I talk to the doctor tomorrow. I'm not expecting good news."

"I'm sorry." He gave her a long look. "Listen, never mind. Obviously this is a bad time. I'll come back another—"

"No, no. It's okay. I don't mind the company. Please, stay."

"Really?"

"Really."

"Well. Okay then." He clapped his hands together. "I'll get started on that window."

"You want to fix it now?"

"No time like the present, as my dad used to say. Your mother's got a ladder in the garage, and I brought my own tools." He unhooked a hammer from his belt and dug a handful of nails from his pants pocket. "Be prepared. Dad used to say that, too, but I don't think these are what he meant."

Finn plugged in an extension cord and rigged an outside light so he could see what he was doing, and an hour and a half later, the upstairs window was securely boarded over with a sheet of plywood and Georgia O'Keeffe was back on the bedroom wall, no worse for the wear. On top of that, he promised to come back and replace the front steps, and he said he knew a local plumber he could call who would come and take care of the leak under the house.

"That would be wonderful," Evie said, feeling ridiculously grateful. "Thank you. Thank you so much."

"My pleasure," he said, holding her gaze for a few moments. He really wasn't bad looking. Not bad looking at all.

Evie got out two beers, opened them, and handed him one. It was a brand she'd never seen before, Bronx Brewery, its label a black-and-white image of the back of a subway car. She saw him eyeing the counter where she'd left the business card that Frank from across the street had left.

"What was he doing here?" he said.

"Asking about my mother. Apparently they were friends."

"Friends." Finn seemed to consider that for a moment before he shrugged and turned his attention to the refrigerator. "Your dad was a firefighter?" He pointed to her father's official firehouse photo that her mother had stuck on the door. "How could I have forgotten that?"

The picture showed her father's big smile, crinkly eyes, and bushy mustache. He had on black turnout gear, the jacket collar pulled up framing his face, a white 3 over the visor of his battered black helmet. He used to let her wear that helmet for dress-up, and whenever she'd put it on, she'd been surrounded immediately by the smell of sweat and smoke. She wondered what had happened to it, whether it was still in the house somewhere.

"Rescue 3?" Finn said. "That's up in Tremont, isn't it?"

Evie nodded, surprised. That wasn't something most people could come up with.

"I remember him pretty well, actually. Looks like he was about my age in that picture. Nice guy."

"Yeah. He sure was." Evie took another swallow of beer, sideswiped by the sadness that welled up in her.

"He used to come to the store every Sunday morning for doughnuts."

"I remember. Best doughnuts ever." It had been years since Evie had eaten a doughnut that came even close to the decadence of the jelly doughnuts of her childhood.

Finn grinned. "The very best. They're from a little mom-and-pop shop. They keep trying to retire, but they still make them for us. Your dad's still a firefighter?"

"Died in '02."

"I'm sorry. I didn't know. I was away." He took a step closer to her. She could smell the tang of his perspiration. "Was he one of the first responders on Nine-Eleven?"

She shook her head. "He retired a year before."

Her dad had died a year nearly to the day after that awful morning when eight of his best buddies boarded the rescue truck and never came back. He'd never gotten over the fact that they'd all perished and he wasn't with them.

Finn didn't say anything, and Evie appreciated that he didn't feel like he had to rush in and fill the silence. "So where were you?" she asked, after a moment.

"In class. Third row." He closed his eyes, like he was visualizing. "Second seat. Civil Procedure. Required class, and they tortured us by scheduling it at eight in the morning."

"You went to law school?" Evie hadn't meant it to come out sounding quite so incredulous.

"Columbia Law, class of '04. Michael Finneas Ryan, J.D., at your service." He took a little bow. "Another lifetime. Different things mattered to me back then." He stared out into space. "I remember that day like it was yesterday. We could see the smoke all the way from the fifth-floor classroom window up at 116th Street." He sighed and shook his head. "A group of us trooped over to St. Luke's, right from class, and tried to give blood."

Evie and her friends had gone to St. Vincent's Hospital in the Village. They'd been turned away.

"What about you?" he asked.

"In the dorm at NYU." Her mother's phone call had woken her up. She almost hadn't answered because she hadn't wanted her mother to know she was skipping her nine o'clock class.

Are you all right? Then, *Turn on the TV.*

Later, Evie had wandered out into the acrid haze, through drifts of paper that turned lower Manhattan into a perverted snow globe.

Finn took a long pull on the beer, and wiped his mouth with the back of his hand. "Listen," he said, "was I kind of arrogant when you first came into the store? I tend to be a bit judgmental." He tilted his head and smiled. "My ex-girlfriend called it something else."

"I didn't notice," Evie said. She had noticed, though, Finn's casual drop of the "ex-girlfriend."

"Ha, ha. Like hell you didn't. I thought maybe that's why you were so . . . quiet when you came in again."

Arrogant and judgmental sure, but also perceptive. "No. Sorry. It had nothing to do with you." She straightened her father's picture under the refrigerator magnet. "So, tell me about Soundview Lagoons."

"You really want to hear? Or are you changing the subject?"

"Yes."

He laughed. "Soundview Lagoons. Well, they are pretty amazing. At low tide, they're transformed into seven acres of mudflat, home to great blue herons, great egrets, blue and fiddler crabs, eastern mud snails, blue-finger mud and hermit crabs, and the ribbed mussel. And it's no joke what's happening around here. Most people could give a rat's ass whether the eel grass comes back. They couldn't care less about what happens to salt-marsh sharp-tailed sparrows and clapper rails."

"I confess, I don't know a sparrow from a clapper rail."

"A clapper rail is the size of a chicken. Long orange bill. Whitish rump. It's all about whether you decide you're going to pay attention."

Evie did a double take. That was something she'd often said herself, that preserving history was about deciding to pay attention.

"I've seen old postcards of Higgs Point," she said. "There was a ferry landing, beaches, a casino, all of them long gone. Wasn't there an amusement park, too?"

"Snakapins Park. My family owned it."

"Snakapins?"

"It's an Algonquin word. Means 'land between two waters.'"

Evie smiled. Leave it to the Algonquin—or the Siwanoy if she remembered her history of the boroughs correctly—to come up with such an evocative name for the place that white men named the far more pedestrian Higgs Point. "And your . . . grandfather borrowed the word for his amusement park?"

"Great-grandfather. His parents used to come over from Queens and camp out by the water. Hard to believe, looking at it now. Anyway, he loved it so much that he bought up what was mostly farmland and swamp. Built the amusement park. The store used to be one of the main buildings. You wouldn't believe the old crap that's still in the basement."

Evie's heart skipped a beat. "Old crap?"

He grinned. "You like old crap?"

"Of course. It's what I do. I'm a curator at the Five-Boroughs Historical Society."

"Really?" He tilted his head and narrowed his eyes at her. "I didn't know that."

Evie felt herself flush. "You never asked."

"My ex-girlfriend accused me of that, too. I'm sorry."

"Apology accepted. So tell me about what's in the basement of the store?"

"All kinds of stuff. It's been moldering down there since the place closed down in the twenties. There's even parts from some of the old rides. Junk, really."

Junk? That depended entirely on who was looking at it. Evie opened her mouth to explain about her job, and that preserving pieces from the past was something she cared passionately about. But instead, all that came out was a huge yawn.

Finn laughed, reached out for her hand, and pulled her to her feet.

He was so close she could smell beer and sawdust and maybe a whiff of turpentine. He put his hands around her waist.

Too fast. The thought was like an alarm going off in her head. But before she could react, he'd released her.

"You need sleep," he said. He walked his empty beer bottle to the kitchen sink, reached across, and tugged the curtains closed.

Evie followed, unsteady on her feet. Even a single beer made her tipsy?

"Thanks. For everything," she said.

"No big deal. I won't forget about the front steps and the leak. Anything else you need?"

"Actually, there is something. That old gas pump outside the store? It doesn't still pump gas by any chance?"

"The EPA would have my head on a platter if it did. Do you need gas?"

"My mother's car won't start, and I'm hoping it's only out of gas."

"I've got a can of gas in the back of my truck. Enough to get you to a service station, anyway. I'll bring it over tomorrow. Around ten? After our morning rush."

"That's perfect. Thanks. I'll be here."

"It's okay if you're not. I've got a key to the garage." Evie's surprise must have shown on her face because he added, "Your mother has us leave deliveries there."

"Really?" She wondered if her mother's deliveries had included cases of cigarette cartons. She could understand her mother not wanting them deposited at her front door.

"Well," he said, taking a step closer. She could feel his body heat. "Guess I better go."

"Thanks for the beer."

"Thanks for the company." He put his finger under her chin and raised her face to his. Her heart felt like it was pounding a mile a minute, but before she could decide whether she wanted to kiss him or not, he kissed her on the nose and headed for the door.

"Don't forget to lock up," he shot over his shoulder. "Sleep tight. See you in the morning."

The instant he was gone, she realized that she did want to kiss him. Wanted to be kissed. But she was also desperately tired and glad he'd known not to press his advantage.

Evie cleared a space in the living room for a twin mattress she dragged down from the upstairs bedroom. The sheets already on it were clean, despite the squirrels. She'd meant to call Ginger and tell her about the envelopes of cash, but it was much too late. Tomorrow. First thing.

She got the money out of the refrigerator and slid it under the mattress, then changed into an oversize T-shirt, brushed her teeth, and got into bed. Before she closed her eyes she took a minute to contemplate the mess that still surrounded her. Why had her mother even bothered to drag in broken aluminum lawn chairs? Had it been drunken inspiration? And had she done that before or after she got the flat-screen TV?

Evie rubbed her nose. She could still feel Finn's lips. Five minutes later, she was sound asleep.

Chapter
Nineteen

The sound track of Mina's dreams that night was the roar of heavy equipment. She saw herself standing helplessly across the street as a wrecking ball slammed, over and over, into the front of her house. She could hear poor Ivory meowing and see a skeletal Angela Quintanilla rapping at the front window, both of them trapped inside.

She woke up, drenched in sweat, to find that Ivory really was mewing and rattling the closed bedroom door. This was Ivory's morning routine, sticking her paw under the door and trying to pull it open. Mina had done everything she could think of to discourage her. Quiet would reign again only after the cat had been fed.

Mina tried to sit up, but she felt like a cement block was resting on her chest. Her heart pounded, and the acrid smell of diesel filled her head. What finally got her up was the cat. Not mews but silence. Like a quiet toddler, that was never a good sign.

Sure enough, when she got out to the kitchen, Ivory was perched on the counter, licking a puddle of liquid that had dripped off the package of chicken parts that Mina had left to thaw on the shelf and forgotten all about. Before Mina could stop her, Ivory sat back on her haunches, tail twitching, and leaped for the shelf, catching the edge of the plate, which came down with a crash.

"Bad cat!" Mina scooped Ivory off the counter and dropped her with a thud on the floor. Ivory gave her a sour look and a reproachful *meow*.

Mina had put the chicken into the refrigerator and was sweeping up the broken plate when she noticed it was nearly eight o'clock. She hadn't slept that late in years. No wonder the cat had been frantic with hunger. As if sensing her advantage, Ivory started to complain again.

"All right, all right already," Mina said. She opened a can of Fancy Feast tuna and mackerel, even though she hated the smell. That was Ivory's favorite.

Mina's breakfast would be her usual instant oatmeal with raisins and a splash of maple syrup and skim milk. She turned on the kettle to start the water, still puzzling over what could have happened to those papers she knew she'd hidden under the seat cushion of the couch. *Well, they didn't just sprout legs and walk.* That's what her mother would have said.

That girl, Evie, could have taken them. But why would she? More likely it was Brian, thinking he'd be so very clever. He could easily have tucked those papers under his jacket. Which would mean that he was onto her little charade. Perhaps it was just as well. *No* would still have been her answer even after slogging through that document and looking up every unfamiliar term.

She opened a kitchen cabinet, reaching for where she always kept the oatmeal. Only it wasn't there. She stared at the empty spot. She'd made oatmeal yesterday morning, and the box still had four or five packets left in it. Had Brian walked off with that, too?

Mina hauled over her step stool and got up on the second step for a better look. There was Raisin Bran cereal that probably needed to be thrown out. Gingersnaps. Minute Rice. Egg noodles. Crackers dotted with sesame seeds instead of the salt that she'd have much preferred but that the doctor told her to avoid. Though why, at this point in her life, did it really matter what she ate?

She pulled everything down, setting the packages on the counter, until the cabinet was completely empty. No oatmeal.

Sighing, she poured some Raisin Bran into a bowl and opened the refrigerator. There, right next to her half gallon of skim milk and the thawed chicken parts she'd just put away, sat the oatmeal.

That didn't bother her so much. Many's the time she'd put ice cream away in the refrigerator, only to find it melted to soup the next morning. What shook her to her core was that, sitting on the refrigerator shelf on the other side of the skim milk, was her pocketbook.

She reached in and touched the hard, cold vinyl, just to convince herself that it was really there. Then she took her purse from the refrigerator and looked around, as if someone might be in the kitchen watching her.

What could she have been thinking? Clearly, she hadn't been thinking at all. If Brian could have seen her now, he'd have had a field day.

She was about to remove the oatmeal, too, when an infernal screeching sound startled her. Instinctively, her hands flew up to cover her ears.

Of course she knew that sound. Her smoke alarm. She spun around to see plumes of smoke billowing from her teakettle. She grabbed for a dish towel, reached for the kettle, and flung it into the sink. Then she turned on the water, full blast.

She jumped back as steam hissed and spat. The air was thick with scorched-metal smell, and the alarm seemed to blare even louder.

Mina turned the water off, switched on the fan over the stove, opened the kitchen windows, and stood there, holding on to the counter, her heart pounding so hard it threatened to burst from her chest. As she gulped in fresh air, the speckled gray and white of the Formica countertop seemed to swirl before her eyes.

She peered into the sink. The kettle lay there on its side, a black char covering the bottom and running halfway up the sides. A scorched hole was burned into the dishcloth. For some reason, the whistle—that infernal whistle that had been her reason for buying that particular teapot in the first place—had not gone off. Or if it had, she hadn't heard it, and how could she have missed that?

Or . . . She poked at the kettle, turning it over. The whistle, that little gizmo that reminded her of miniature organ pipes on the end of the spout, was gone. She didn't even know that it came off, and yet somehow it had.

Finally, the smoke alarm stopped. Mina sat down. An incinerated teakettle she could rationalize. It could happen to anyone, and after all, she'd been distracted. But coming right on top of leaving her handbag . . . *in the refrigerator*? That went beyond misplacing and uncomfortably a few steps beyond what her doctor referred to, in that patronizing tone that fortysomething doctors used to address their elderly patients, as "benign senescent forgetfulness." There was nothing benign about senescence.

Mina stood, straightening her bathrobe and tucking her hair behind her ears. She'd be damned if she'd let herself be swallowed up by self-pity. All she had to do was put things back in order. She took a deep breath. And then keep them that way.

She placed a quilted placemat on her kitchen counter and set her purse on it. From now on, she promised herself, that was where she'd leave it. Then she lined up everything she'd taken down from the cabinet, sorting the packages—cereal, cookies, crackers, grains, and beans—and checking the expiration dates before placing them back in the cupboard.

While she was at it, she reorganized her canned goods in the adjacent cabinet, wiping tops that had become dusty and tossing anything past its use-by date. Then she double-checked the shelves in the refrigerator to be sure that everything that was there belonged.

Later, after eating the stale bran cereal, she boiled herself a cup of water in the microwave, dropped in a tea bag, and carried the cup and the morning paper out onto the back porch. There, she settled into the glider and opened to the obituaries, determined to start the day afresh.

Chapter
Twenty

Cocooned in blankets on the mattress she'd dragged down from upstairs, Evie woke up thinking: *jelly doughnut, jelly doughnut, jelly doughnut.* She'd completely forgotten about those doughnuts, and how her dad used to make what he called his "doughnut run" on Sunday mornings. Coated with velvety powdered sugar, the light cakey doughnut left not a trace of the usual greasy film that said "store-bought." Sparkles' doughnuts had been literally jam-packed, front to back, so every bite risked spurting some of the filling out the other end—filling that was in a league of its own, too, thick and tangy and intensely raspberry. Not that pallid, sugary-sweet, gelatinous stuff that doughnuts were filled with these days.

Could the doughnuts Finn said they still sold be anywhere near as good as the ones she remembered? It was worth a trip to find out.

Evie rolled off the mattress onto the living room floor. She ached from all the lifting and bending she'd done the day before. Still wrapped in a quilt, she made her way to the bathroom. After washing her hands, she opened the medicine cabinet looking for toothpaste. No toothpaste, but the medicine cabinet was stocked: Nyquil, Excedrin, a few bottles of bright red nail polish and nail polish remover. Plus numerous bottles of various shapes and sizes, all with pale-green NaturaPharm labels. Vitamin A. Thiamin B_1. Riboflavin B_2. Niacin B_3. Vitamin C. Calcium. And more. It was an impressive collection.

Evie found a tube of Crest in the drawer. As she brushed her teeth, she wondered when her mother had started taking vitamins. Even more surprisingly, given the complete disarray of the rest of the house, she'd kept them lined them up in her medicine cabinet in alphabetical order.

Evie didn't bother changing out of the plaid flannel pajama bottoms and NYU sweatshirt she'd slept in, though she did take a moment to brush her hair into a ponytail and wash her face, checking that she didn't have flecks of sleep still in her eyes. She was about to leave when she paused. If Finn saw her sorting the mail in the house, anyone could have. She went back inside, took the envelopes of cash from under the mattress, stuffed them into her purse, and took her purse with her.

As she locked the front door, she remembered how her parents and all their neighbors used to leave their doors unlocked. It didn't really surprise her that her mother had given a garage key to Finn. That way, she wouldn't need to worry about being there when the deliveries arrived; more to the point, she wouldn't have had to worry about being sober or even awake.

Evie was out on the sidewalk before she realized that the steps hadn't creaked. She went back to inspect them. New planks were already in place. Finn must have come over at the crack of dawn to do the work.

Evie started for Sparkles at a brisk clip. The morning was chilly, but with each stride away from the water the air grew warmer, and she slowed her pace. She checked her phone on the off chance that she'd missed any calls. Nothing from the hospital. Nothing from Seth. She was as relieved by the latter as by the former.

She'd been surprised that Finn had known instantly where her father's fire station, Rescue 3, was located. She hoped he wasn't one of those fire freaks—sparkies, her dad used to call them—men who chased the apparatus and were so obsessed with the spectacle that they didn't have the good sense to get out of the way. When Evie's parents' house had burned, a group of them had come to watch, eager to add the Ferrantes' address to the list of fires they'd witnessed first-hand. Meanwhile their mother tried to comfort Evie and Ginger, who were crying hysterically, knowing the dogs were still in the house.

That day, news vans and police vehicles had parked at Sparkles. Now the half-dozen parking spaces outside the store were filled. She went inside, taking a deep inhale of rich coffee aroma. Two checkout lines were operating to handle the morning crush. She got in Finn's line. She caught his eye and mouthed *Thank you!* He flashed her a thumbs-up.

As Evie waited her turn at the register, from outside she heard the polite *toot-toot* of a car horn. Through the plate-glass window she caught a glimpse of the outside parking area. A dark Mercedes was pulling out. A moment later, a Land Rover pulled in.

Land Rover? Mercedes? That made her take a second look at the other people in line. They were more racially mixed, and some were speaking Spanish, but otherwise they were not all that different from the clientele who lined up at Dunkin' Donuts in her quickly gentrifying Brooklyn neighborhood.

Finally she was at the front of the line. But by then only a few plain cake, chocolate iced, and glazed doughnuts remained in the glass case. No jelly. It was ridiculous how disappointed she felt.

"I saved you one," Finn said, reaching under the counter and bringing out a little paper plate holding a single perfect powdered-sugar-covered jelly doughnut.

Chapter
Twenty-one

It was an exceptionally clear morning. Mina buttoned her sweater and folded her arms against the chill as she rocked on her back porch. The sun was already high in the sky, making the water sparkle, and the Manhattan skyline was in sharp focus. Mina picked out the Chrysler Building and the Empire State Building, both still distinctive amid the surrounding welter of box-top skyscrapers.

The girl had wanted to talk to her about what it had been like working at the Empire State. Did she remember? she'd asked. How could Mina not? Steadying herself with her cane, she stood and stepped to the porch railing. Every day she looked out at that building and was reminded. Maybe talking about it would be a good thing.

A loud *smack* startled her as something solid caromed off the porch column, inches from her head. Far too late, Mina cried out and ducked. With a gentle *whoosh* the missile landed in the marsh grass beyond her narrow strip of neatly mowed lawn.

Idiotic. Pea-brained. Had to be that man from across the street using the narrow strip between her house and the one next door as his own private driving range. Had he been at it all morning?

Mina took cover at the edge of the house, imagining him teeing up another ball, lining up his shot, swinging . . . Nothing. She waited a few moments more before stepping to the side of the porch and daring a glance back between the houses. There was no one there. Frank Cutler and his trusty nine-iron must have beaten a hasty retreat when he heard her cry out.

She had a good mind to march over there and confront him. But she knew what he'd say. Golf ball? What golf ball? Then he'd shake his head at her delusional, overactive imagination.

He could scoff at her all he wanted, but she knew what she knew. And now—she gazed speculatively out to where clumps of marsh grass that had been planted by city workers two years ago along the shoreline were now filling in nicely—she'd have proof. This time, if she wasn't mistaken, the ball had landed just a few feet in.

She looked down at her feet. She had on bedroom slippers. What she needed were boots. Rubber boots. Like the tall fishing boots that her father used to wear back when you could cast your net into the river and pull out healthy, foot-long herring.

Mina found her father's old boots, dust covered but intact, in the back of the hall closet behind the set of matching luggage that she'd used only once when she and Henry went to Niagara Falls. She pulled them on over her slippers. The boots came up over her knees, and even with the slippers they were too big, but they'd do the job. She tucked her pant legs into them. This time, Frank "Sam Snead" Cutler was not going to get away with it.

Cane in hand, Mina clomped back outside and down off the porch to the edge of the marsh. There she paused for a moment, closed her eyes, and replayed the sound of the ball landing. Envisioned the spot. Then she opened her eyes, took a breath. She waded into the tall grass at the edge of the marsh, poking her cane ahead of her as she went.

It was high tide, and the muddy water quickly closed over the tops of her feet. Each time she took a step her boot came out of the muck with a sucking sound. When she reached the spot, she used the cane for balance as she nudged apart the reeds.

There was an empty beer can. A little farther on, a plastic grocery bag. She tucked the can into the bag and tossed them onto her lawn.

A few more steps in, she was over her ankles in mud. The ball had probably sunk beneath the surface, too. If only she'd thought to pull on a pair of rubber gloves, but it was too late for that now. Reluctantly she pushed up her sweater sleeve, bent over, and began rooting around, feeling through the nasty root-clogged slime for something solid. She tried not to inhale the sulfurous marsh gas that wafted up as she disturbed the mud.

She found snails, stones, bits of shell. She was about to give up when she felt something hard and round. Triumphant, she dug it out. A golf ball!

She straightened, swiping aside tendrils of hair with the back of her arm, rage beating in her chest. What did he think, that a golf ball was going to dissolve like a lump of sugar in a cup of hot tea? It would be there for decades, centuries even, assuming it didn't end up down the gullet of one of the majestic great blue herons that were returning to the marsh in record numbers.

With each step out of the marsh, it felt as if the mud were trying to pull those old boots off her feet. Finally she was back on the grass. Speechless with fury, she marched around her house and stood on her front lawn, leaning on her cane and shaking her fist at the house across the street. He was probably inside, behind drawn shades, laughing at her.

Mina crossed the street and up her blasted neighbor's front walk, trailing wet footprints up those fancy granite steps he'd installed, each one bigger than a tombstone. She marched across the narrow porch he'd slapped on the front and up to that fancy walnut door with its stained-glass insets on either side. The doorbell was the old twist kind but in shiny, brand-new brass. Ridiculous. She turned it. Heard chimes ringing—the opening notes of "Goodnight Irene."

No answer. No footsteps. No sounds at all from inside the house. She raised her cane and rapped it against the door. He had to be in there. It couldn't have been more than fifteen minutes ago that he'd driven that ball.

Mina gave an anxious look behind her. No one was watching. She reached for the doorknob, turned it, and pushed. To her amazement, the door opened.

Chapter
Twenty-two

Mina had just started to peer into Frank Cutler's house when a light in the darkened front hall started flashing and a blaring Klaxon nearly blew her off the steps. She fought her first impulse, which was to scramble off the porch and race home. But scrambling and racing had long ago dropped out of her repertoire, and besides, it was too late for any of that. Two neighbors had come out and were looking on, and a dark car with a bubble light going in its windshield was already tearing up the street toward her.

She covered her ears to muffle the blaring alarm and waited. The sedan pulled over in front of the house. A man in a dark uniform got out. Well over six feet tall and whippet slender, his skin a rich reddish-brown, he reached back through his car window for a cap and set it on his head.

"Ma'am," he said, touching the visor of his cap. Above it was stuck a silver badge.

That's when Mina realized he was eyeing her less than respectfully. Not disrespectfully, really. More like he was looking at a suspicious package. His gaze lingered on her feet, those oversize rubber boots coated in mud.

Mina straightened and cleared her throat. Before she could explain what her neighbor had been up to, and how this time she had the evidence to prove it, he tilted his head and *tsk-tsked.* "We have to stop meeting like this, Miss Mina."

Miss Mina? She wasn't about to play Driving Miss damned Daisy to his Uncle Tom. "Excuse me, but do I know you?"

"Breaking in. Again?" He reached for her arm.

Mina didn't like that. Not one little bit. She backed away. "Don't you lay a hand on me. I was not trying to break in. That man . . . he was—" She held up the ball and realized she had an opera-length coating of mud up her arm. She switched hands and held out the ball. "I found this in the salt marsh. It's a protected area, isn't it?"

But the officer was looking past her. She turned to follow his gaze. Racing—much too fast, if you asked her—up the street toward them was a red sports car like the one that belonged to Frank Cutler. As it got closer, she could see the man himself, sitting right there at the wheel.

Another car pulled to a stop behind him. Brian's. She might not have recognized the gray car as a Mercedes, but the '60s peace sign in the front grill had always struck her as a hilarious irony.

"You'd better come with me." The officer grabbed for her arm again.

"I'll do no such thing." She wrenched away.

Frank Cutler got out and charged over to the house and up onto the porch. "What in the hell is going on?" he demanded.

Brian got out, too, and stood on the sidewalk, gazing up at her from beneath the red brim of a blue baseball cap. "What on earth is she up to now?" He put his hands on his hips, like he was the grown-up in the room.

"Everything's under control," the officer said. "Caught her trying to break in—"

"Again? You stay off my property," Frank Cutler said, taking a menacing step toward Mina. They were like cartoon characters, all of them, and Mina almost expected a blast of steam to erupt from the top of Frank Cutler's head.

"Well?" the officer said to Mina.

"I . . . He . . . It's not . . ." Mina took a deep breath and tried to gather herself. "I was not trying to break in."

"So you're *not* responsible for setting off my alarm?" Frank Cutler said.

"I am. I guess. But it wasn't my fault. I—"

"For the third time, it's not your fault?"

Third time? What on God's green earth was he talking about?

"You've been warned and warned again," the officer said. He reached into his pocket and removed a pair of handcuffs.

That frightened her. "Put those fool things away. Brian? For heaven's sake, say something."

But Brian stood there staring at the ground like he was examining the roots his feet had grown. Frank Cutler's jaw was clamped in a grim, satisfied smile. And the man in uniform advanced. When he grabbed her arm, Mina's cane went flying.

Mina couldn't think what else to do, so she screamed.

Chapter
Twenty-three

Saving her a jelly doughnut had been a small thing, silly really, and yet so incredibly sweet, Evie thought as she walked back to her mother's house licking the last of the raspberry jam from between her fingers. She only wished Finn had set aside two. She smiled, remembering that crullers were Ginger's passion, and Finn hadn't set aside a single one of those. That reminded her that she needed to call Ginger and tell her about the money she'd found.

She was almost back to the house when she heard a woman scream. She turned the corner to find cars blocking the street. A dark sedan with a blue light flashing in the windshield was parked in front of Mrs. Yetner's house; behind it was Frank Cutler's red sports car, and behind that was a dark Mercedes. Frank Cutler was up on his front porch. So was Mrs. Yetner. Another man, wearing a dark uniform, was up on the porch, too. A cop? Mrs. Yetner's nephew Brian tipped back his red-brimmed baseball cap and looked on from the sidewalk.

As Evie watched, the uniform stepped between Frank and Mrs.

Yetner. He put his arm around Mrs. Yetner and tried to herd her off the porch. Mrs. Yetner looked bewildered. Then angry. "Take your hands off me," she said. "What do you think you're doing?"

But the officer kept right on pushing, practically lifting the poor woman off her feet. Tendrils of white hair were flying loose from what was usually a neat bun at the nape of Mrs. Yetner's neck, and her glasses were askew. Her nephew obviously wasn't going to help her out. He stood there in stony silence.

"Stop!" Evie cried.

The officer must have let go, because Mrs. Yetner collapsed like a marionette on the steps of Mr. Cutler's house. Evie dropped her coffee and charged up the steps. She sat down and put her arms around Mrs. Yetner, shielding her from the men. Cold seeped off the stone steps through the flannel of her pajama bottoms and she could feel Mrs. Yetner's birdlike bones through her thick sweater.

"Ridiculous . . . pea-brained . . . ticket-writing nitwit." Mrs. Yetner sputtered the words, hand to her chest as she panted for breath. "Trying to put me away."

That's when Evie noticed that one of the old woman's hands was coated in mud and she had on knee-high black rubber boots pulled on over her pant legs. The boots were coated with fresh mud, too, well up over the ankles.

"Honestly, Miss Mina," the uniformed man said, the brim of his hat pulled low over his forehead. "No one's trying to put you away." He rolled his eyes at Evie and tapped a finger to the side of his head.

"Fiddlesticks." Mrs. Yetner straightened her glasses and gave him a steely look. "I'm not your *Miss Mina*. And I'm not nuts."

"Of course she's not," Evie said, shading her eyes to get a better look at the man. A yellow shield-shaped patch was sewn to the shoulder of his dark gray zippered jacket. A silvery badge was pinned over the brim of his cap. She could make out the word SECURITY.

"Sorry, ma'am," he said to Mrs. Yetner, though from his tone it was clear that he didn't mean it, "but three times in the last month?" He shook his head. "Or has it been four?"

Mrs. Yetner didn't answer. She looked frightened.

"You know it's against the law, breaking and entering," the officer added.

Evie felt Mrs. Yetner stiffen. She took a breath. "Now you listen to me. I was not breaking in. And I never entered. The door was open." Mrs. Yetner jabbed a finger in the direction of Frank. "He's the one you should arrest. He was hitting his golf balls. See?" She held out what looked like a muddy golf ball. "Into the salt marsh."

Frank guffawed—an ugly sound. "Please, would you give me a break. If that isn't the most absurd—"

"Absurd? Exactly. And dangerous, too," Mrs. Yetner said. "Not to mention that the marsh is a protected area. Isn't polluting against the law?"

"Polluting? For Chrissake, I wasn't even here. You saw me drive up," Frank shot back. "What's it going to take to get you to stop harassing me?"

The officer heaved a heavy sigh. "You can always press charges."

Frank glared at Mrs. Yetner. Then his look slid over to Evie and he wavered, the anger bleeding from his face. "I guess not. But she'd better keep off my property. I don't want to have to file a restraining order."

"Just you try," Mrs. Yetner said under her breath.

"Oh yeah? And you'll do what exactly?" Frank crossed his arms and scowled down at her. "I don't like being threatened."

"Neither"—Mrs. Yetner held his gaze, and as the seconds ticked by she seemed to grow calmer and calmer while he looked more and more like a balloon getting too much air blown into it—"do I."

He was the first to look away. "Stupid cow."

"Pardon me? What did you say?" Mrs. Yetner asked, calmer still. Frank gave her an uneasy look. "Nothing."

Mrs. Yetner took a deep breath. "All right then." She straightened her back and rose to her feet. Evie stood with her. "I'm going home now. I think I've made my point."

Evie retrieved Mrs. Yetner's cane from the grass and handed it to her. But Mrs. Yetner's first step was a stumble.

"Here," Evie said, taking her arm again, "let me help you." Evie could feel the men watching as she helped Mrs. Yetner cross the street.

Brian at least hurried over and took Mrs. Yetner's other arm. "Aunt Mina, doesn't this prove the point that I've been trying to make? You didn't even remember the other times this has happened. I can only imagine what other little mishaps you're covering up, or worse still, forgetting."

Mrs. Yetner's grip tightened on Evie's arm and she blanched. The scar down the side of her face and neck was livid.

As they continued across the street, Brian went on in a quiet voice that Evie could barely hear. "You may not like it, but it's time to start looking seriously at nursing—"

"I am not going into a nursing home," Mina spat back at him.

"Fine. Elderly housing then. Assisted living. Call it whatever you like. Some kind of residential setting where they can give you the help you need and not make you feel like you're being a bother."

That stopped Mrs. Yetner in her tracks. She stared at Brian, her mouth open.

Brian went on. "Look, I know you're not feebleminded. That's not what this is about. But let me call around and make some appointments so you can at least see what your options are. I'll try to set up some visits for tomorrow. Monday afternoon. All right?"

Mrs. Yetner sagged, and in a quiet voice, she said, "Oh, all right. If you must."

Chapter
Twenty-four

It wasn't until Mina was inside her house with the door firmly shut that she let go of Evie's arm. Feeling utterly defeated and trembling with humiliation, she sank down on a bench in the entryway and stared at the mud she'd tracked across the threshold. Mina could hear herself panting like she'd been running.

"Are you all right?" Evie asked.

"Of course I'm all right," Mina said. How could her own nephew talk to her that way? And in public?

Evie made a murmur of sympathy. What would have happened, Mina wondered, if the girl hadn't shown up? That man was going to handcuff her and haul her off to jail? And Brian, standing right there and not lifting a finger to help.

As if she couldn't take care of herself. She'd been taking care of herself for—

"Here, let me help you off with these." Evie squatted down in front of her.

"It's all right. I can do it." Mina bent over and strained to reach the boot. Tried to take a deep breath, but that made her back ache. She needed to slow down, to breathe, and get the pounding in her chest to ease.

Reluctantly she gave up, leaned back, and let Evie pick up one of her legs then the other, tugging off the tall rubber boots like her mother used to do when she was in first grade. Her feet came out bare. Mina reached into each boot and pulled out the bedroom slippers that were stuck inside. She dropped them on the floor and slid her feet into them.

Evie set the boots on the mat by the door. Then she went into the kitchen and came back with some paper towels. She wiped away the mud Mina had tracked into the entryway.

"Are they still out there?" Mina asked.

Evie stood and looked out through the window in the front door. "They're talking."

"Having a jolly postmortem on my behalf, no doubt."

After a long pause, Evie said, "They're leaving now."

When she heard the sound of a car engine catching, Mina felt the tension finally drain from her back. "I'm quite sure they think I'm a complete nitwit. Delusional. But this thing nearly hit me in the head." She set the golf ball on the hall table. "As if I could make up something like that."

Evie picked up the ball and examined it.

"He said it was"—Mina continued, lowering her voice though she knew no one but Evie could hear her—"the third time that I've set off that alarm."

"But it's not?" Evie offered Mina her cane.

"Could someone forget a thing like that?" Mina took the cane and stood. "With that alarm blaring? You tell me." She pushed away the supporting hand Evie offered. She'd be damned if she'd let herself be treated as an invalid.

She made her way to the bathroom where she washed the mud off her hands and arm. Afterward, she stared at her reflection in the mirror over the sink. The scar had turned bright pink. She ran her fingers along its rippled surface. Pink or not, it was completely numb. A blessing, really.

She moistened a washcloth and wiped away streaks of mud from her face. Then she turned her head so she could no longer see the scar.

When she'd turned forty, Mina's face had started to remind her of her mother's. But her mother hadn't made it past seventy. Now the person in the mirror was a complete stranger. The loose skin on her cheeks looked like antique vellum, foxed with age. Pouches sagged under her eyes. Deep lines were incised from the corners of her mouth to her chin. It was odd. Though she was physically transformed, she felt like exactly the same person she'd been when she was twelve.

She could take looking older. Feeling older, even. But losing her memory and her mind? Turning into a person that people talked about but never to? Mina swallowed a knot of fear in her throat and left the bathroom.

"You're the one who sold me on the therapeutic effects of a nice cup of tea," Evie said as Mina sank into her chair in the living room. "How about I fix one for you now? I know where everything is."

Mina sighed. Yes, a cup of hot tea would be lovely. Especially one that she didn't have to make herself. She was about to say so when she remembered the incinerated teakettle. She felt a new flush of humiliation creep up her neck.

"No, thank you, dear. You're kind to offer. But really I'm perfectly fine. Don't worry about me. You already have your hands full. Are you going back to the hospital today?"

Evie checked her watch. "Oh, shit." Her face colored. "I mean sheesh. How'd it get so late? The doctor's only there until noon, and I have to take the bus again unless Finn has put some gas in the tank."

"Well, you certainly don't want to miss the doctor." Mina pushed off the afghan and heaved herself to her feet. "Take my car keys. I'm not going anywhere, and in case you can't get your mother's car started, you'll have a backup."

"You sure?"

"Oh my, yes. I should have offered earlier. Besides, I haven't driven it in days and it's like an old dog that needs to be walked every once in a while. As soon as I find my purse—" Mina glanced around the living room. Where had she left it?

"I saw it. Hold on." Evie disappeared into the kitchen. She came back a moment later with Mina's handbag.

Of course. Now Mina remembered setting it carefully on the quilted placemat on the kitchen counter, determined not to lose it again. What on earth was the matter with her?

"Thank you so much," Evie said when Mina handed her the car keys. "This is so generous of you. You really are a peach." Evie started to go but turned back. "You sure you're okay? Is there anyone I should call to come stay with you?"

"Stay with me? *Pshaw.* If there's anything I know how to be, it's alone. You go. Hurry."

"Thank you."

As Evie started out through the dining room, Mina noticed for the first time that she had on loose red-and-blue-plaid flannel pants. Were those pajama bottoms?

"You're going out in those?" she asked.

Chapter
Twenty-five

You're going out in those? Mrs. Yetner's parting shot was a zinger—a gibe masquerading as an innocent question. Evie would have bristled had it come from her own mother. But she loved it coming from Mrs. Yetner. She gave her startled neighbor a quick hug and chuckled as she hurried back to her mother's house to shower and dress for the hospital.

When Evie pulled the shower curtain, two roaches ran down the drain. In the shower, she let hot water run hard, pounding her sore shoulders and neck. Was that man really going to arrest Mrs. Yetner? More likely he'd said that to rattle her. If that had been his intention, it worked.

Right after Evie had helped Mrs. Yetner off with her boots, she'd looked out and seen the officer and Frank Cutler talking, their heads bent. The man had acted like a police officer, but since when did police badges say SECURITY? Maybe he was a private security guard.

The golf ball was no figment of Mrs. Yetner's imagination. When Evie had picked it up and scraped dried mud off its dimpled surface, she could tell that it was no ancient relic, either. Still, it could have been lying in the marsh for months, and there was no way to tell whether Mr. Cutler had been the one who'd launched it.

Before Evie left for the hospital, she made sure all the windows were shut and set up roach bombs on the bathroom and kitchen floors. SUPER FOGGER, the label read. PRO GRADE. The bomb didn't just have a warning label. It had a warning booklet that peeled off the can: Hazards to humans and domestic animals. Environmental hazards. Danger of explosion. Leave the premises for at least four hours. Ventilate thoroughly before reentering.

The label almost talked her out of it until she noticed on the kitchen ceiling four translucent wormy creatures, which sadly she recognized as moth larvae. As she rushed out of the house, bombs activated, locking the door behind her, Finn was in the driveway raising her mother's garage door. He waved to her.

"Hey," she said, heading over to him.

"Everything okay?"

"We had a little excitement." She hadn't realized, but she was out of breath.

"I heard. Something about a golf ball." He shook his head and picked up a red square gallon gas can from the ground by his feet. The contents sloshed. "This should be enough to get you to a gas station. And the fix to your front steps is only temporary, but at least you won't kill yourself coming and going." He unscrewed the gas cap and inserted the can's long yellow spout into the opening.

As he started to pour, Evie smelled the pungent gasoline odor. She glanced at her watch. She had just enough time to stop for gas on her way to the hospital.

"There," he said, pulling out the spout. "Hop in and give it a whirl." He came around, pulled open the driver-side door, and gestured with a welcoming hand. Then he hesitated. "Hold on. Stay back." He crouched alongside the car. Unhooking a flashlight from his tool belt, he played the light under the car, around and behind the rear wheel.

"What?" Evie stepped closer. Then she smelled it. The odor of gasoline had gone from strong to overwhelming. She put her hand up over her face.

"Your mother's car didn't run out of gas." Finn stood and faced her, brushing his hands off on his pant legs. "Gas ran out of it."

Chapter
Twenty-six

Long after the girl had gone, Mina could feel Evie's strong arms around her and a faint fruity smell that Mina finally placed. Raspberry.

It had been a while since Mina had been properly hugged. Not since her sister. Mina sat at the kitchen table as memories flooded back. She and Annabelle, young, walking arm in arm to Sparkles. Annabelle supporting her in the shallows, helping her learn to float on her back. Buttoning the long row of tiny mother-of-pearl buttons on the back of Annabelle's wedding dress.

Their last embrace might have been one of the last times that Mina visited Annabelle in the nursing home, a few weeks before her sister slipped into a coma and was moved to the hospital where Mina had promised her she'd never end up.

Mina had arrived that day and found Annabelle parked in the corridor outside her room, hunched over a locked-in tray-table in what the nurses called a geri-chair. Asleep? Mina couldn't be sure.

Her sister's once lustrous auburn hair, now white and wispy, was neatly pulled back into a bun at her neck. Her eyeglasses were anchored with a band that went around her head. The blouse and pants Mina had bought for her a few weeks earlier were already swimming on her.

When she'd stepped closer, she heard Annabelle muttering. She had to stoop to make out the words. "Don't say that." A pause. "You already . . . had your chance." The words came out in short intense spurts, on puffs of breaths like Annabelle was trying to blow out a match. "You just be quiet."

"Hello, dear," Mina said, laying her hand gently on her sister's arm. She kissed the top of her head and breathed in shampoo scent. Even if the staff couldn't keep Annabelle from sliding into oblivion, at least the attention to hygiene was excellent.

Annabelle lifted her head and blinked, an unfocused look in her eyes, then coughed weakly. Mina could hear her labored breathing. Pneumonia and heart failure would eventually be the official cause of death.

Mina lifted her sister's hand and pressed it against her own cheek. "Hello, Annabelle."

Finally her sister's gaze connected with hers. "Hello, dearest," Annabelle said. The flicker of recognition was still there, thank God. That sweet smile. Then Annabelle raised her arms and gave Mina what she didn't know would be her last hug.

"Who were you talking to?" Mina had asked.

"Talking to talking to talking . . ." Annabelle gave a vague wave of the hand. Her once long, tapered fingers were knotted with arthritis, the way that Mina's were becoming. "Friends." Annabelle blinked twice, her gaze wandering until it anchored once again on Mina. "Imaginary friends."

"You know they're not real," Mina said.

"I know, I know." Annabelle put a finger to her lips, *shhh,* and added in a stage whisper. "But they don't."

Mina had laughed, and then stopped laughing because it was clear that Annabelle didn't get her own joke, and she wasn't about to start laughing *at* her sister. Not then. Not ever.

Later, after Annabelle was back in bed, Brian had arrived at the nursing home. "Hello, Mother," he'd said, standing in the doorway like a cigar store Indian.

"Hello, Gilbert," Annabelle had said. She raised her eyebrows in Brian's direction and asked Mina, "Is he imaginary, too?"

Fortunately Brian never heard that. He wouldn't have found the comment amusing, not the slightest bit.

He came over to the bed and kissed Annabelle's cheek.

Every once in a while, even then near the end, Annabelle had surprised Mina, as she did at that moment when her gaze sharpened. "Oh!" She pursed her lips, tilted her head, and narrowed her eyes. Then she licked her thumb and wiped his cheek. Annabelle never had been much of a doting mother, but she had liked her things spotless.

Brian had drawn back. "Mother, please."

The familiar sound of her car engine turning over brought Mina back to the present. Apparently Evie needed to borrow her car after all.

Mina remembered the chicken she'd thawed. Chicken cacciatore was a simple recipe. Chicken, chopped green and sweet red pepper, a can of Hunt's tomato sauce, plus an onion, which Mina left out. These days, onions of any kind gave her heartburn. She hoped the chicken, having been thawed and then refrigerated, wasn't going to kill her.

A short time later Mina had put together the ingredients. She set the lid on the pot and turned the burner low to simmer. She could leave it there for hours because she liked her chicken well cooked, to the point where the meat was falling off the bone. With rice and a green salad, she'd have dinner for at least four nights.

Before she sat down again with the paper, she pulled her calendar from the kitchen wall. Three baby burrowing owls were pictured for

May—not anything she was likely to see out her window. She wrote BRIAN in Monday's block. She could hardly forget the reason he was coming back.

Annabelle's had been a slow decline. In the early days, she'd felt her marbles slipping away. Then, even those were gone. If Mina hadn't been there, she'd have forgotten to eat. Forgotten to clean herself. Eventually she completely lost track of what she'd lost track of.

Mina was determined not to let her present slip away. In today's box in tiny printing she started a list.

1.   Burned teakettle
2.   Purse + oatmeal in icebox
3.   Lost legal papers
4.   Set off C's alarm

To the last item she added a question: *For the third time?*

Chapter
Twenty-seven

Evie had gratefully accepted Finn's offer to call a local mechanic, a buddy of his, he said, and get the car towed. Once it was up on a lift, Finn assured her, they'd find the leak and patch the tank. It shouldn't cost much at all.

Evie barely had to turn the key for Mrs. Yetner's Mustang to roar to life. She shifted into reverse, released the emergency brake, and backed out of the driveway. In seconds she was past Sparkles and on her way.

Like the house, Mrs. Yetner's car was in its own spotlessly clean time warp. Not even a corner of the faux wood laminate on the dash was curled or missing. But it wasn't perfect: the springs in the driver seat were shot, and Evie needed three of the four cushions Mrs. Yetner had piled on the deep bucket seat to see over the leather-clad steering wheel. She hand-cranked the window down and reached out to adjust the side mirror.

A tow truck passed her, going the opposite way. She wondered if it could be heading over to pick up her mother's car already. How long had it been, she wondered, since her mother had tried to drive it?

Evie was lucky that Mrs. Yetner had pressed her car keys on her.

What would have taken forty minutes by bus took ten, and still she was going to get to the hospital barely in time to catch the doctor. Halfway there it started to drizzle, and by the time she pulled into the parking lot, rain was coming down hard. She parked and ran into the building.

When she got to her mother's room, wet and out of breath from running, she found the curtain drawn around her mother's bed. From within, she heard voices. She backed out of the room and waited in the open doorway.

Finally the curtain drew back. A woman in a white lab coat turned around. Beyond her, Evie's mother lay propped up in bed, unblinking, staring off into space. Her skin was tinged yellow against the white linen.

"Dr. Foran?" Evie said.

"You must be Sandra's daughter." Dr. Foran offered her hand. Her nails were cut short, polished clear, and she wore a thin gold wedding band. She had a file folder tucked under her other arm.

"Evie Ferrante," Evie said, shaking the doctor's cool strong hand.

"I'm glad you're here." Dr. Foran's voice was low and her direct look unnerving. "Let's go somewhere we can talk."

Evie followed her down the hall, anchoring her gaze on the long dark ponytail that snaked down the back of the doctor's white lab coat.

Dr. Foran led Evie to a visitors' lounge and pulled up two chairs opposite each other in a corner. Evie sat in one. Dr. Foran sat in the other and leaned forward. She looked very young, no older than Evie. In the harsh artificial light, the dark circles under her eyes grew even darker.

"You know, of course, that your mother has late-stage liver disease."

Late stage. That was what Ginger had said. Evie's pulse pounded in her ears, and she wished Ginger were there.

"It's cirrhosis," Dr. Foran continued. "Her liver function is very compromised. The liver detoxifies the body, and your mother's is no longer doing its job. That's what's causing the fluid buildup in her abdomen. Her mood swings and agitation. Weight loss. Jaundice. Fatigue. Nausea."

Jaundice. Fatigue. Nausea. The words seemed to float in front of Evie. She opened her bag and found a little notebook and a pen. "I'm sorry, what did you say? I need to write this down."

As Dr. Foran repeated the symptoms, Evie copied them down. Dr. Foran added, "She shows signs of chronic malnutrition, that much is obvious. But her liver function tests turned up additional abnormalities. Whenever a patient presents with liver failure, we compare the levels of two liver enzymes, AST and ALT."

"AST. ALT." Evie wrote the acronyms.

"Aspartate aminotransferase and alanine aminotransferase."

Evie didn't even try to write that down.

"Her AST and ALT would be between two hundred and four hundred if she had liver failure from alcohol alone. But they're over a thousand."

Evie wrote down > *1000* and circled it. "What does that mean?"

"It's an indication of paracetamol overdose."

"Paracetamol."

"Acetaminophen. Same thing. It's in a lot of over-the-counter drugs. People take a Tylenol and a Nyquil and a Coricidin, not realizing they all have acetaminophen. More than two grams a day can be lethal for someone with a compromised liver. That's just three Extra Strength Tylenol. You can see how easy it is to overdose."

"Especially if you're drinking and losing track of time."

"Especially. Acetaminophen toxicity is the second-most-common cause of acute liver failure requiring transplantation."

A liver transplant? "Would my mother be a candidate for that?"

"We do many of them here. But your mother is so weak she might not survive the operation. More than that, she'd have to really *want* to stop drinking. Make a serious commitment." Dr. Foran tilted her head and gave a tired smile.

No, Evie didn't think her mother could stop drinking either, not even if she realized it was a question of life or death. "Is there no other treatment?"

"What we can do is keep her calm and comfortable. That's what we're doing now. She's taking medication for anxiety and delirium. There's more we can give her as the disease progresses." Dr. Foran put her hand on Evie's arm. "But you know of course, no one survives without a functioning liver. The damage is irreversible."

Irreversible. Evie wrote the word down. Read it. And even though it was what she'd expected to hear, she felt as if she'd been sucker-punched.

"Does she know?"

"It's difficult to tell what your mother"—Dr. Foran drew quote marks in the air—"*knows.* I've scheduled a brain scan for tomorrow. I'm guessing that will show that she's already suffered significant brain damage."

"Significant brain damage," Evie murmured. She couldn't bring herself to write down those words.

"The problem is that we have no baseline to compare. Your mother hasn't been seeing a physician regularly. But a decline like this is generally gradual. Up to a point."

Since when had her mother been beyond that point? Evie wondered. Years ago when she'd shown up drunk at Ginger's wedding? Or ten years before that when she'd fallen down the stairs? Or what about when she'd run the family station wagon into a tree?

No one had put a gun to her mother's head and forced her to drink. At first it had to have been a choice. At some point, though, Evie knew it hadn't been.

"How long does she have?"

"You'd think with all the cases like this that we handle, we'd know the answer. But it's surprisingly variable. Maybe a few months. Maybe weeks. What often happens is that the kidneys fail and the patient falls into a hepatic coma. After that, it's usually a matter of days, depending on whether the patient wants us to use extreme measures to prolong life."

"Extreme measures?" Evie's voice was barely a whisper.

Dr. Foran shook her head and pursed her lips. "There's no easy way to say this. There's a good chance that she'll linger. Possibly for weeks. It will be up to you and your sister to determine the course of treatment at that point." She handed Evie some stapled pages. COM-PASSION AND TREATMENT CHOICES was printed on the cover sheet.

Evie tried to swallow the lump in her throat. She'd known that this moment was coming, but now that it was here, she wasn't ready for it. "What should we do?"

"Get her affairs in order. Be here for her. Watch and wait. She may surprise us all and rebound. But you need to prepare yourselves. Now is the time for you and your sister to talk to your mother about what will happen when she can no longer tell us what she wants. And this is important. Write down exactly what she says. It will make it easier for you later to respect her wishes."

After Dr. Foran left, Evie stood at the window of the lounge, alone with her thoughts. As fat raindrops pelted the glass, the doctor's words sank in. She and Ginger were not going to be able to prop their mother up on her pins this time. There'd be no miracle cure. No liver transplant. Not even a temporary reprieve until the next emergency, drop-everything-right-now phone call.

She called Ginger.

"So you talked to Dr. Foran?" was the first thing Ginger said.

"Yes, Ginger, I talked to Dr. Foran." The words came out sharp. "I'm sorry. Yes. Just now. She says—" Evie's insides wrenched, and a sob escaped from nowhere.

"Evie? Honey?"

"Hang on." Evie put the phone down for a few moments until she could breathe again. Then she started over. "It's not good." She told Ginger what Dr. Foran had said, glad that she had taken notes.

"Significant brain damage," Ginger said. "But I thought you said she recognized you?"

"Yesterday she did."

"So how can they tell? I mean, they've got her on all kinds of drugs. And she's in withdrawal. She's got the DTs. How can they be sure that whatever this is isn't temporary?"

"They're giving her a brain scan."

"When?"

"Tomorrow."

"And what if—"

"Ginger, she's dying. And Dr. Foran says it could be soon."

"Oh, God. How soon?"

Evie stared at her notes, the words swimming on the page. "Weeks. Maybe only days."

"Days? I don't believe it."

"Ginger—"

"Oh, God. We should have done something. Dragged her to AA meetings. Gotten her a sponsor."

"You know it doesn't work like that."

"Insisted that she see a therapist, then. I don't know. Done *something*." Ginger paused, then added, "And maybe, just maybe if you hadn't checked out months ago—"

"Stop right there," Evie said, suddenly furious. "And maybe if her father hadn't been such a shithead. Maybe if her mother hadn't been depressed. Maybe if Daddy hadn't died. And you're right. Maybe if I'd been a better daughter." She stopped and took a deep breath, counted to five, then added, "Do you really think anything either of us could have done would have made a difference? She'd have had to want to stop drinking."

Ginger didn't say anything, but Evie could hear her raspy breathing.

"Ginger?"

"You're right. I'm sorry. Of course it's not your fault."

"It's not yours, either." Evie stared out the rain-streaked window. Cars were still going up and down the street. The red light on the corner turned green. As if nothing had changed.

"And I'm sorry, too," Evie said. "Even if I couldn't be there for her, I should have been there for you."

Ginger sniffed. "Yeah, you should have been."

"All right already, I get it, Gingey Wingey."

"Sticks and stones, Fungus Face."

"Oh, very original."

"Brat," Ginger shot right back.

"I'm rubber, you're glue." Evie tried to laugh, but she just couldn't make it happen.

"So," Ginger said, taking a long, audible inhale, "moving forward."

"Moving forward," Evie repeated. "We need to talk to her. Both of us. Together. And find out what she wants. For now. For later. The doctor said we shouldn't put it off for even another day."

After a long silence, Ginger said, "I wish Daddy were here."

"Me, too."

"I'll be there as soon as I can."

Chapter
Twenty-eight

When Evie got back to the hospital room, her mother was staring off into space. She looked small and frail lying there in the big hospital bed. A lunch tray that had been left for her was untouched. Evie hadn't eaten anything since the jelly doughnut this morning, and it was well past two. She should have been hungry, but the sight of food turned her stomach.

"Mom?" Evie touched her mother's cheek. "Mom?"

Her mother gave her a tight smile. "Ginger?"

Evie didn't know whether she was asking where Ginger was or thought Evie was Ginger. "I talked to Ginger. She's on her way over."

Her mother blinked, taking that in.

"How are you feeling?" Evie asked. "Can I get you anything?"

"Water." The word came out a whisper. Her mother licked her chapped lips.

Evie gave her a drink from a glass of water on the table by the bed. Sandra took a few sips from the straw and gave a weak cough. When Evie dabbed at her chin with a Kleenex, her mother winced.

"Mom, I need to ask you something."

Her mother gave a vague nod.

"I found checks and a lot of cash just lying around."

Her mother gave a faint smile.

"The cash. Where's it from?" Evie asked.

"My—" Her mother mumbled something.

"Your what?"

Her mother's hand tightened on the sheets. "Safety net."

That made Evie sad. As if a few envelopes of cash were all it took to make her mother safe. "Where is all that money coming from?"

"A friend."

"What friend?"

Her mother pinched her lips shut. Evie knew that expression. It said, *None of your business.* Fair enough.

"There's also some uncashed checks. Mom, I need to use some of that money to repair the house and pay your bills. Okay?"

Her mother's brow wrinkled, and she stared off into the space between them. Evie touched her arm and she snapped back.

Evie tried again. "I want your permission to use that money to pay your bills. And repair the car. And the roof—there are shingles all over the lawn. And you need a new upstairs window."

"Window?" Her mother was staring hard at Evie, like she was trying to penetrate a dense fog.

Exasperated, Evie said, "I don't want to spend your money without your permission. Can I use the money to pay the bills and repair the house?"

Her mother nodded, not so much *yes* as *whatever.*

"Okay. So I brought the checks with me." Evie pulled them and a pen from her purse. "Can you endorse them to me so I can deposit them? Do you feel up to that?"

Her mother pushed herself up and took the pen. Evie moved her mother's lunch aside to clear a space on the tray.

Her mother began endorsing checks, signing each one over to Evie without a pause. Each signature was a little more shaky and illegible than the last. When she'd signed the last one, she collapsed against the pillow, as if the effort had exhausted her.

Evie was putting the checks into her bag when her mother said, "Ginger?"

Evie turned back, thinking her mother was mistaking her for Ginger again. But when Evie followed her gaze to the doorway, Ginger really was there.

"Hi, Mom," Ginger said. She had a long cardigan sweater wrapped around her. Her dark hair was loosely anchored with a banana clip. Their father used to say that Ginger had the face of an angel, and she still had big lash-fringed eyes and pale skin that almost seemed to glow.

Ginger came into the room and gave Evie a hug. She smelled of rose water. "I got this off the Internet from the IRS," she said under her breath, handing her a two-page printed form that said POWER OF ATTORNEY, before sitting on the edge of the bed. Evie stood next to her.

"My baby girls." Their mother looked back and forth from Evie to Ginger. "I'm so happy to see you." Her eyes welled with tears.

Evie bit her lip to keep from crying, too.

Ginger leaned forward and kissed her mother's cheek. "So how's your shoulder?"

"My . . . ?" Their mother looked down at her swaddled shoulder, as if seeing it for the first time. "It's nothing. Just a nuisance. I'll be fine." She gave a tight smile that didn't reach her eyes. "Everything will be fine."

"Of course it will," Ginger said.

Evie nudged her with her knee.

"Mom—" Ginger started.

"I know," their mother said, her voice barely a whisper. She closed her eyes, and a tear squeezed out and ran down her cheek. She opened her eyes. "I know it's not going to be fine."

"No," Evie said, handing her mother a tissue.

"Not this time," Ginger said with a sob, taking a tissue for herself.

They hung there for a few moments. Finally Evie broke the silence. "The doctor says that the prognosis isn't good. And that we should talk to you so we'll know what you want if we have to . . ." It was so hard to put this into words. " . . . make choices for you. It's hard to even think about. But Dr. Foran said we shouldn't put it off."

Her mother swallowed and grimaced.

Evie took out the pages about treatment choices that Dr. Foran had given her. She turned to the end, where there was a list. "Your doctor gave me this to help us talk about what you want and what you don't want."

Ginger picked up the thread. "If there are choices. You know? And you can't communicate what you want." She leaned forward. "Please, please, tell us what you're thinking."

"No . . . transplant." Their mother's voice was clear, even if it was barely a whisper.

"No transplant," Evie said, writing it down. She was relieved that she didn't have to tell her mother that a transplant was probably not an option.

"If we have choices, where do you want to go if they release you from the hospital?" Evie said, reading off the first item on the list.

"Home." Her mother sounded so definite. As Evie wrote it down, she had to wonder if her mother had even the slightest idea what a mess home had become or how complicated it would be to honor that simple request.

"Okay. Pain medication?" Evie said. Her mother's gaze drifted to the ceiling. "Mom? Can I say that you want the doctors to do whatever it takes to keep you comfortable? Are you okay with that?"

Her mother nodded.

Evie went on, asking her about sedation, hydration, a feeding tube, and on through the endless-seeming list. In response to each, her mother managed to say a few words, or just nod or shake her head.

Finally, the hardest question. "Mom, if you crash, do you want the doctors to try to resuscitate you?"

Her mother shook her head.

"Do you want to be kept on life support?" As she said the words, Evie winced. It sounded so cold and brutal.

Her mother's "no" was barely a whisper. Then she turned to Evie. "Write it down."

Evie did. "And what about after?"

"Cremated," she said.

"Of course. Like Daddy?"

Her mother smiled.

Evie remembered the windy day she and Ginger and their mother powered up the motorboat that her father kept moored at the scruffy Point Yacht Club, driven it a mile or so out, and scattered his ashes on the swells of the Sound.

Evie read the checklist back, item by item, and at the end her mother signed it. Finally Ginger took over, explaining the document she'd brought in, power of attorney, and how it would allow her and Evie to take over their mother's finances and later her estate. Ginger held the paper while their mother signed without a murmur. Then she let the pen drop onto the bed. She whispered something that Evie didn't catch.

"Not afraid of what?" Ginger asked.

"Dying," their mother said. The tension lines in her forehead deepened. "But the house . . ."

Ginger said, "Is there something you want us to do with the house?"

Their mother gave a weak wave and muttered something that sounded like *I'm sorry.* The tension lines faded. Then, "It's too late."

After that, her mother sank back again into the pillows, and she turned her head away from Ginger and Evie. Minutes later she was asleep.

Evie followed Ginger out into the hall.

"That was so hard," Ginger said. She looked pale and drawn. "But not as hard as I thought it would be. And I'm glad we didn't wait." She glanced back toward the room. "I can't believe it's happening so fast. I wish there was something—"

"I know," Evie said. "You're so used to fixing things, but this isn't something that can be fixed."

Ginger sighed and bit her lip. Her eyes welled up again with tears. Evie put her arms around her, thinking how glad she was that she didn't have to go through this alone.

"I'm sorry, excuse me." It was a nurse pushing a medication cart. Evie and Ginger stepped aside so she could take it into their mother's room.

Ginger wiped her eyes with the side of her hand. "Her insurance is kicking in. I called to check. So that's okay for now."

"And just like she said, it turns out there really is money to fix the house."

"Really?"

"I found months of uncashed pension checks that I got her to endorse. And envelopes of cash."

"What?"

"Five of them. Like this." Evie pulled one of the envelopes from her purse. Ginger took it and riffled through the hundred-dollar bills. She whistled. "What on earth?"

"I have no idea. And here's the other weird thing. I went through all of her papers. Her credit card? In March she owed eight thousand dollars. In April? Zero. Paid in full."

"But how—?"

"That's what I'd like to know. She's not writing checks. She's not depositing or withdrawing money. So how's her credit card bill getting paid off? And who paid for her new HDTV?"

Before she left the hospital, Evie made a copy of the signed checklist with her mother's wishes and left it for the doctor. The rain let up long enough for Evie to sprint through the parking lot to where she'd parked Mrs. Yetner's car without getting soaked. But as soon as she got in, a brilliant flash of lightning and a clap of thunder made the steering wheel vibrate. Raindrops came down like ball bearings.

Ginger had invited her to come home with her and stay overnight in Connecticut, and Evie wished she could have accepted. It had been a long, hard day, and she really didn't want to be alone. But Mrs. Yetner was expecting her car back, and there was so much to do at the house.

Evie turned on the car and cranked up the defrost. The wipers, thunking back and forth at top speed, could barely keep up with the rain sheeting down the windshield. Carefully she backed out of the space and pulled out of the parking lot.

She had to concentrate to keep the car on her side of the road. The white lines that divided the lanes were nearly invisible on the wet pavement. Ordinarily she would have pulled over and waited out the storm, but today it was good to have something other than her roiling insides to focus on. Fortunately, Sunday traffic was light, and it took only a bit longer than the usual ten minutes to drive back to Higgs Point.

After she'd backed the car into Mrs. Yetner's garage, unclenched her hands from the steering wheel, turned off the ignition, and set the emergency brake, Evie sat there in the dark, keys in her lap, listening to the engine tick. She could have closed her eyes and gone to sleep right there. Instead, she got out, locked the car, and hurried through the rain to Mrs. Yetner's door. Rain dripped down the back of her neck as she stood under the porch overhang, ringing the bell. A pungent, sweet, burning smell hung in the air. Like someone was barbecuing. In the rain? Not likely.

Evie knocked and waited some more, but there was still no answer. Maybe Mrs. Yetner was napping. She pushed the keys through the mail slot and ran back to her mother's house. She was starting up the front steps when she realized that her mother's garage door was raised and the light was on.

Evie ran to the garage and ducked inside. Mrs. Yetner was scooping kitty litter from a giant bag and sprinkling it on the floor where the car had leaked gasoline. An open umbrella was dripping on the floor beside her.

Mrs. Yetner looked over at her and waved the scoop. "A gas leak. Imagine that? Car's not even five years old." It was nearly ten years old, but Mrs. Yetner had a point. "There. That should take care of it. Let that sit, and then sweep it up in a few hours."

"Thanks."

Mrs. Yetner peered at Evie, her eyes magnified through her glasses. "What's happened? Is your mother all right?"

"She's the same, really." Evie forced a smile and tried to swallow. There was no point pretending that everything was fine. "She's dying. I guess it's just starting to hit me."

Mrs. Yetner looked sad, but not surprised. "I am so sorry." She dropped the scoop into the bag and looked hard at Evie. "Have you eaten?"

"No. I'm sure that's part of the problem. I'll go in and make myself something to eat."

"Would you like me to—"

"No. I'm fine. Really."

"You're sure?"

"Absolutely."

Mrs. Yetner went to pick up the bag of cat litter.

"Here. Let me." Evie picked it up.

Mrs. Yetner turned back and clicked her tongue at the pile of cat litter. "One spark and the whole garage could have gone up in flames. Could have jumped the driveway and heaven knows what."

Evie remembered watching from the sidewalk, so many years ago, as fire shot through the roof of this very house. It had never occurred to her how terrified her neighbors must have been that the fire would spread to their houses, too. She followed Mrs. Yetner across the driveway and up to the front steps of her house. The rain had turned to barely a drizzle.

"Fire," Mrs. Yetner said, pulling open her storm door. "Funny how that odor sticks in memory. It's almost as if I can smell it right now."

That same smell was stuck in Evie's memory, but the sweet burning she smelled at that moment wasn't in her imagination. "Hang on," she said, setting the cat litter on the bottom step. "Let me."

She nudged Mrs. Yetner to one side and eased open the front door. A smoky haze filled the entryway.

"Oh dear." Mrs. Yetner's hand flew to her mouth. She stood there, stunned for a few seconds. Then, before Evie could stop her, she hurried past her into the house.

Evie grabbed the handset from the rotary phone on the table in the front hall and dialed 911. From the kitchen she heard a crash. Water running. A loud *hiss* and the smell of steam.

The 911 operator had answered and Evie was about to give her the address when Mrs. Yetner came out of the kitchen, her face bright pink. "It's all right. It's under control."

"You're sure?"

"Yes, yes." Mrs. Yetner waved away her concern.

The operator was asking for the address again when Evie interrupted with, "Never mind. Sorry. My mistake. No emergency after all." It took her a few more assurances to allay the operator's concerns. When she hung up, she asked Mrs. Yetner, "What happened?"

"It's nothing. Really." Mrs. Yetner smoothed her hair in place and took a breath. "Just some chicken I left on the stove."

"Can I help you clean up?" Evie asked, wondering if this was another one of Mrs. Yetner's "little mishaps" that her nephew had been going on about.

Chapter Twenty-nine

Mina turned down Evie's offer to stay and help clean up. It was the last thing the poor girl needed after the day that she'd been through. Besides, Mina was far too embarrassed by what had happened.

With all the windows and doors open, the smoke began to clear, though the odors of burned chicken and tomato were still pungent in the air. She scraped what she could into the garbage. Filled the pot with hot water and a few squirts of dishwashing liquid. Maybe it was salvageable. She stood there, staring into suds that rapidly turned black. Maybe not.

How could this have happened? She always, always, always set the burner to low when she made chicken cacciatore. But when she'd fought her way through the smoky kitchen to turn off the burner, she found the dial cranked well past medium.

On top of that, despite thick smoke, the alarm hadn't sounded. Hadn't it gone off yesterday when her teapot went up? Wasn't it supposed to reset itself automatically? Mina took out a broom and jammed the end of the stick up into the smoke alarm's test button, expecting to hear the shrill alarm sound. But nothing happened.

Maybe the battery had run down, though that made no sense either. It was supposed to at least chirp for a while before it died. She was sure she had a replacement battery, and she knew exactly where it was in the storage closet in the bag where she kept lightbulbs. But even standing on her kitchen step stool she wasn't nearly tall enough, never mind steady enough, to reattach the wires and replace the battery. Tomorrow, she'd get someone—Brian or Finn—to give her a hand.

She wrote a reminder on a Post-it and stuck it to her refrigerator door. Then, wearily she took down her calendar and continued the list she'd started, writing more items in today's block:

5. Burned chicken
6. Smoke alarm dead

She hung her calendar back on its hook. Maybe it was just as well that she'd broken down and agreed to visit nursing homes with Brian. She hated the idea that she'd end up in one of those places, but at least there she wouldn't be burning down the neighborhood.

Back when Annabelle was still lucid most of the time, Mina had taken her to visit several nursing homes that took care of people with dementia. Annabelle had chosen Pelham Manor. True, it was a bit shabby, but it was clean and well run, and she'd wanted to be nearby, so Mina could get there easily. Annabelle had been fortunate to have had particularly kind caregivers.

Mina remembered the day she'd moved Annabelle into a freshly painted room. She'd loaded her sister's few meager suitcases and some boxed-up framed photographs and personal items into the trunk of her car. Even though it had been swelteringly hot that day, Annabelle insisted on riding with the car windows rolled up. She had sat bolt upright in the passenger seat, her eyes bright as buttons, to use one of their mother's expressions, as their old neighborhood streamed by.

"Are you sure there's enough gas?" Annabelle had asked. She asked the same thing every time she got in the car with Mina—or in a cab, or even on a bus, for that matter.

"We're going to run out of gas," Annabelle said for the third time as they passed a gas station. A half block later, "Shouldn't we get gas?"

"Look," Mina said, pointing to the needle that showed well over half a tank. "There's plenty. Relax."

But *relax* was one of the many things that Annabelle could no longer do. Sitting there in her coat, sweat streaming down her face, she'd clutched the armrest and twisted in her seat, watching the blue-and-yellow Sunoco sign recede behind them, so agitated that the knuckles on the hand Mina could see turned white. With the other hand, she pulled at her hair, yanking out pins that Mina had so carefully put in not twenty minutes earlier.

Irrational anxiety—the doctor had already warned Mina about that and told her that it was likely to increase as dementia deepened. Mina had learned from experience that it was immune to reasoning or hard evidence. Distraction was the only strategy that seemed to work, even temporarily.

So, when they came to a stop at a red light, Mina pointed to the opposite corner. "Oh Annabelle, look. What happened to the movie theater that used to be over there on that corner?"

It took Annabelle a few seconds to refocus—as if gears were shifting and cogs falling into place. But when she did, her expression softened, and the lines of tension eased from around her eyes. "Oh yes, the Halcyon."

Mina had forgotten that the movie theater, with its gilded ceiling and massive crystal chandelier, had been called the Halcyon—from halcyon days, how appropriate. The light turned green, and Mina accelerated.

"Popcorn," Annabelle said. "Can I get a large?"

At least Annabelle had died first, as Mina had hoped and prayed she would, with Mina sitting by her side and holding her hand. Would anyone be there with Mina to hold her hand at the end?

Chapter
Thirty

Getting old sucked, Evie thought as she crossed back to her mother's house. She left behind wet footprints in the tall grass, already flattened by the heavy rain. Would she go out flailing and dwindling like her mother or fighting—she noticed the open garage with the light on—and sweeping up cat litter like Mrs. Yetner?

She detoured to the garage. The pile of litter was mounded on the floor near the back, and the smell of gas had completely vanished. She'd deal with it tomorrow. She turned off the light, pulled down the door, and returned to the house. The minute she'd unlocked the front door and pushed it open, an overpowering smell, both acrid and sweet, sent her reeling back. Roach bombs. She'd forgotten all about them.

She took a deep breath before plunging in and racing from window to window, throwing them open. When she got to the back door, she pulled it open, stepped outside onto the back porch, and gasped for breath. The light mist and stiff breeze that whipped off the marsh felt good on her face. She stayed out there for a few minutes, giving the house and her own lungs time to air out before going back inside.

In the bedroom she found a sweatshirt and sweatpants in her mother's bureau and a pair of warm socks. She shucked her damp clothes and changed. Returning to the living room, she stood there, looking around. Something felt off, but she couldn't put her finger on what.

The photos were still in their places on the mantel. The pattern of dust on the coffee table showed where Evie had cleared away ashtrays and papers. The TV was still on the wall. Still, she couldn't shake a feeling of unease.

Her neck prickled as she realized what it was. The TV's shipping box with the SONY logo was no longer leaning against the side of the sofa. It was gone. What else?

Evie walked through the dining room and into the kitchen. Slowly she did a 360. Cabinets and drawers were open. She'd left them that way. The bills and statements were still in orderly rows on the kitchen table. Or . . . not quite. The rows looked as if they'd been slightly disturbed. She could easily have done that herself when she went crashing through to open the windows.

But when she looked more carefully at the piles, she realized it was more than that. The phone bill on the top of one of them was six months old. When she'd finished sorting, the newest one would have been on top.

Someone had been in the house, and it only now occurred to her that it was just possible that the person was still there. Evie grabbed her purse, ran out of the house, and dialed 911.

Evie waited outside in a light drizzle for the police, wondering if the officer who'd rousted Mrs. Yetner off Mr. Cutler's porch would show up. But the two officers who climbed out of the cruiser that arrived after a ten-minute wait were strangers. One, barrel chested and straight backed, was not much older than Evie. She followed his gaze as he took in the house, reminded again of how appalling it looked: graffiti, sodden bags of trash, and a soiled mattress leaning up against the side, and landscaping that belonged in a vacant lot.

The other officer, an older man, tall with a stiff gait, went into her mother's house while the younger one came over to talk to her. Evie felt silly telling him about the missing packing box and that papers had been rearranged. But he didn't seem to think it was silly at all. He wrote down everything she said.

The older officer emerged from her mother's house and strode over to them. "It's okay. No one's inside. There's no sign of a forced entry. You sure you left the house locked?"

"Absolutely."

"When did you leave?"

"At around eleven this morning."

"Anyone else have keys to the house?" he asked.

"My sister. She's in Connecticut. And"—Evie swallowed a twinge of guilt—"the man who runs the convenience store up the street has keys to the garage. Maybe to the house, too. I don't know. He was over here this morning, helping me with my mother's car."

"You were right to get out of there and call us," the older officer said. "I'm going to talk with your neighbors. See if anyone saw anything."

He strode next door where Mrs. Yetner was peering out from behind her screen door.

The younger officer said, "So a cardboard box is missing?"

"I didn't really have time to check. There might be more."

"Why don't we go in and you have a look around?"

Evie agreed, glad not to be going back inside by herself. The officer hung back, following her from room to room. In her mother's bedroom, she checked her jewelry drawer. There, amid a jumble of rhinestones and fake pearls, were her grandmother's diamond wedding ring and the sapphire earrings that her dad had given her mother on their twentieth anniversary. In the dining room, her mother's few pieces of good silver were still there. Beyond that, there wasn't much of value to take. Not any longer.

"Up until this morning," Evie told the police officer, "there was a fair amount of cash in the house."

That got his attention. "Really?"

"Thousands of dollars. I'd taken it with me."

"Lucky thing you did. Who knew your mother was keeping cash in the house?"

"Obviously whoever gave it to her. But I have no idea who that was, and she's not telling."

"She didn't have any friends?"

"There's the man across the street. He came over to ask me if he could do anything to help. I got the impression that he and my mother were good friends."

"What about the man with the keys to her garage? Was he a good friend, too?" he asked, raising his eyebrows.

Evie felt herself flush. "Not that kind of friend."

When they got back outside, Evie glanced across the street to where the second officer was ringing Frank Cutler's bell. That house was dark, and the garage was open and empty. The officer gave up and tried the house next door.

"Okay, then. I guess that about wraps it up," the younger officer said, handing her his card. He put away his notebook and looked as if he was anxious to be off. "Call if you discover anything else missing. And if I were you, I'd get the locks changed immediately."

The older officer came back. "Just the old woman living next door is around. She has an interesting theory. She says the man who lives over there"—he indicated across the street toward Mr. Cutler's house—"was out in front of your house earlier today. Talking to a tow truck driver who picked up a car. She thinks she saw a box in the driveway. Says she's sure the man took it with him. But you can take that with a grain of salt. She calls us all the time, almost always with some complaint about that neighbor."

Evie looked next door. Mrs. Yetner was still standing in her doorway, the screen pushed open. Was she a reliable witness or did she see what she wanted to see?

"Besides," the officer added, "I'm not sure her eyesight is all that good."

Evie waved at Mrs. Yetner. Her neighbor certainly saw her well enough to wave back.

Chapter
Thirty-one

Mina had been surprised to see the police officers next door talking to Evie. Even more surprised when one of them came over to talk to her. As often as she called the police, she couldn't remember the last time they'd actually stopped and questioned her. She was lucky if they slowed down when they rolled by.

Now she watched as the pair got back into their cruiser and drove off. Sandra Ferrante's daughter was still out on her mother's front steps, standing there like the poor thing didn't have the good sense to come in out of the rain.

Mina pulled an umbrella from the stand and walked next door, picking her way across the wet lawn. "You had a break-in?"

"That's what it looks like. Did you see anyone trying to get into the house?"

"I didn't. But I was busy." She'd gotten the chicken started, sat down to read, and then fallen asleep. The rain had woken her. When it let up, she'd taken the kitty litter over and sprinkled it over the gasoline spill. Young people had no idea how easy it was for a fire to get started. "What did they take?"

"Nothing, really."

"What kind of nothing?"

The girl squirmed under Mina's gaze. "A brown shipping box. Who'd bother with that?"

The girl must have been talking about the box that Mina had seen sitting at the end of the driveway getting rained on. Or maybe it had been in the grass. Weeds, really. Mina doubted if there was even a single sprout of actual bluegrass or fescue left in that yard. Then she'd gotten distracted by the sound of the winch raising the car and the spectacle of the truck driving off with the car in tow. After that, Frank had disappeared and she couldn't recall seeing the box again.

"A big box?" Mina stretched her arms wide. "And flat?"

"Where did you see it?"

"Out in front of your house when he"—she tipped her head in the direction of the house across the street—"was out there chatting up the tow truck driver. I don't know what he's up to but he's a schemer, that one." Mina felt her face grow warm. "And he's been hanging around your mother." Like smell on a dead fish, as her father liked to say. "Helping out." Mina sniffed.

As if that man were capable of helping anyone other than himself. Oh, he'd been pleasant enough when he first moved in. Brought her a bottle of sweet sherry that she'd never even opened. Even her grandmother hadn't had a taste for sherry. Offered to clear the leaves off her lawn when she'd complained about the infernal noise of his leaf blower.

"He thinks I haven't heard him, going through my trash in the middle of the night." Mina caught the girl's skeptical look. "More than once."

"I know you don't like him very much." The girl had her arms folded in front of her as she pinched and tweaked her sleeves. "Are you sure you saw him actually walk off with that box?"

"Well." Mina dropped her gaze. "Maybe not walk off with it."

"Mrs. Yetner, whoever got in didn't break in. I know Finn has a key to the garage. But maybe you know if my mother gave house keys to anyone else."

Mina fastened the top button of her blouse and pulled her sweater around her. The question flustered her, because somewhere, deep in the recesses of her memory, she did recall that Sandra Ferrante had, once upon a time, given her a key to her front door. It was years and years ago, when the girls were little and sometimes locked themselves out. Mina had a vague memory of slipping the key into an envelope and writing *Ferrante* on it. But where it had gotten to, she had no idea.

"You don't think I—" Mina started. "Because I would never—"

"You? Of course not," the girl said, her cheeks blazing. "It's just that whoever got in must have a key. Which means they can get in whenever they want to. And I might not even have noticed except the papers were—" Her voice cracked and she took a breath. "And I don't know if it's random or what." The poor girl was trembling.

"Shhhh," Mina said, putting her arm around her. "The thing to do is get the locks changed. Right away. And why don't you stay overnight with us? Ivory will be delighted." She could read Evie's guarded look. "I promise not to leave a pot on the stove and burn the house down."

Chapter
Thirty-two

It had been so sweet of Mrs. Yetner to invite Evie to stay over, and though Evie had no intention of taking her up on it, knowing that she had the option made her feel safer and less alone. It was chilly and damp when she got back inside. The insecticide smell hadn't vanished completely, and in the kitchen a single pantry moth fluttered drunkenly about. With her bare hand, she smacked it against the wall.

It took four calls to locksmiths listed in her mother's 2008 copy of the Yellow Pages before she found one that was still in business and taking calls on a Sunday night. In return for payment in cash, the woman who took her call promised someone would be there in an hour.

Evie hung up and called Ginger. "The house got broken into," Evie said as soon as Ginger picked up, "but they didn't take anything valuable."

"Oh my God. What next? Are you okay?" Ginger asked, her voice rising. "Did you call the police?"

"I'm fine. Of course I did."

"Did they make a mess?"

"No. In fact, if I wasn't so anal about the way I sorted Mom's papers, I never would have realized the house was broken into. And before you ask, I've got someone coming to change the locks."

"Tonight?"

"In an hour."

"You sure you're okay?"

"Other than a headache—" Evie put her hand to her temple and massaged the spot that had started to throb. Headaches that started that way usually turned into doozies. She started for the bathroom where she'd seen some Excedrin in the medicine cabinet. "—I'm fine."

"It's a good thing you had all that money with you," Ginger said.

"Good thing," Evie said as she ran water in the bathroom sink and splashed her face with one hand. "I'll deposit it first thing tomorrow."

"You're sure nothing else is missing?"

"Ginger, I checked everywhere." Evie opened the medicine cabinet. "I'm sure—"

But the words died on her lips, and the phone dropped into the sink with a clatter. Except for the tube of Crest toothpaste that she was sure she'd left on the sink, the bottom shelf of the medicine cabinet was empty.

She picked up the phone. "You're not going to believe this. Everything that was on one shelf of Mom's medicine cabinet is missing."

"That's weird. Were there any prescription drugs?"

"I don't remember anything like that." Evie conjured a visual image of what else she'd seen. "She had Excedrin. Vitamins. Maybe some cold medicine. I can't remember what else."

"Excedrin and vitamins?" After a long silence, Ginger added, "You know, I'd find it more reassuring if whoever broke in *had* taken her jewelry and her goddamned TV. Because this is just plain creepy. I don't think you should stay there."

"I can't leave now. I've got a locksmith on his way over. At least when he's done, I'll be the only one with a key."

"Then I'm coming to stay with you."

"You are not." The doorbell rang. "That's the locksmith. Don't worry. Mrs. Yetner invited me to stay with her, and I will if I need to."

"How do you know she wasn't the one who broke in?"

"Don't be ridiculous," Evie said and disconnected the call.

Chapter
Thirty-three

Brian arrived the next morning, hours earlier than Mina expected him. She was still eating her breakfast and reading the paper.

"You remembered I was coming, didn't you?" he said. "You're up to looking at residences?"

Of course she did. Of course she was. She took a drink of tea, scraped up a last mouthful of oatmeal, and walked the dishes to the sink.

"I've arranged for us to see a few places." He read from a piece of paper. "Pelham Manor. Golden Oaks—"

She took the paper from him and adjusted her glasses. "I can read, for heaven's sake."

He had four addresses written down. Pelham Manor was where Annabelle had spent her final days. Golden Oaks was also in the Bronx. Briarfield Gardens was on Saw Mill River Road, over into Westchester. The fourth place she'd never heard of. Visiting four in a single day seemed awfully ambitious.

She handed him back the paper. "Have you eaten? Can I get you anything?"

"I'm fine." He looked at his watch. "We've got to step on it, Aunt Mina. They're expecting us at Pelham Manor in thirty minutes."

Mina folded the newspaper, slapped it down on the table, and stood. "All right then. I'll be ready in a minute."

She closed herself in the bathroom, even though she didn't need to go. Then she sat on the closed toilet seat trying to calm herself. She'd thought she'd be fine, visiting old age homes. But she wasn't. She did not want to leave her house. Her neighborhood. Her marsh. Besides, she was nowhere near that far gone. *Or am I?* she wondered as she stared down at the backs of her hands, the veins popping beneath skin that was shriveled like loose latex.

"Aunt Mina, you haven't forgotten I'm out here waiting for you, have you?"

"Not yet." Mina reached back and flushed the toilet.

"Do you need any help?"

"Don't be ridiculous." She stood and checked her face in the mirror, relaxing the frown lines as much as she still could and smoothing her chins. She splashed her face with warm water and dried it.

From the other side of the door, Brian called, his voice sounding more urgent, "I'll go start the car and meet you—"

She banged out of the bathroom. "Don't bother. I'll drive." She found her purse sitting on the placemat in the kitchen, snagged her cane, and stumped out the door. Immediately she realized it had started to rain again. She should have picked up an umbrella, but she'd be damned if she was going to go back for it now.

She waited until Brian got in the car and had shut the door, too, before releasing the brake and slamming the car into drive. Let him sulk. He'd been doing that since he was three years old, whenever things didn't go precisely his way. Once on the street she accelerated, holding on to the wheel to pull herself up a little taller to see over the steering wheel. Had she shrunk more? With relief, she noticed a cushion from the seat was on the floor. The girl must have left it there.

When they'd emerged from her little pocket of residential streets, Brian said, "So you know where you're going?"

She harrumphed. Did he think she could forget how to drive to a place she'd gone every day for two years? When Brian put in an occasional appearance there, he'd acted as if he deserved a medal.

She bypassed the highway on-ramp, and he asked again if she knew how to get there.

"This is the way I go." She wanted to say, *Shall I let you off and you can take the bus?* She chuckled to herself, imagining him standing on the street corner and receding in her rearview mirror.

Mina didn't take highways. Not anymore. Whenever she tried to, it seemed as if they'd repainted the lines to make the lanes even narrower, while those big rigs that rumbled along at top speed and tailgated her had grown longer and wider.

She didn't drive at night, either. Ever. It wasn't so much that she couldn't see, though that was a piece of it. She could swear that some oncoming headlights on new cars were brighter than brights. Apparently those new blue headlights were legal, though she couldn't imagine why, because they were blinding. Those seconds it took for her eyes to recover from them were terrifying. Plenty of time to run someone over or give herself a heart attack.

No, she'd stick to daytime driving, thank you very much. As Mina drove up the street, the phantom smell of yeast teased her nose. A Wonder Bread factory had once been nearby.

"You'd better lock your door," she told Brian as they passed a row of derelict houses. Those had been brand-new when she was in elementary school, but now their perimeters were surrounded by battered chain-link fencing. A stout dog, tied to a front porch railing, barked as they drove by.

It was a little farther to Pelham Bay Park, where her mother used to take Mina and Annabelle to play when they were little. There, in the distance, were the Co-op City towers, standing on the banks of the Hutchinson River on land that had been a broad flat expanse her father used to call "the dump." He'd taken them there to swim back in the day when you still could.

Mina pulled into Pelham Manor's familiar entryway. Could it be only six months since she was there? Her last visit had been a week after Annabelle died. Mina had gone in to remove what remained of Annabelle's few possessions. She'd given away most of Annabelle's clothes. Donated her unused medications. And left with a few forlorn cardboard boxes.

Chapter
Thirty-four

When the alarm went off that morning, Evie felt as if she were pushing herself up from beneath a pile of cinder blocks. The locksmith hadn't arrived until after ten, and he hadn't finished until nearly midnight, far too late for Evie to change her mind about where she was going to sleep. For hours she'd lain awake on the mattress on the living room floor, jumping at the slightest sound. No matter how many times she'd made a circuit of the house, demonstrating to herself that the doors and windows were secure, anxiety had returned the minute she lay down again.

On the way to work, she stopped at the bank. The minute she deposited the cash and checks, she felt as if some of the burden had lifted. But now, as she stood in front of a whiteboard in the Historical Society's conference room and stared at a chart outlining everything that had to be done before *Seared in Memory* opened, the weight was back.

While she waited for her staff to arrive, she took a red marker and wrote *E* beside each of the tasks that were her responsibility. The workload, even spread over three weeks, was daunting. She'd never get it done if she had to be on watch for her mother.

"Hey, are you all right?" Nick's voice startled her. She looked over as he entered the conference room. He held a cup of coffee out to her. "You look like you could use this."

"Thanks," Evie said, taking it. She did need coffee. She inhaled and took a sip. It had a hazelnut edge.

The other two members of her team filed into the conference room and took their places at the table—Maia, whom she'd hired last year, fresh out of graduate school, and Marie-Christine, who was a Barnard College intern. Now they were all looking at her.

"I'm sorry if I've seemed distracted. My mother is seriously ill," Evie told them, starting the little speech she'd practiced on the ride in and trying to sound as businesslike and unemotional as possible. "I don't know exactly what's going to happen, but I might need to cut back on my hours. My sister and I are trying to take it one day at a time. With the opening so soon, I'd like us to put together a backup plan just in case."

They had started to go through, figuring out which of them could take over which of her tasks, when Evie's phone went off. The number on the readout was her mother's neighborhood. The hospital? Evie's stomach did a flip-flop. She excused herself and stepped out into the hall to take the call.

"Mrs. Ferrante?" The man's voice was unfamiliar.

Evie swallowed. "This is her daughter."

"Oh, right. This is Jack, from Egan's Sunoco. We've got your mother's Subaru up on the lift?" Evie sagged against the wall, relief sweeping through her. Of course. That's who Finn must have called to tow the car, the gas station where her mother had always gone to have their car tuned. "We thought it would be an easy repair, but it turns out it's not. The fuel tank needs to be replaced. The fuel pump and filler pipe, too."

Fuel tank. Fuel pump. Filler pipe. Evie heard the words, but she wasn't really processing them.

"The rest of the car looks fine. And with a little luck we can probably have it fixed for you in a day or two. But I didn't want to start the work until I checked with you first. Run you about eight hundred."

So much for an inexpensive repair. For a moment Evie felt paralyzed. Did it make sense to repair a car her mother would never drive again? Still, it had to be fixed or she and Ginger would never be able to sell it.

"Go ahead," she told him as she imagined a flock of her mother's hundred-dollar bills sprouting wings and flying out the window.

When she returned to the conference room, she was confronted with the worried faces of her staff. No, she told them, the call wasn't the hospital.

When her phone rang an hour later, it was. Her mother had lost consciousness while she was undergoing a brain scan. She was in intensive care.

Chapter
Thirty-five

The parking lot at Pelham Manor was nearly full. Even the handicap spot where Mina always used to park whenever she visited Annabelle was taken. Mina had to zigzag back a few rows to find a spot. Brian came around and made a show of offering her his arm, but she ignored him. She started toward the building, trying to ignore the persistent drizzle and Brian's inane remarks about the weather.

In the circular drive by the entrance, a van was parked, its side door open and a hydraulic lift raising an old man in a wheelchair. Annabelle had taken a few van trips to the mall when she'd first moved to Pelham Manor, but on one outing she'd wandered into the basement and gotten lost. It had taken security hours to find her, and after that the staff at Pelham Manor had put a stop to her trips.

Mina got to the front entrance first and rang the bell. As she waited, Brian caught up to her. There was a buzz and a click, and he pulled the door open for her to go inside. Then he went to the front desk and talked to the receptionist.

Mina looked around the familiar space. Plastic forsythia bloomed in a vase on the table by the elevator. Last time she'd been here, there'd been sprays of autumn leaves and bittersweet. Fortunately the bittersweet had been fake, too—she remembered reading somewhere that the real thing was poisonous, and more than a few of the patients on Annabelle's floor were as likely to eat floral arrangements as look at them.

Mina heard a discreet throat-clearing and turned to find a woman in a light blue suit with a staff badge hanging around her neck standing beside her. Smiling, tall, and elegantly silver-haired, she reminded Mina of Mrs. Weber, her fourth-grade teacher, who told her students she'd once been a fashion model.

"Good morning, Mrs. Yetner," the woman said. She gave Mina's hand the gentle squeeze of someone who knew better than to put pressure on arthritic fingers. Brian came over to join them. "And Mr. Granville. It's good to see you both again. Celeste Hall."

Mina squinted at the badge the woman wore. It was easier for her to remember names if she saw them in print. But the print side of the badge was twisted around, facing the woman's chest.

The woman turned back to Mina. "It was good to get your call."

"My what?"

"Here." She gave Mina a large envelope. A sticker on the front said THE MATERIAL YOU REQUESTED, which she most certainly had not. But it was the name written on the front, *Wilhelmina,* that gave her a start. The last person who'd called her that was Annabelle, and only when she was annoyed.

"I'm happy to show you around our independent living tier," the woman went on, leading the way to the elevator. As Mina trailed behind in her wake, she smelled tangerine and ginger. Now Mina remembered. This was the woman who'd been there when Mina had checked Annabelle in on that hot summer day, efficient, calm, and frequently glancing at the large man's watch she wore on her wrist then as she did now.

The woman pressed the elevator call button and turned back. With a sympathetic smile on her face, she said, "Independent living is quite different from assisted living, and of course Memory Care where your sister stayed with us is something else entirely. We have three hundred and fifty . . ."

Mercifully, the elevator doors had opened. The annoyingly cheerful woman, whose name Mina had already forgotten, rattled on with her canned speech as they rode the elevator up one floor, so slowly that it felt as if they were barely moving at all.

Instead of a locked door with a nurses' station beyond, as there'd been on Annabelle's floor, the elevator doors opened onto a spacious, brightly lit room littered with sofas and wing chairs that looked as if they'd lost their way en route to a furniture showroom.

When Mina and Annabelle had first visited, Annabelle had said, "But everyone is so old." Mina had laughed, but now she was thinking the exact same thing as a woman shuffled past, pushing a walker tethered to an oxygen tank. An old man sat nodding off in a chair.

But it wasn't all shuffle and nap. A woman who sat reading a *USA Today* lowered her paper and gave Mina a sharp appraising look as the energetic guide led them down a hall to a library where all five computer stations were in use. Maybe Mina would finally get around to learning how to use one. Past that was a room set up like a den with a big TV and card tables. Four women there were playing mah-jongg. Another foursome, men and women, were playing poker, betting with nickels.

"Are you a card player?" their cheerful guide asked with a treacly smile. Lipstick was smeared on her front tooth.

Mina said she wasn't, but she wondered if anyone still knew how to play whist. She'd passed many a pleasant evening playing that with her grandmother.

Past the card room was an exercise room where women and a few men sat in two rows of chairs. According to Mina's guide, they were "enjoying a session of chair yoga." As Mina watched them look up at the ceiling, down into their laps, curl and stretch, she realized that she'd probably enjoy it, too.

All in all, it wasn't so bad, really. It didn't smell terrible. No one was muttering, or marching along like a zombie, or disrobing in the hallway. Mina had witnessed all three on the floor where Annabelle had been installed.

Continuing on, they passed a hall table, its top strewn with flower petals surrounding a carefully calligraphed card that read *Dearly Departed*. Beside the card was a framed photograph of a woman smiling and looking directly at the camera, her hand to her cheek. Perched on her head was a party hat in the shape of a tiara—just the kind of goofy thing Mina would never be caught dead wearing. But from the woman's lively expression, it looked as if she was in on the joke.

Below the picture was a name and a room number and the date, May 17. Three days ago.

Farther down a corridor and beyond double doors were the rooms. The woman walked ahead with Brian at her side. They were chatting. Brian turned and motioned for Mina to hurry up. But just then a young woman came out into the corridor from one of the rooms. She turned back, holding the door open, talking and nodding.

Inside, Mina could see a cozy room with ruffled white curtains, a well-worn leather lounge chair, and a bed neatly made with a finely crocheted spread like one tucked away in Mina's linen closet that she didn't dare use for fear Ivory would have at it. Which reminded her, would they let her bring Ivory? It gave her a stomachache imagining Ivory being dumped at an animal shelter.

A woman in a wheelchair sat facing the door, so stooped she was bent near double, her thin white hair tucked into a bun at the nape of her neck. Beside her was a piecrust-top table crowded with framed photographs and porcelain figurines. The young woman at the open door said something to her, and the old woman craned her neck in order to look up. Her face reminded Mina of a shriveled apple. Eyes sharp. She was starting to say something when the young woman let go of the door and walked off down the hall.

It seemed to Mina as if the door closed in slow motion with the old woman sitting there, talking to no one, until finally she was shut in that room, utterly alone with only a television, pictures of loved ones, and a window overlooking a parking lot. In a few weeks or months, a picture of her smiling gamely at the camera would be sitting on the Dearly Departed table. And the cozy room she was in would be filled with someone else's memories.

It was the thing no one wanted to talk about. People came to places like this to die. Even after they'd finished their tour and were riding down in the elevator Mina was still shaken, thinking about the woman in the wheelchair.

Assisted *living*? *Pfff.* If she came here, it would be to die, tidily and off camera, as inexorably as the elevator she was in was going down.

Chapter
Thirty-six

"Next stop, Golden Oaks. It's not far," Brian said in a cheery, much too loud voice back in the lobby. He held Mina's coat for her, and dutifully Mina threaded her arms through the sleeves. But her mind kept replaying the door closing on the old woman.

Brian handed Mina her cane. "You know, I think I'd like to go home," she said.

"Home? *Home?*" The word exploded from Brian's mouth and echoed in the empty space, and Brian looked around guiltily. "But you promised," he continued more quietly. "We've made appointments."

"*You* made the appointments. You keep them. I am going home." And before Brian could protest, Mina started for the door. On her way out, she tossed the envelope with the material she'd never requested in a trash bin.

She assumed Brian would come chasing after her, shouting and struggling to put on his own coat. Offering to bring the car around and putting his hand out like she'd just fork over her car keys. But when she turned and looked back, there he was, still inside, talking on his cell phone. Gesturing with his free hand like he was explaining something, or maybe apologizing. That was the one thing that, at her age, Mina rarely felt the urge to do.

The pavement outside was wet. She stepped out from under the front awning and into a steady drizzle. A car stopped so she could cross the circular drive and continue at a brisk pace into the parking lot and down the center aisle, her cane tapping sharply on the macadam. Three rows in, she turned right and walked past car after nondescript car. When she was nearly at the end of the row, she realized her car wasn't there. She turned around, and around again, checking the adjacent row for her car's distinctive silhouette.

Keys clutched in her hand, she started to retrace her steps more slowly now. Stopped. She remembered exactly where she'd parked—right in that spot where a dark red van was now parked. Or was it the spot next to it where there was a black pickup truck?

She looked up and down the row. Or maybe it was farther along? She took a few steps in that direction.

"Aunt Mina!" It was Brian, calling to her from the start of the row. "Don't you remember? You parked over here." He pointed in the opposite direction.

What? Mina could have sworn this was right. Could she have gotten completely turned around?

"Come on!" Brian gestured for her to follow him.

Mina had started toward him when she heard an engine rumble. Startled, she turned and stumbled, barely catching herself from falling. All she could see was the bed of the pickup truck coming at her, white backup lights glowing in the rain.

Mina put her hands up, as if she could actually stop a two-thousand-pound vehicle with her bare hands. In a flash of coherence, as she went down hard she thought, *Please, not my other hip.*

The next thing she knew, she was on the ground. Somehow she'd managed to get out of the truck's path. The truck peeled out without so much as slowing down, leaving behind the smell of exhaust. Through the side of her head she felt more than heard running footsteps.

"Aunt Mina, are you all right?" Brian's voice came from a blurry figure standing over her. Mina realized she'd lost her glasses, and she patted the ground around her. Her cane and purse and car keys had gone flying, too. "What kind of idiot backs up without even looking? Asshole."

Watch your language, young man. The voice in Mina's head was her mother's, but she knew it was exactly what Annabelle would have said, too.

Brian knelt beside her. "Aunt Mina? Are you all right?"

Her hip throbbed, and her heart was banging like a jackhammer. Each time she tried to breathe, it felt as if a fist pressed against her breastbone.

"You're white as a sheet." His words came to her slowly, as if pushing their way through a fog.

Mina tried to say, *I'm fine.* But she couldn't get the words to come out of her mouth.

"I'm calling an ambulance."

Mina did not want to go to the hospital. Nine times out of ten, you came out sicker than you went in, if you came out at all. She gasped for breath, still unable to say a word. Finally, she managed to croak out a small, weak, "No!"

"Hello? Emergency?"

"No!" This time she sounded louder. Mina wiped a strand of hair from across her eyes. She took a breath.

"Lie still," Brian said. "You might have broken something."

"Don't you think I'd know if I'd broken something?" Mina snapped. Her elbow and knees felt raw, and she thought she might be bleeding. But she'd survived plenty of skinned knees and elbows. Gingerly she flexed her wrists. Rotated her shoulders. Lifted her head off the wet pavement. "Put that fool thing away," she said, "and help me find my eyeglasses. I'm fine."

But the minute she tried to shift her legs, she knew she was not fine. The pain in her hip was white hot and excruciating. She felt a bulge where there shouldn't have been one, right where the ball of her titanium hip joint was supposed to snap into the pelvis.

The blurry figure that descended over her had to be Brian. He barely touched her, and she screamed in pain. Then the world went mercifully black.

Chapter
Thirty-seven

As Evie's taxi drove up the East Side on the way to the hospital, meter ticking, Evie called Ginger to tell her that their mother was in intensive care; then she scrolled through her calendar of meetings for that day and the next and sent out regrets that she'd be unable to attend.

"Ma'am?" the taxi driver said. Evie looked up. The driver was looking back at her. The taxi had pulled up in front of the hospital. "That's fifty-six dollars even."

Moments later she was inside, following the signs to intensive care.

The glass double doors of the intensive care unit were locked. Hanging on the door was a clipboard with a sign-in sheet. Evie wrote her mother's name and her own. Then she pressed the nearby buzzer. A nurse came to the door. She looked tired, her eyelids puffy and sagging.

"I'm Sandra Ferrante's daughter," Evie said.

The nurse led her to one of the beds in the back where Evie's mother lay completely still. An IV tube was attached to her arm, and what looked like an oversize clothespin was clipped to her index finger.

Evie pulled up a chair to her mother's bedside. "Mom?" she said. Her mother's closed eyelids quivered. "Can she hear me?" Evie asked the nurse.

"Maybe. It's always a good idea to assume they can."

Evie looked at one of the monitors to which her mother was attached. There were numbers—85 and 72—on the readout. Evie had no idea if that was bad or good, but the steady iridescent-green wave pattern that laid itself out over and over again on the screen was reassuring.

"That's showing us her oxygen levels and her heart rate," the nurse said. "Right now she's good. Much better than when they brought her in a few hours ago. An alarm will sound if—"

A high-pitched alarm sounded from a monitor several beds away. "That's my cue," the nurse said, hurrying off.

Evie turned back to her mother. "Mom? It's me, Evie. I'm right here. And Ginger is on her way." She touched her mother's arm and gently brushed hair off her forehead. Her mother's eyelids didn't even flicker.

Evie had never been in an intensive care unit before. She glanced at the bed closest to her mother's. A very old woman lay there, her cheeks and eyes sunken into her skull. She was hooked up to a ventilator that wheezed and hissed and thumped as she breathed in and out, along with an entire bank of additional monitors. No one was by her side except a nurse, bending over her and raising her eyelid.

Evie looked away, then around at the rest of the unit. Every other bed was occupied, every patient connected to devices in what felt like some kind of purgatory. How long did the hospital keep patients here before giving up? she wondered. How many of these people would bounce back?

Chapter
Thirty-eight

"Easy does it," a woman's soothing voice said. As Mina was turned over and lifted onto a stretcher, she gasped for breath. The pain in her left side was excruciating. The world around her shorted out and went dark.

"I'm sorry. I know it hurts." The same voice pulled her back. Mina blinked up at the figure who was blocking a pulsing light. "Can you hear me?"

"Yes," Mina managed to gasp out. She could feel the woman gently wiping grit from the side of her face.

"Good. Hang on now." A sheet was tucked under her arms. "You've dislocated your left hip. We're taking you to the hospital."

Something was being wrapped around her upper arm. Tightening. A blood pressure cuff.

"You're going to be fine." The woman's voice again as the cuff was removed.

They were moving now. Into an ambulance? A hand came down over her face. Mina fought it. Pushed it away.

"It's oxygen. It will help you breathe." That woman, this time with the pressure of a reassuring hand on her shoulder. "Your blood pressure is dropping so we want to be sure you're getting enough. Don't worry, I've got your purse and your cane."

Mina grabbed the woman's arm. She tried to say, "My glasses."

"Excuse me?"

Mina stared up into the face bending over her, just able to make out the features. She tried again. "Glasses. Please." She could feel the woman's long hair tickling her face. "I can't see."

"Hold on." The woman raised her voice. "Hey, watch where you're stepping. Anyone find this woman's glasses?"

After a pause, Mina heard a man's voice growl, "Yo. Got 'em."

A few moments later, Mina's glasses were slipped over her face, and she could see sky. There was a small break in the clouds and the fresh, unlined face of the young woman standing over her. Long dark bangs hung over her eyes. Mina resisted the urge to push the hair back. How could the girl see? Mina craned her neck to find the waiting ambulance. A police officer was standing by its open doors, talking to Brian.

Mina didn't struggle this time when an oxygen mask was fastened over her face. The stretcher she was on started to roll. Every bump felt like an electrode jabbed into her hip.

Through a blur of pain, Mina could hear Brian's voice. "Y-e-t . . ." He was spelling her name for the police officer. "Ninety." She was ninety-one, but she didn't have the strength to correct him.

The stretcher stopped at the back of the ambulance. The sky and parking lot disappeared as Mina was lifted inside. It was warm and dry and quiet, and she could just hear Brian's voice. "No, I didn't get the license plate, but I saw it peel out of here. I don't think the guy even realized he'd hit her."

The policeman's response was barely a rumble.

Brian's voice again: "I got a pretty good look. It was a dark red Dodge minivan."

"But it wasn't," Mina said, the words caught in the oxygen mask. It had been a truck, a black pickup truck that was parked next to the red van.

The EMT was crouched beside Mina. She put her hand on Mina's arm. "Shhh. Just try to relax. We'll be at the hospital in a few minutes, and soon you'll be right as rain."

The ambulance doors slammed shut, and a moment later, the siren started to wail, and they were in motion.

Chapter
Thirty-nine

Evie sat back and closed her eyes. The smell in the ICU was pure hospital, but with all the clanking and hissing and beeping, and beneath that the rush and squeak of rubber-soled shoes, Evie could easily imagine she was in the belly of some huge machine. She'd been there for less than an hour when Ginger arrived.

"I got here as fast as I could," Ginger said. She was wearing a stretched-out T-shirt and yoga pants, and her hair was damp, like she'd come over right after taking a shower.

"She's been unconscious since I got here," Evie said. The numbers on the monitors were still frozen at 85 and 72.

Ginger bent over and kissed their mother on the forehead once, twice, three times. As she did so, one of the numbers changed. 74. 75. 76.

"Look at that!" Evie pointed to the readout. "I think that's her heart rate. It jumped when you kissed her." As she and Ginger watched, it dropped back to 74.

"She knows we're here," Ginger said, pulling over another chair. "Mom?" she said, taking their mother's hand, her eyes glued to the numbers. "It's Ginger and Evie. Can you hear me?"

But nothing happened. Evie sat there with Ginger, taking turns talking to their mother and trying to make the number spike again. Minute after minute dragged by, but Sandra Ferrante just lay there, her eyes half closed, unmoving.

"I'm glad we talked to her yesterday. At least we know what she wants," Ginger said, yawning and stretching.

"She never even opened my birthday card," Evie said. In spite of herself, she could feel tears rise and her throat close up.

"Oh, Evie. You know you're being ridiculous." Ginger gave her a sympathetic look. "And you look awfully pale. Have you had anything to eat?"

"Just coffee at work."

"No wonder. Let's go downstairs and grab a bite."

"Shouldn't we take turns?"

Ginger turned and looked at their mother. At the numbers that weren't moving. A nurse went by and Ginger stopped her. "Would it be okay if we went downstairs, just for ten minutes or so, to get something to eat?"

"Of course," the nurse said. "Give me your cell number and I'll call if there's a change, though I doubt there will be."

A few minutes later, they stepped off the elevator in the lobby. In the café, Evie grabbed a packaged ham-and-cheese sandwich, a bag of chips, and a bottle of water and got in the cashier's line to pay.

"I'm sorry," the cashier was telling the man in line in front of her, "we don't have lattes. Just coffee. Caf or decaf."

Ginger got in line behind Evie. She'd ladled herself what looked like a cup of pea soup so thick that the plastic spoon was standing straight up in it.

"Ma'am?" Evie turned. The cashier was holding out her hand so she could scan Evie's purchases. Evie handed them to her.

The man in front of her had stepped aside. She noticed he had a black vinyl woman's purse tucked under his arm. That made her sad. There was only one reason why a man would be carrying an old-fashioned and well-worn woman's purse in a hospital cafeteria.

She gave the cashier a ten-dollar bill. That's when she recognized the man. "Excuse me," she said to him. "You're my neighbor's nephew, aren't you?"

The man gave her a startled look. Some of his coffee sloshed onto his hand from the open lid and he jumped back.

Evie said, "My mother. She lives"—she took the two quarters and a penny change from the cashier and dropped them into a tips cup—"I mean, lived—I mean—" Which was right? Evie had no idea. She teared up.

The nephew looked at her in dismay. "Oh, right. Of course," he said. "Next door to Aunt Mina. Is your mother here in the hospital?" He glanced past her, uneasily shifting from foot to foot like he was afraid to ask how her mother was doing.

Ginger had paid for her soup and stepped out of line. She elbowed Evie. Evie took the hint. "Ginger, remember Mom's neighbor, Mrs. Yetner? This is her nephew. I'm sorry, I've forgotten your name."

"Brian Granville," he said. "I'd offer to shake, but I've managed to spill coffee all over myself." He snagged a napkin and wiped his hands.

Ginger said, "Your aunt is the one who called to tell us that Mom had been taken to the hospital. She left a message on my voice mail, and I remembered who she was right away. It was very thoughtful of her to call me. Otherwise we'd never have known."

"My aunt." Brian blinked three times. "Actually, she's why I'm here."

"What?" Evie's stomach turned over. "She's here? She's all right, isn't she? I mean, I saw her just last night."

"She lost her bearings in a parking lot. Fell. It was a miracle that a truck didn't back right over her. At her age?" He shook his head, his face somber. "And, well, you know how headstrong she can be. Did not want to come to the hospital. Not one bit. She's in surgery now."

"Surgery—?" Evie started to ask, but Brian's eyes focused on something behind her, and something in his expression made Evie turn to look. There was Mrs. Yetner's favorite neighbor, Frank Cutler. He'd probably come over to visit Evie's mother.

Evie went over to him. "Frank?" she said. "It's Evie Ferrante, Sandra's daughter. Did you come to see her?"

"I . . ." Frank Cutler glanced between Evie, Ginger, and Brian. "Yes, of course. I was about to go up."

"She'd be so pleased. And we'll let her know, but I'm afraid she's had a setback and she's been moved to intensive care. They only let family in."

"Family. Of course. I didn't realize."

"I'm sorry you had to make the trip for nothing."

"You'll tell her I was here and asking after her, won't you?" He started to turn to go.

"Did you know someone broke into her house yesterday?" Evie asked.

"Really? I'm sorry to hear that. Another burglary? What did they take?"

A shipping box. Vitamins. That sounded so lame. "You were around during the day, weren't you? Because Mrs. Yetner saw you out in the rain, talking to the man who came for my mother's car. What I wondered was, did you see anyone letting themselves into the house? Because there was no sign of a break-in. Do you know who my mother might have given keys?"

"Keys?" A muscle worked in Frank Cutler's jaw.

"Maybe she gave you a set?"

"You think I had something to do with this break-in?"

"No," Evie said quickly. "I'm asking, because Mrs. Yetner saw you—"

He held up his hands to stop her. "That woman. Busybody. Far too much time on her hands. Nothing to do but interfere." He looked across at Brian. "Sorry, but that's the truth. And yes, I was there. I wanted to know what had happened to Sandy's car. If there was anything I could do to help. If there was more vandalism or another break-in. The police told you that, didn't they?"

It wasn't until Evie and Ginger were back in the ICU, sitting with their mother and finishing their food when it occurred to Evie that the police hadn't said anything about a rash of vandalism or break-ins. Seemed like the kind of thing they should at least have mentioned.

Chapter Forty

Mina felt warm, buoyant, like she was floating in bathwater, oddly out of kilter and misconnected like one of those Picasso portraits with the drooping eyes. She was surrounded by people in white. Angels? The joke would be on her if there turned out to be any.

Beep, beep, beep. Beyond the figures huddled over her she caught glimpses of neon-green lines tracing out wave patterns.

One of the figures was bending over her now. She felt pressure on her side. A pull on her leg. Stronger pulling. *Pop.* She felt it ripple down her leg and across her pelvis. A moment, just a moment of what she diagnosed as pain. Lightning zapping through her.

Beep-beep-beep. The sound accelerated.

"There. It's back in." A man's voice.

"Blood pressure's a hundred and thirty-five over eighty." A woman's voice.

"I've got it." A man's. Pressure on her arm. A pinch.

There. Moments later Mina settled. Her Picasso eye was in alignment now. She felt her leg being lifted, bent, straightened.

"Looking good." The man's voice again, the words reaching her as if through wads of cotton batting. Like the soft diapers her mother used for years to dust the furniture, until they turned to shreds.

Mina felt herself moving now, ceiling lights streaming overhead like the white lines on a highway. Into the elevator. Doors closing. *Home.* Mina was sure she could hear her own voice. *Take me home.*

But when she woke up later, who knew how much later, she was in a hospital room.

"Mrs. Yetner?" Was that Brian's voice? Why would he be calling her that? "Can you hear me?"

Mina opened her eyes. A man was stooped over her and silhouetted against the sun, which was low in the sky and shining in through a window. A hospital window. The man had on a white coat, but his face was a blur. All Mina could make out was that he had a full beard.

"I'm Dr. Milner. How are you feeling?"

Mina's tongue felt thick, and her throat was raw. She reached out a hand, groping for her glasses on the table by the bed.

"Here. Let me help you with those." He slid on her glasses and smiled down at her. White teeth. The beard was neatly clipped. He couldn't possibly be more than twenty-five. "Are you in pain?" he asked.

Was she? She'd felt worse. She gave her head a tiny shake.

"Can you tell me your name?" he asked.

That made Mina smile. She remembered the many times she'd watched the staff at Pelham Manor ask Annabelle that question, and the day when she'd answered, "Anne Shirley." Not too long after that Annabelle couldn't come up with an answer to that question at all.

Mina cleared her throat. "Wilhelmina Yetner." It came out weak but clear.

"Excellent. Do you know what happened to you?"

Of course she knew what happened. "I fell. In the parking lot. Idiot driver." She looked around and made a guess on the answer to the question he'd be asking next. "Bronx Memorial Hospital."

He chuckled.

"Your turn," she said. "How am I?"

"Dislocated your hip, I'm sorry to say."

Mina knew which hip it was. The one that had been replaced. The one on the side that was starting to throb. Her arms were scraped raw, too, she could tell, but it could have been much worse.

"Has that happened before?" the doctor asked.

"Never." She was always careful not to overflex, to never go beyond the ninety-degree angle as her surgeon had warned her.

"Well, it's back where it belongs now. You took a nasty tumble, but I don't see why you shouldn't expect a full recovery. We were concerned about your blood pressure. It was very low when you came in. Then it spiked during reduction. We're pretty sure that was from the shock of the accident, but we're going to keep you overnight to monitor your vital signs and make sure it's all systems go."

Just overnight? Well, thank goodness for that. "So I'll live?"

"Absolutely." He unhooked her from a monitor, lowered the mattress, and cranked up the back. "And now, we need to get you up and about. The sooner the better."

The royal "we." The staff in the home talked to Annabelle like that, too. Like she was a toddler.

He brought over a walker. Another milestone on the slippery slope to infirmity.

She pushed back the covers, took the hand he offered her, and pulled herself up. Slowly, gingerly, she inched her legs over the side of the bed. Her feet dangled inches from the floor, and for a moment she could see Annabelle's feet and legs, the way they'd grown child-like and slack from disuse near the end. Better to die than waste away like that.

Mina summoned her strength and pressed her feet to the floor. She half expected the doctor to say *upsadaisy* as she shifted her weight to her good leg. Holding on to the walker, she shifted her weight gradually to the other side, too, worried that the ball would slip out of the socket again. But it held, and though it was sore, the pain was tolerable.

"No deep knee bends, now," the doctor said, backing up so she could move forward under her own steam. "But normal movement shouldn't be a problem. If we need to, we can get you fitted with a hip brace."

A hip brace? She'd just as soon not. Mina leaned into the walker and stepped forward with one foot. Then the other. Lifted the walker and moved it forward, thinking all the while of the old people at Pelham Manor tethered to their walkers and oxygen tanks. She gritted her teeth and took another step forward. The walker did make her feel more stable.

"Terrific," the doctor said, watching her with a critical eye.

What was terrific was that she could shuffle her way to the bathroom and take care of her own business. When someone had to wipe for her, she'd be ready to check out.

By the time Mina was back in bed, she was sweating from exertion. She collapsed, shivering against the pillows. Accepted some pain medication. The doctor was tapping at a computer when she closed her eyes for what she thought would be a few moments.

"Aunt Mina?" This time it *was* Brian's voice.

Mina opened her eyes. The bed was still cranked up, but now it was dark out. Brian was standing by her bed. Her purse sat on the tray table. Beside it Brian set her key ring. Mina squinted at it. Something looked different. Then she got it. Her car keys had been removed.

"How are you feeling?"

"Sore. A little shaky. Not so bad, considering. Where are my car keys?"

"I drove your car home and left it parked in your garage," he said, eyeing her coolly and taking a sip from a paper coffee cup.

"I want my car keys." She extended her hand, palm up. "Now." No matter how hard she stared at it, her hand still trembled. Damn him. She was not about to beg.

"That car isn't safe. What is it, thirty years old? And you shouldn't be driving it."

Mina felt her jaw trembling as she tried to stare him down. "I have never gotten a speeding ticket. Ever. Or had a single accident. And *I* don't drink." What did he think, that she'd forgotten the DUI that got his license suspended a while back? Or maybe he was still insisting that the police had singled him out, that he'd barely tested intoxicated after his car spontaneously accelerated and that fire hydrant took out the front quarter panel of his precious Mercedes. He'd had to "borrow" money from her to make the repairs—money that she'd long ago kissed good-bye.

"Facts are facts, Brian," Mina went on. "I am a safe driver—"

"—who can't remember where she parked her car."

"Well . . . that . . ."

"Who walks oblivious behind parked cars."

"Really, Brian, I don't think you're being fair."

"Fair? I'm sorry, Aunt Mina," Brian said, though there wasn't a drop of remorse in his tone. "But, as you are so fond of saying, facts are facts. Seems crystal clear to me. If you can't find your car, you shouldn't be driving one."

Mina pushed herself upright, wincing at the dull ache that pulsed through her side. She shifted to find the least uncomfortable position.

"Thank you very much for your concern, Brian, but I can take care of myself. I'm not a child, you know."

For a moment, he actually looked wounded. "Well, neither am I, in case you haven't noticed." He pulled over a molded plastic chair and sat in it, crossing his arms over his chest and rocking the chair back on two back legs. Of course he was doing that deliberately. He knew she'd remember the time he'd leaned back like that one Thanksgiving dinner and cracked her mother's dining room chair legs.

He stared down his nose at her. "There will come a time, and I'm afraid it's not in the too distant future, when you're going to want . . . *need* to move somewhere more appropriate."

Appropriate. *Appropriate?* Mina seethed. "You are not in charge of my life."

Brian gave a heavy sigh. "Sadly, no one is. That's what scares me." The chair creaked ominously as he leaned back still farther, as if taunting her.

"Sit properly, Brian," Mina said. She plucked a tissue from the box by the bed and blew her nose. "It doesn't matter. Keep the keys. You should probably have a set anyway. I have copies."

"Of course you do." He leaned forward, setting the chair straight and narrowing his eyes at her. "But do you remember where you put them?"

Mina's vision blurred and her throat started to close, but she refused to cry. Absolutely refused. She could hear her mother's voice: *There is a little bit of good in the worst of us and a little bit of bad in the best of us.* She wasn't sure if Brian was one of the worst, but he was a boatload of arrogant, smug, and annoying.

Brian's look softened. "Aunt Mina, let's not fight. I don't want you to hurt yourself. Or worse, for you to hurt someone else. Imagine how you'd feel."

She wanted to slap that smirk off his face. "I am not going to live in one of those . . . places. If you think I am, then you've got another think coming. As soon as I'm fit again, I am going home."

"Fit? You've got to be—" Brian stopped. He pinned her with a hard look, and after a moment of stony silence, he said, "Yes. Fine. I agree. You're going home."

Mina was too stunned to reply.

"Tomorrow, most likely," Brian continued into the silence. "I'll arrange for someone to stay with you and help out for a while. Until you can get around on your own."

Mina felt breathless, as if a closed door she'd been pressing against had suddenly been pulled open on her and she'd gone tumbling, like Alice down the rabbit hole.

"What's the matter?" Brian said. "I thought that's what you wanted?"

"It is. Of course it is."

"I know when to stop beating a dead horse." Mina winced at his analogy. "Besides, it's your life. And who's to say, maybe you're right." He glanced at his watch. "I've got to go." He stood, fished Mina's car keys from his pocket, and threaded them back on the key ring. "Here," he said, tossing the key ring on the tray table. "Drive, if you insist. Be my guest."

Mina snatched the keys before he could change his mind. She knew he was up to something.

Chapter
Forty-one

It was dark out by the time Evie left the ICU with Ginger. Now she knew what "serious but stable" condition looked like. They left their phone numbers stuck to their mother's chart at the nurses' station.

As they rode down in the elevator, Ginger said, "I feel so awful about saddling you with all this. Insisting that you come and take charge. I didn't realize it would be like this. That she'd . . ." Ginger swiped at her cheek with the back of her hand and fished a tissue out of her purse. She dabbed at her eyes, then continued. "It was me that Mom especially asked Mrs. Yetner to call. And now she's in a coma that she may never come out of. And I can't remember what the last thing I said to her was." She blew her nose. "It was weeks ago, and I'd been so relieved she wasn't calling and waking us up in the middle of the night that it never occurred to me that something might be, you know, wrong."

They got out in the lobby. Evie looked around the cavernous

space, so much emptier and quieter now than it had been when they arrived. A siren wailed outside.

"Love you, Ma," Evie said. She felt exhausted.

"What?"

"That's what I'm sure you said to her. It's what you always say last."

"Oh, God, I hope so."

"I know so. Because you're the good daughter." Evie hooked her arm in Ginger's and gave her a zerbert on the cheek. "You go home. I'm going to find Mrs. Yetner. She's been so kind to me and she doesn't have much family, only a nephew. Then I'll go back up to check on Mom to see if anything's changed before heading home."

"Promise you'll call me if there's anything?"

"Promise." Evie went to the information desk to find Mrs. Yetner's room number. When she got back, Ginger was drying her eyes.

"I'm coming with you," Ginger said.

"You don't need to do that."

"Yes, I do. Mom told Mrs. Yetner to call me."

Evie and Ginger took the elevator to the third floor, General Medical. As they got closer to the open door, a man Evie recognized as Mrs. Yetner's nephew backed into the corridor. "I'll see you tomorrow." He turned and almost ran smack into Evie and Ginger.

"How is she?" Evie asked.

"Feisty as ever." Brian glanced over his shoulder into Mrs. Yetner's room, then back at Evie. "I guess I'd be a lot more worried if she wasn't." He strode off down the hall.

Evie went to the open door and peered inside. Mrs. Yetner was lying in the raised hospital bed, facing away from the door.

"Hello?" Evie said. "Can we come in?"

Mrs. Yetner turned her head. "Oh! It's you." She gestured Evie into the room. She was as pale as the bedsheets, but her eyes were as clear and sharp as ever.

Evie went over to the bed. "I ran into your nephew. He said you fell? That you had surgery?"

"Surgery?" Mrs. Yetner seemed to summon her dignity, sitting straighter, but a spasm of pain stopped her. "Not exactly. They put me out and snapped me back together. My artificial hip."

Evie winced, thinking of the pop beads she and Ginger used to play with.

"Painful but not life threatening. Unfortunately for Brian."

"Hi, Mrs. Yetner," Ginger said, coming from behind Evie and approaching the bed. Gently she took Mrs. Yetner's hand. "You remember me?"

Mrs. Yetner's eyes widened. "Ginger? Of course I remember you. Miss Root Beer Popsicle. I used to keep some in the icebox, just for you." Under Mrs. Yetner's appraising look, Ginger smoothed her rumpled T-shirt and patted her hair.

Mrs. Yetner's gaze shifted back and forth from Evie to Ginger. "Oh, girls, don't look at me like that. I'm not ready for last rites. And I've already been up and around."

"You have? That's wonderful," Evie said, wiping away an unexpected tear.

"And I'll be going home soon. As long as that thing"—she pointed at the monitor by the bed—"doesn't misbehave."

Ginger pulled over a chair. "Thank you for calling me about Mom. We'd never have known otherwise."

Mrs. Yetner smiled. "How is she?"

"She's okay." Ginger mouth quivered as she exchanged a look with Evie. "She's not okay. She's in a coma. She's never going to be"—Ginger hiccuped—"okay. Oh, I don't mean to burden you with all this. You've got your own problems to deal with. But the message you left me? You said she wanted me to know something, but then you didn't get a chance to say what it was."

"Oh dear." Mrs. Yetner blinked. "What did she say? Something about don't tell him—"

"Who?"

"She didn't say. I wrote down her exact words. I'm sure I did. Because I knew I'd forget." She looked at Evie. "You'll find it in the house. It was"—Mrs. Yetner strained to find the memory—"on a slip of paper that the ambulance person gave me. She wrote down Ginger's phone number, and when I got in the house, I wrote down exactly what your mother said because my brain is a sieve these days." She pushed the key ring that was on her tray table over. "Here. Evie, you go in and see if you can find the note. And please. I've been so worried about Ivory. Could you feed her and let her sit in your lap for a bit? She won't eat dry food. There's tins of wet food in the cabinet. Tuna and mackerel— that's her favorite. And could you see that she has fresh water and scoop out her litter box?"

"Should I let her out?"

"Let her out?" Mrs. Yetner looked horrified. "As in *outside* out? She wouldn't know what to do with herself. She's used to being inside, and she's used to having company."

"I could take her home with me."

"Heavens, no. She's never lived anywhere but with me and she's a bit high-strung. If you get there and can't find her, she'll be hiding under the living room sofa."

"I'll feed her as soon as I get back," Evie promised. "And I can check in the morning and feed her before I leave."

"Or . . . why don't you stay in my house? Would you?"

Evie had mounds of trash yet to deal with, and she wasn't sure it was a good idea to leave her mother's house empty overnight. "Why don't we play it by ear?"

"The upstairs bedroom is all yours," Mrs. Yetner went on. "There's fresh towels and sheets in the linen closet. Just until I'm back, of course. And then, when I get home"—Mrs. Yetner cleared her throat—"we can have that talk about what it was like. You were right. I was working at the Empire State Building on that terrible morning."

Chapter
Forty-two

Before Evie left, Mrs. Yetner told her to leave the keys under a white-washed rock by the back porch where she could find them when she got home. As Evie sat in the passenger seat of Ginger's minivan for the short ride from the hospital, she called work and left a message that she'd be out but checking e-mail.

When they pulled up at their mother's house, Ginger sat there for a few moments staring out the car window. "Dear God," she said. "You told me, but I really had no idea how bad it was."

"Believe it or not, it was worse when I got here," Evie said.

Headlights strafed the house, and a dark pickup truck pulled up alongside them. Ginger hit the automatic door locks. The driver-side window on the truck rolled down. Finn leaned out.

"That's Finn Ryan," Evie said. "His father owned the convenience store. Remember him?"

"I do." Ginger rolled down the window.

"Hey," Finn said. Then, "Oh, excuse me. I thought you were—" He did a double take. "Ginger?"

"Here I am," Evie called across to him before Ginger could muster a response. "What's up?"

"I came by to see if you wanted a ride to tonight's meeting."

For a moment Evie's mind went blank. Then she remembered. His neighborhood conservancy group. "I'm sorry, Finn. I can't make it tonight. They've moved my mother to the ICU, and I'm completely wiped."

"ICU? I'm sorry." After an awkward silence, he said, "Okay. Of course. I understand. Another time then?" He revved the truck engine and shifted into gear.

"Another time," Evie called over the noise.

He smiled at her, winked, and took off.

"Finn," Ginger said. "I certainly do remember him. He's the kid who used to hang out in the back of the store. Kind of a geek." She gave Evie a speculative look. "He turned out cute, don't you think? What meeting?"

"Marsh preservation. A neighborhood group he belongs to. Actually, I get the impression that he started it."

"Sounds like he thought you had a date to go with him, or—" Fortunately for Evie, Ginger's cell phone chimed. She fished it out to read a text message. "Uh-oh. I've got to get home. Tony's running a fever."

"Tell him I said feel better soon," Evie said as she started to get out of the car.

Ginger put her hand on her arm. "You sure you're okay here alone? You could come home with me."

"You have your hands full. Besides, I don't want to catch whatever Tony's got and then give it to Mom. That's all she needs. And Ivory would be very annoyed if I left her without her salmon."

"Tuna and mackerel."

"Exactly."

Ginger waited in the car as Evie went around to the back of Mrs.

Yetner's house and tried to fit Mrs. Yetner's key into the back door in the dark. Piteous reproachful yowls came from inside the house, and Ivory jumped up on the windowsill and stared out at her. When Evie finally got the door open, she came around and waved to Ginger.

"You sure you're okay?" Ginger called.

"Go!" Evie said, shooing her away.

As Ginger drove off, Evie went inside. The cat kept right on squalling until Evie picked her up. She settled briefly in Evie's arms, then turned back to complaining as Evie put her down and hurried into the kitchen to find the cat food. Ivory was up on her back legs, begging, when Evie bent down and put the full dish on the floor.

While the cat ate, Evie rinsed out the can and tossed it into Mrs. Yetner's recycle bin. There were already a half-dozen empties in there. Fancy Feast. That was the same brand as the empty cat food cans she'd found in her mother's house.

Evie put fresh water in the cat's bowl and crouched to set it on the floor by the food. While Ivory lapped some up, Evie noticed there was still a slight burnt smell in the air. She remembered—Mrs. Yetner had burned some chicken.

Sure enough, there in the sink a blackened pot was soaking. Otherwise, the room was in perfect order. Evie hadn't noticed before that the kitchen had a wall-mounted phone with a rotary dial. The calendar beside the phone caught her eye. Calendars were one of those things people rarely saved, but were in their own way a Rorschach that said as much about the person as the era. She remembered Farrah Fawcett in that famous swimsuit on the calendar that hung on the wall at her father's fire station. Mrs. Yetner's calendar was from the Nature Conservancy, and April's picture featured a trio of tiny owls, their bright green eyes wide open.

In some of the date blocks, Mrs. Yetner had written notes in her neat, precise hand. But in the last few days she'd written much more.

Burned teakettle, the list began and went on, spreading over into later date blocks.

The poor thing. Maybe her nephew did have her pegged.

Evie picked up Mrs. Yetner's keys and got ready to leave. But when she got to the back door, Ivory was pacing back and forth in front of it and yowling piteously. When Evie bent down and scratched the cat behind the ears, Ivory blinked, yelped once, and with a graceful leap landed on Evie's shoulder. Then she stuck her nose in Evie's ear and purred like a truck engine.

The message was clear. And why not stay overnight? This house was so much cleaner and cozier than her mother's. Besides, Ivory wasn't the only one who needed company.

Chapter
Forty-three

Mrs. Yetner's upstairs bedroom was long and narrow, stretching from the front of the house to the back, just like the bedroom where Evie and Ginger had slept as kids. Two simple iron twin beds were shoved under sloping ceilings at one end on either side of a window. The beds were covered with quilts, hand pieced from patches of soft 1930s cotton printed in distinctive period designs rich in creamy pastels. Hooked area rugs from the same period in gray, black, and pale green were scattered on the floor.

Evie stepped to the window that looked out over the water—the same view as from her mother's—but this window and the one at the opposite end of the room felt grander than the windows in her mother's upstairs. They were trimmed in oak carved in the Eastlake architectural style that predated the house by at least forty years. Evie ran her hand over the sill and its distinctive sawtooth trim. It wouldn't have surprised her if the woodwork had come from the house where Mrs. Yetner's father had found that marble mantel.

At the opposite end of the room were a pair of dark mahogany bureaus, one low and one high, 1940s vintage. She came closer. Among the perfume bottles on the lower bureau sat quite a large blown-glass paperweight with lovely millefiori flowers of red, white, and blue. A single framed picture was on the wall behind the bureau. It was a page from one of those massive old street atlases and was dated 1911.

Evie took the map down to get a better look. The neighborhood was rendered in detail typical of maps from that period. There was the Bronx River running into the East River with piers jutting out into the water. A few blocks inland was Snakapins Park, the amusement park Finn said his great-grandfather had owned. In the middle of the park was what looked like a black hole labeled INK WELL. Probably the park's swimming pool. One of the bigger structures had to be what was now Sparkles Variety.

Apparently in 1911 Mrs. Yetner's father hadn't started building the houses in what was now Higgs Point. The crescent of land bounded by water—Evie estimated about a hundred acres—had no structures, but narrow lanes were indicated with parallel dashed lines running east-west, some of them extensions of streets farther in from the water. Over the area, in print so small that she could barely read it, the words *Snakapins Park Bungalows* were spelled out. Evie wondered if that was the waterfront where Finn's great-grandfather's family used to come summers and camp out. A pier marked Ferry Point, just south, must have been the landing point for the ferry from College Point in Queens, where there really had been a college once upon a time, in the early 1800s. So interesting how old maps like this one were historical snapshots.

Later, Evie went back to her mother's house to get clothes and her toothbrush. When she came back to Mrs. Yetner's, she washed out Ivory's food bowl, added some fresh water, turned out the lights downstairs, and headed up to the bedroom.

She took the bed on the right, the same side that had been hers growing up. The bed had old-fashioned springs that squeaked when she got into it, and her instinct to duck her head so she didn't hit the sloped ceiling was ingrained. Immediately the cat jumped up, circled, kneaded her claws into the quilt, and curled up. Evie hoped it was all right to let Ivory sleep with her. The cat's back felt warm up against Evie's.

Even with Ivory's comforting presence, it took Evie what felt like hours to fall asleep. When she finally did, she dreamed she was trying to fall asleep in her own childhood bedroom. A cold breeze swept through the room, from front window to back window. The door to the room opened and her mother stood there.

But the mother wavering on the threshold of the room was the wraith mother Evie had left in the hospital. *It's just a dream, it's just a dream, it's just a dream,* Evie told herself. She knew that because the silk robe this mother had on had been thrown away years ago.

Her mother stepped into the room, pointed her finger at Evie, opened her mouth, and emitted an unearthly yowl.

Evie sat bolt upright in the bed, sweating and shaking. The bedroom really was cold, and outside the sky was dark. The room was familiar and not familiar. It took a moment for her to remember where she was.

And then the sound came again. A yowl. Definitely an animal. Then a thump. Then a hiss. The empty spot beside her on the bed was still warm, and the sounds were coming from downstairs.

Evie wrapped the quilt around her, stepped to the window, and looked out into the marsh. Far off, the lights of Manhattan barely glowed through a thin fog. Below, light poured out onto the backyard from the living room window. She was sure she'd turned out the lights downstairs.

Evie held very still and listened, her heart pounding in her chest.

Those creaking footsteps didn't belong to any house cat. Someone was in the house.

She looked for a phone in the room but there was none. Her cell phone was downstairs in her purse, though she couldn't remember where she'd left it. She remembered there was a phone at the foot of the stairs.

Casting about for some kind of weapon, she grabbed the glass paperweight from the bureau and crept to the top of the stairs. In the gloom, she could make out the telephone sitting on the table by the front door. She started down the stairs, tiptoeing, holding the heavy paperweight like a baseball. She'd almost reached the table when she heard a man's voice call quietly, "Here, kitty kitty kitty."

Evie froze. There was a hiss and, again, that preternatural howling. That had to be Ivory.

Evie used the sounds as cover to take the last few steps. She grabbed the phone and darted back up the stairs, as far as the cord would reach. She sat on a step and, by feel, she found the 9 hole and dialed, cringing at the sound as the dial ratcheted back.

"Shit." The man's voice again. She heard him grunt. Footsteps on the kitchen floor. A cabinet door opening, then closing. Then footsteps receding from the kitchen and onto the carpet. Another grunt.

She dialed 1 and was about to dial another 1 when she heard, "Come on out of there, Ivory."

Ivory? A burglar who knew the cat's name? How likely was that?

Evie hung up the phone and set it on the step. Still holding the paperweight, she crept down to the kitchen door and peered in. No one was there. Beyond the dining room, lights were on in the living room. A man dressed in dark clothing and a baseball cap was crouched in front of the couch, holding a broom. As Evie watched, he got down on his belly. "Shit," he said again and turned his baseball cap to face the back. The brim was red, and the team insignia above it looked familiar. "Come on. Get out of the way, you stupid cat." Now Evie recognized the voice. It was Mrs. Yetner's nephew.

Ivory hissed and yowled as Brian poked the broom under the couch. He reached under, groped about, and then jerked back. "Ow. Damn you." He reached in again, grunting. "Now I've got you. Just you—"

"Hey," Evie cried.

Brian kept right on grunting and reaching and Ivory kept right on screeching and hissing.

Evie came up behind him. "Hey!"

Brian froze. He let go, sat up, and twisted around. "What are you doing here?"

"Your aunt asked me to stay over and take care of the cat. She didn't tell you?"

"Obviously not," Brian said. "I came over to take care of the cat, too."

Evie folded her arms across her chest. "In the middle of the night? With a broom?"

He struggled to his feet and dropped the broom. "The cat got spooked. I was trying to coax her out from under there so I can take her home with me."

Coax? Drag was more like it. And in what? Evie didn't see a cat carrier sitting open.

"Well, you didn't need to. Your aunt asked me to stay here with Ivory while she's gone. So I am. And when your aunt comes home—"

Brian rocked back on his heels and squashed his chins into his neck. "Who said she's coming home?"

"She did." Evie pulled the quilt tighter around her as he narrowed his eyes.

"I'm sure you mean well," he said, tugging on his lapels, "but you don't even live here. I don't want to see my aunt hurt. I don't want her to start depending on you and then you disappear." He took a breath.

"Anyway, never mind about the cat. I can see Ivory doesn't need me."
He started for the door, then paused and turned around. "Thank you."
He stomped off.

"No problem," Evie murmured to his receding back.

Evie heard the front door open and shut. Moments later a car
engine started. By the time she got to the kitchen and looked out the
window, his car was gone.

She dropped the quilt and hurried back into the living room. She
got down on her hands and knees and looked under the couch. Ivory
was there, a shadowy lump glowering back at her.

"Hey, Ivory. It's okay. You can come out now." Evie made kissing
sounds. "Come on. Come on out." She reached under the couch, but
the cat backed farther into the saggy underbelly of the sofa. Evie's
hand brushed against a piece of metal on the floor and she pulled it
out instead of the cat. A small piece of shiny brass that fit in the palm
of her hand. She turned it over, recognizing the fused tubes—it was
the little whistle attachment that had been on Mrs. Yetner's teakettle.

From under the sofa came the sound of rustling paper. Evie lay
down on the floor and raised the sofa's skirt to let in more light. It
looked as if Ivory was backed up on top of some papers. Evie reached
in, grabbed a corner of a page, and tugged it out.

She sat, legs crossed, to see what she'd found. It was a sheet from
some kind of legal document. The header on the page read "Life
Estate Deed." There was a line for signature by a "Grantor," and
below that, a block of text that began:

> Grantor makes no warranty, express or implied, concern-
> ing the property's condition, need of repair, existence or
> absence of any defects, visible, hidden, latent, or otherwise.

As Evie went on reading, Ivory crept out from under the sofa. She stretched, yawned nonchalantly, rubbed her forehead against Evie's knee, and curled up on the discarded quilt.

Evie had to move the sofa away from the wall to reach the rest of the papers, including a cover letter to Wilhelmina Yetner. These looked like the papers Evie had seen Mrs. Yetner shove under a sofa cushion when Brian had come to visit the last time—probably the legal document that he'd been pestering her about. A few words popped out at her. *Life tenant. Remainderman.*

As she was getting up from the floor, a small slip of blue paper fluttered from between the pages. She picked it up. What caught her immediate attention were the words, written in the same handwriting as on the calendar:

Tell Ginger. Don't let him in until I'm gone.

Chapter
Forty-four

"That's the message?" Ginger said when Evie had gotten her on the phone the next morning and read her what Mrs. Yetner had written down. "What's it mean?"

"Beats me. Too bad we can't ask her," Evie said, staring at the words written on the scrap of paper.

"You're sure that's all?"

"I'm looking at it right now. It was under the couch. I never would have found it except that Mrs. Yetner's nephew let himself in last night to get the cat. Ivory hid under the couch and put up such a fuss that it woke me up."

"He didn't know you were there?"

"Apparently not."

"How creepy is that?"

"Scared me half to death until I realized who it was. If I'd gotten up in the morning and found the cat missing, I'd have been beside myself."

"Read it to me one more time, would you?"

"'Tell Ginger. Don't let him in until I'm gone.'"

"Right."

Right. What Evie couldn't help wondering was whether she'd already let "him" in.

After Evie got off the phone, she fed Ivory, straightened Mrs. Yetner's upstairs bedroom, and packed up her things. She planned to spend the morning cleaning her mother's house, but as she was leaving, she picked up the document she'd found under the couch. Life estate deed. What exactly was that?

Evie sat down and made herself read it through once, then again to be sure. It was just what it said, a deed. The property was 105 Neck Road—Mrs. Yetner's house. Properly signed and executed, it would have transferred ownership. Instead of payment, it gave Mrs. Yetner the right to continue living there. She'd be responsible for property taxes and "maintenance and upkeep." But the minute she kicked it, Soundview Management, or the "remainderman," in legalese, would receive the property. No muss, no fuss, and no need to go through probate. Their logo was so innocuous, a double row of wavy lines beneath the outlines of a crab and a fish.

The reason why anyone would sign away property like that was prominently laid out. The "life tenant"—in this case, Mrs. Yetner—would receive a regular income, twenty-four thousand dollars a year in monthly increments, a sort of reverse rent. Sounded like a great deal for someone who had a good long life ahead of her—someone, say, in her sixties.

The thought left Evie ice cold. Her mother was sixty-two. And she'd told Ginger that she was getting a new monthly income. That would explain those cash-filled envelopes. The sooner her mother died, the better the deal was for the remainderman.

Could an agreement like that be nullified or was it already too late? Evie needed legal advice, and she needed it fast. Too bad she didn't have a friend who was a lawyer. Then it occurred to her. She did.

When Evie got to Sparkles, the store seemed empty. Her "Anyone here?" got no answer. She helped herself to a jelly doughnut from the glass case by the register and left a dollar and a quarter on the counter. When she got outside, she noticed Finn's pickup parked behind the store. He couldn't have gone far.

Evie was walking back to her mother's house when she realized what she'd thought at first was the omnipresent roar of a jet on its approach to LaGuardia was much louder and more uneven. As she turned onto Neck Road, a big flatback truck roared past her on the narrow street. Riding on its platform was a yellow bulldozer. Close behind came two dump trucks, their beds filled with debris. One of the drivers gave his horn a friendly toot, and Evie raised her hand to wave.

Standing in their dust, it occurred to Evie to wonder where they were coming from. Her mother's street, which ran along the water, only went on for about another half mile before it came to a dead end at the lagoon.

Evie followed the trail of grit and glass the trucks had left in their wakes past her mother's and Mrs. Yetner's houses, past blocks she had ridden her bike up and down when she was little. The trail ended at an empty lot. There was Finn, crouched amid the rubble, staring out into the marsh.

"Finn?" Evie said, coming up behind him.

He jumped to his feet. "Oh. It's you." He gestured toward the empty lot. "Can you believe this? Yesterday there was a house here."

Evie looked around. There was another empty lot two houses farther along. "And over there?" She pointed.

"Up until a few months ago, there was a house there, too." He hadn't shaved and looked like he hadn't slept, either. He seemed so distraught, and she wondered if he'd been up all night, witnessing the destruction.

Finn walked across what had been the front lawn of the recently demolished house, his sneakers crunching the debris. He bent over and fished out a foot-long piece of what looked like windowsill, its bright red paint flaking. "Must have brought in the equipment yesterday after dark. While me and anyone who might have tried to stop them were at the neighborhood meeting." He gazed somberly out across the water.

Evie walked over to him and took his arm. She didn't know what to say.

"What kills me," he said, "is that I might have been able to prevent this. Mrs. Yetner brought me a demolition permit she lifted off the house that was here." He took a folded yellow card from out of his jacket pocket. "She must have told you about it."

"She didn't," Evie said. Occasionally the Historical Society would get similar documents, a last remaining vestige of a building that someone had deemed too historically insignificant to be left standing.

This house, and the one two doors up, had hardly been historically or architecturally noteworthy—none of these houses in Higgs Point were. Unlike brownstones in Greenwich Village or Brooklyn Heights, the history of Higgs Point was not steeped in entitlement. But taken together, this neighborhood with all its little shotgun houses on lanes too narrow to be called streets, built within a few years of one another, was a one-off. There was nothing like it anywhere else in the five boroughs. Evie could easily make a case for preserving its unique flavor.

"Listen, even if you'd been here, what could you have done?" Evie said. "Were you going to lie down in front of the bulldozer?"

"I could have called the Preservation Board. Or the Department of Environmental Protection. And yeah, I could have gotten some volunteers together and blocked the bulldozer. Called the newspaper first of course. The thing is, I didn't do anything. Not a goddamned thing." Finn rubbed his grizzled chin with the back of his hand. "I didn't think it was going to happen this fast."

Evie walked into the debris and poked her toe through it. She kicked up what looked like the rim of a plate. She squatted to get a closer look. The piece was white bone china, hand-painted gold. Poking around nearby she found the metal screw cap of a lightbulb and an undamaged ceramic salt shaker in the shape of a miniature lighthouse. Farther in was the shiny, black-and-chrome beehive-shaped base of a blender. It was labeled OSTERIZER. It was so old it would have been worth something on eBay.

"This really is outrageous," Evie said, returning to Finn's side. Houses were supposed to be emptied out before they were bulldozed. This one looked more like it had been hit by a tornado. Like whoever did the job hadn't a clue what he was doing. "Can you believe what a mess they left behind?"

"Looks like they even pushed a shitload of debris into the marsh. Knuckleheads."

"Someone ought to file a complaint. Or threaten a lawsuit. Make them come back and do the job properly." The more Evie talked, the more worked up she got. "Let me see that permit." Evie snatched the card from Finn's grasp. She flattened it and read.

The permit for demolition was all properly signed and sealed. SV Construction Management. Evie recognized the name immediately.

"Have a look at this." She dug in her bag and found the life estate deed she'd pulled out from under Mrs. Yetner's couch. "Here. See? Here's Soundview Management. And here?" She held up the work permit. "SV Construction Management. Got to be the same outfit."

"Where'd you get this?" Finn asked, taking the life estate deed from her.

"I found it at Mrs. Yetner's, shoved under the couch."

Finn paged through the document, his face growing darker. He muttered under his breath and then stood there, staring off into the water.

"Pretty clever, if you ask me," Evie said. "It's the perfect scheme for taking over properties without their ever going on the market. Without anyone being aware. The owner signs away the house before he or she passes away. Don't you think that's what happened here?"

"I don't know, but I aim to find out. Can I keep this?" Finn folded the document and shoved it into his jacket pocket, but not before Evie made yet another connection: the crab and fish logo.

"Wait a minute. Isn't their logo like the one your preservation group uses?"

"You noticed, too?" Finn said, looking chagrined. "One of the members told me that a developer had appropriated our logo, but I hadn't gotten around to doing anything about it. Now I know where to send a cease and desist letter."

Just then a cell phone rang. Finn slipped a phone from his hip pocket and shook his head. "Must be yours."

Evie was afraid to look. But it wasn't the hospital. It was the gas station. Her mother's car was ready to be picked up.

Chapter
Forty-five

Evie accepted Finn's offer to drive her to the gas station. All the way over, her mind was racing. Had her mother accepted the same deal that Mrs. Yetner had been offered? Was that why she was getting those envelopes of cash that she'd apparently been too out of it to open? Was a bulldozer waiting to swoop in and crush her mother's house and everything in it the minute she died?

"So do you still want to see the stuff from Snakapins?" Finn's question interrupted her thoughts.

"Sorry. Do I what?"

He pulled to a stop in front of the gas station, yanked the emergency brake, and shifted in the seat to face her. "Remember, the stuff I told you about that's in the store's basement from Snakapins Park, the old amusement park?"

Snakapins Park and Snakapins Bungalows had been on the map in Mrs. Yetner's bedroom. She hadn't forgotten Finn's comment that there were remnants of the park in the store's basement, and of course she wanted to see them.

"A night later this week?" he said. "After I close the store? By then I should have some answers about what's going on."

Later in the week? Would she still be there? Already what she'd thought would be a few overnights had turned into nearly a week.

"What? Don't tell me your nights are all booked," he said.

"No, it's not that—"

"Good. You know, I always thought all that stuff moldering down there was nothing more than junk that no one had gotten around to tossing out. You can tell me if any of it is worth preserving. I don't even know what's in half the boxes. "

"How many boxes?" Evie asked.

"Lots."

Probably they were filled with decaying junk, Evie told herself. Still, the prospect of being the first to open up a cache of storage boxes that had been closed for decades? It was the kind of thing she lived for.

"Besides," Finn went on, reaching across for the passenger door handle, "you look like you could use a real meal. Aren't you sick of those chicken potpies?"

"You cook, too?"

"I make a mean chili. Do you like chili?"

She nodded and got out of the car.

"Good," he said through the open door. "See you then."

"See you."

He made a U-turn and waved through the window. As she watched him drive off, she caught her breath. She was excited about seeing the remnants of a 1920s amusement park. But even more, she liked that Finn wanted to know if the material was *worth preserving,* not how much it was worth.

As if on cue, her cell phone rang. Seth.

"Hi, babe."

Evie grimaced. She'd told him she hated when he called her that. "So how was the game?" she asked.

"They lost. Insane defense. Minor screwups, lousy offensive rebounds, throwing the ball out of bounds, jumping off the court and diving on the floor. I mean, what's that all about? Sorry about changing plans on you," he continued, barely missing a beat. "I know you're not crazy about basketball. But, hey, great seats. How could I not go? How about we go out for Chinese tomorrow? I'll make a reservation at the Shun Lee Palace."

"Seth, I doubt if I'll be back tomorrow. Besides, I wanted to go to Chinatown for soup dumplings."

"I'm sure they have soup dumplings at the Shun Lee."

They probably did. Four miniature ones for the same price that you could get two bamboo steamers full of them at the Soup Dumpling House.

"I hear they have a sensational Peking duck," Seth said into her silence, his voice coaxing.

They probably had Seth's favorite Polish vodka, too. "Are you going to ask about my mother?" she asked, not bothering to soften the annoyed edge in her voice.

She could hear him breathing on the other end of the line. Finally, "I'm sorry. Of course. How is she?"

"She's dying, Seth. And the house is a complete wreck. And I'm holding it together, but basically I'm a complete wreck, too. Which I know isn't what you want to hear when you're making dinner reservations."

"Hey, babe, it's not your fault."

Not her fault? Was he really that clueless?

"And you know," Evie said, taking a quick breath before plunging on, "there's something I've been meaning to tell you. I don't really like steaks. Or martinis. Or the smell of cigar smoke, even when you smoked hours ago and brushed your teeth."

After that, a pit of silence before Seth exploded with, "Is that so? Well, while we're on the subject, I don't like soup dumplings. Chinatown is dirty. And I could care less about an old airplane engine lying at the bottom of an elevator shaft."

"I guess it wouldn't make much of a tie tack, would it?" Evie shot back, and she disconnected the call. She stared at the phone for a few moments before shoving it back into her purse. As if mocking her, a shiny black Lincoln town car rolled past, as out of place in the neighborhood as Seth had been in her life.

Squashing the teeny-tiniest pang of regret, she turned to face the gas station. It looked nothing like it had when Evie used to ride there with her dad to fill up their car. Back then there'd been a single island with gas pumps on either side, serviced by a pair of nimble gas jockeys who cleaned and squeegeed windshields and offered to top off the oil. Now there were four islands with two pumps each, all but one of them self-serve, and a single attendant who pumped gas if someone actually pulled into the "full serve" spot.

But one thing was still there. Over the garage doors was a wonderfully detailed bas-relief of the front end of a 1930s car that seemed to emerge from a medallion of concrete. With its muscular fenders, exposed headlights, and distinctive grille, Evie guessed it was supposed to be a DeSoto.

Evie walked into a little glassed-in office tucked into the front corner of the garage. When she gave her name at the desk, the man whom she recognized as one of the brothers who'd inherited the business pulled out a bill. *Jack* was stitched over the pocket of his work shirt.

"I used to come in here years ago with my dad," Evie told him. "It looks so different out there, but in here it's exactly the same."

He looked at the bill. "Ferrante?" Up at her. "You're Vinny's girl?"

"One of them."

"Fine man, your dad. Though we used to kid him about that heap he drove around in."

Evie laughed, remembering her father's Chevy Caprice woody wagon that he'd driven until the axle rusted apart. He loved that old car. It was so big that they'd once loaded a double mattress into the back of it.

"Must have gotten my love of old things from him," she said, handing Jack her card. "If you ever tear this building down, the Historical Society would be very interested in that bas-relief over the doors." She took him outside and showed him what she meant. "We'd come in and drill it out of there. Wouldn't cost you a penny."

He stared at her card for a moment, then looked up into the roof peak and scratched his head. "Really? What's it worth?"

"It's worth preserving."

After Evie paid, Jack said, "Got a minute?" He led her out into the garage, which smelled of axle grease and cigarette smoke. Her mother's car was being lowered on one of the hydraulic lifts. He went over to what looked like an enclosed broad shallow metal pan sitting on a sheet of plastic. With his toe, he lifted it. The underside was corroded and riddled with holes.

"This is the gas tank we took out of your mother's car. It's not unusual for gas tanks to corrode little by little over time. And of course around here we've got more than our share of moisture and salt. But this car's not superold, and you can see the gas tank failure is massive. Thing is, it's rotted from the inside. We had your mother's car up on the lift a couple of months ago for brake work and there was nothing like this."

"So what are you saying?"

"This isn't normal wear and tear. To do this much damage this fast, some kind of strong acid had to have been poured directly into the tank."

Evie stood there for a moment, blinking at the ruined gas tank and feeling sick to her stomach. The most benign explanation she could come up with was vandalism. More insidious: sabotage.

Evie drove her mother's car from the gas station directly to the hospital where Ginger was waiting for her to take over. "She hasn't woken up," Ginger said when she met Evie outside the ICU. Evie had the impression that Ginger was barely holding it together. "Dr. Foran says she's in a hepatic coma. She might have some awareness but probably not. I keep talking to her anyway. I want her to know she's not alone."

Evie knew it wouldn't be much longer. Dr. Foran had said patients fell into a hepatic coma days before the end.

"At least she's breathing on her own," Ginger said. "She seems calm. They're giving her pain medication, so I hope she's not uncomfortable."

Evie hoped Ginger was right. "Speaking of sick, how's Tony doing?"

"His fever is down, and he's not throwing up." Ginger gave a tired smile. "Life goes on. Which reminds me, did you pick up the car?"

"I did. They couldn't just patch the tank. They had to replace it. The failure was so massive the mechanic thinks someone must have poured acid into the gas tank."

"What? But why?"

Evie had been asking herself that same question all the way over. Her mother was an easy target—an alcoholic, already alone and isolated. Take away her car and provide her with an endless flow of vodka, and it was a good bet that she'd go on a prolonged bender.

"I think it's about the house," Evie said.

"You've got to be kidding."

"Not the house exactly. The property. Two houses near Mom's have been leveled in the last few months, the last one right after the owner died. And Mrs. Yetner's nephew has been trying to get her to sign a life estate deed, signing over her property to the same people who are tearing down houses. You said Mom was excited because she was getting a regular income? That's part of the deal."

To Evie's relief, Ginger didn't even suggest that she sounded crazy. Still, she seemed a bit skeptical. "So where's this estate deed, or whatever you call it, that Mom signed? There'd be a record, wouldn't there?"

Evie wondered why she hadn't thought of that. Tracing property ownership was a routine part of her work at the Historical Society. "It's something I can find out."

"And you say Mrs. Yetner's nephew is trying to get her to sign one of those agreements?" Ginger said.

"I don't think he's getting much traction. Mrs. Yetner is pretty sharp. But I wanted to ask her what she knows about that deed. Do you mind staying with Mom a little bit longer while I go talk to her?"

But when Evie got to Mrs. Yetner's room, two floors up, she found the bed was empty and the sheets stripped. A nurse was inside, closing the closet door. She turned and saw Evie. "Can I help you?"

"I'm sorry. My friend, Mrs. Yetner? She was in this room? An older woman. She'd dislocated her hip?"

The nurse narrowed her eyes at Evie. "Did reception tell you she was still here?"

"No, no. Nothing like that. I'm sorry." Evie felt as if she'd been caught wandering the school hallway without a pass. "She's my neighbor. I visited her here yesterday and I just assumed . . . and today I was here to see my mother and I thought . . . She is all right, isn't she?"

At that, the nurse finally smiled. "Yes, she's fine. She left a little while ago. She couldn't find her glasses and she was very upset, so I came back to see if she left them here."

While the nurse looked in all the drawers and cabinets, Evie checked under the bed and in the trash can. She knew how frantic Mrs. Yetner would be without her glasses, even for a few hours. That, coming on top of dislocating her hip? It was too much.

"Maybe they got wrapped up in the bedding," the nurse said. "Otherwise I can't imagine what happened to them. Glasses." She shook her head. "That's not the kind of thing anyone would steal."

Evie took one final look around the room before following the nurse out. She'd stop over at Mrs. Yetner's house later that night when she got home. Now she had to get back and spell Ginger.

Evie was waiting for the elevator, pressing the down button a third time even though she knew it would do no good, when a bit of sparkle in the base of a potted plant caught her eye. Using her fingers like tweezers, she reached into a mound of fake moss and pulled out a pair of white cat's-eye glasses with rhinestones in the corners.

Chapter
Forty-six

"For heaven's sakes, we'll get you another pair of glasses, Aunt Mina," Brian said. "Would you stop fretting about them already? It's not a big deal."

It was a big deal. Mina was belted into the front seat of Brian's car, her handbag clutched in her lap. The world whizzing by through the window was a blur. Brian, sitting not three feet away from her, was featureless. If she hadn't recognized the voice coming out of his mouth, and that distinctive smell of whatever cologne it was that he slathered on himself, she'd have had no idea who was driving.

The car came to a halt. "Where are we?" Mina asked.

"Stopped at a light."

As if she didn't know that. After a minute, the car accelerated up an incline, fast. Mina assumed they were on the highway now.

"Now we're on the Bruckner," Brian confirmed.

Mina held on to the door handle as the car moved into the left lane and sped along. The car shuddered rhythmically over seams in the pavement. The vibrations made her hip ache. She could feel the changes in pressure as they passed cars and trucks.

By the time Brian pulled up in front of her house, Mina was wrung out. She was desperate for a quiet cup of tea, her own chair, and another of those painkillers they'd given her in the hospital.

A medium-sized white box truck was parked in front of the house. Brian pulled up parallel to it and rolled down the window. "Yo! How's it going?" he called out.

"We should have it done by the end of the day," the answer came back. A man's voice, though to Mina the man himself was nothing more than a tall dark shadow.

Brian pulled his car into the driveway. Mina squinted. It looked like another man was carrying something inside.

"What's going on?" Mina said.

"The social worker at the hospital told me that the house— the bathroom in particular—isn't properly set up for you. With the walker, you can barely get in the room. If you end up in a wheelchair, you wouldn't be able to get through the door. That got me thinking about turning the upstairs into a master suite with its own bath. So that's what they're building for you. Wide doorway. Roll-in shower. Grab bars. Slip-proof floor."

Mina snorted. Sounded like the spiel she'd heard when the woman in the blue suit had shown them one of the rooms at Pelham Manor.

Brian ignored her. "Once it's done, your health aide can sleep downstairs. We'll see how it goes, and if we need to install a lift on the stairs, we'll do that."

Second-floor bath? Live-in health aide? Stair lift? "How much is all this going to cost?"

"A lot less than the cost of a residential setting, and your insurance will pay for most of it. They'll be using a prefab unit for the bathroom so it won't take long to finish the work. Dora will sleep upstairs until the new bath is done and you can move up."

"Dora?"

"The hospital referred her. Dora . . . Fleischer I think is her last name. I hired her to help you." Without waiting for a response, Brian got out of the car, popped the trunk, and came around to her side and opened the door. He unfolded the walker and set it up for her. "What's the matter? I thought you'd be pleased."

Well, she was and she wasn't. She was pleased to be home. But strangers were in her house. Leaving the door wide open. Tramping up and down her staircase in their work boots. Breaking apart the upstairs bedroom. Had Brian forgotten he didn't own the house? Not yet, at least.

But Mina didn't say anything. Just pushed against the dashboard and shifted her feet out, tried to stand, and then grudgingly took Brian's offered hand and slid out of the car. She gritted her teeth against the pain. The doctor had said she'd feel a lot better a week from now when the swelling went down. As it was, it was slow going pushing the walker up the front walk. Brian helped her climb the front steps.

Inside, the house smelled of plaster dust and overworked electrical tools. As she shuffled across the kitchen floor, Mina felt as if her feet were leaving streaks in a coating of dust. Just as well that she couldn't see. She'd have been desperate to clean, and until the work was done, "clean" would be an uphill battle. Besides, the doctor had said in no uncertain terms there was to be no stooping or bending, not until the physical therapist who'd be coming to the house gave her permission.

"Where are my rugs?" Mina asked as Brian helped her across the bare floor to the living room.

"Rolled up and put away," he said. "You can bring them back when the construction is finished and you don't need to use the walker any longer." They'd reached her chair. He helped her turn around. She felt behind her for the seat cushion. Then, holding on to him, she lowered herself into the chair. This was going to get old fast.

Mina shivered with cold. Brian found her sweater and helped her on with it. Later, even with a mug of hot tea, the crocheted spread piled over her, and the sun shining in through the windows, Mina still felt chilled. She wished Ivory would come out of hiding.

All day long, Brian kept going upstairs to *supervise,* as he called it, the construction. Noise went on unabated, banging and sawing and drilling and hammering, with workers—there had to be at least three of them—marching in and out. It sounded as if they were taking the house apart. Brian explained that the banging and clattering she heard was a chute they'd set up to carry away rubble and debris. They had better not be burying her lovely lacecap hydrangeas.

She'd had to remind Brian to call and order her another pair of prescription glasses. She listened as he made the call, gave them her name and her prescription number. Of course they no longer carried anything like her old frames, but Brian said the woman he talked to on the phone had promised to do her best to come close. Fortunately, '50s fashions were apparently back.

While Brian was on one of his supervisory forays upstairs, Mina made her way to what she was already thinking of as the "downstairs" bath. He was right. She had to leave the walker in the hall.

She washed her face. All that noise had given her a headache, and the hot washcloth felt soothing. Then she took a capsule of pain medication—Brian had filled the prescription at the hospital and the container was on the sink. She'd had a dose before breakfast in the hospital. She couldn't read the label, but she remembered what the doctor had said: no more than once every six hours and take it with food.

In the kitchen she started to put together a light lunch for herself. But as she stood there waiting for the toast to pop, the room felt as if it was spinning. By the time Brian found her, she'd collapsed in the kitchen chair and the toast had gone cold in the toaster.

"What are you doing in here? I could have gotten you lunch. I told you, let me help you."

He walked her into the living room and settled her in her chair again. A while later he brought her lunch on a tray. Mina had taken a few nibbles of cottage cheese on toast and a bite of what she'd thought was canned peaches but turned out to be apricots, when she started to feel warm and drowsy. The headache had gone from sharp to fuzzy.

She took a few more bites and set the tray on the table. Brian plumped a pillow behind her and, despite all the noise coming from upstairs, she nodded off.

Chapter
Forty-seven

Evie had spent the rest of the afternoon sitting by her mother's bedside talking quietly. When she ran out of things to say, she read to her
mother from a copy of Tina Fey's *Bossypants,* which Ginger had left.
If her mother got the jokes or felt any pain, she showed no sign of it.

Now Evie backed the car into her mother's driveway and pulled
to a stop before the closed garage door. Sitting on the passenger seat
were Mrs. Yetner's glasses and a bag of takeout she'd picked up at El
Coquí, a little bodega she'd passed on the way home. The rich aroma
from chicken soup, a double order of sweet plantains, and garlicky
black beans and rice filled the car.

She got out of the car and opened the garage, intending to pull the
car in. Instead, she turned on the light and gazed around.

The kitty litter Mrs. Yetner had sprinkled on the floor was still
there. Evie swept it onto a newspaper and dumped it in one of the
garbage bags she'd left outside. Then she went back into the garage.

When she was growing up, her parents had kept the car parked
in the driveway. The garage had been her father's domain. Inside, it

always reeked, not of gasoline but of his cigars, the ones her mother wouldn't let him smoke in the house.

The shadowy interior seemed so much smaller without a car filling it. Without her father. At least her mother hadn't packed the garage with garbage and debris the way she had the house.

Against the back wall was her father's fireman's locker—a tall, narrow wooden cabinet with FERRANTE stenciled on the front of it. His captain had let him take it home when he retired. It was one of the few things she'd really want to keep when her mother died. *When her mother died.* The phrase brought her up short, no longer a hypothetical.

Beside the locker stood her father's worktable. How often she'd sat perched on the edge, watching her father sand down a tabletop or cane a chair seat. His coveted set of red metal tool drawers was tucked in the back of the garage, too. She understood now how he must have used the garage as a refuge.

But as Evie looked around she wondered what had been poured into her mother's car's gas tank that had been strong enough to rot it out within a few weeks. Paint stripper? Toilet cleaner? Drain cleaner? Or what about muriatic acid? She knew forgers often used that to make new metal look old, sometimes so convincingly that even experts couldn't tell.

But nothing like any of that was lying around. Besides, the more toxic the material, the more likely that it would be sealed inside something else. Like mercury in a fluorescent bulb. Or acid in a battery.

It wasn't until she'd backed the car into the garage and got out with Mrs. Yetner's glasses and the take-out bag that she realized. Of course. There had been several car batteries sitting on the floor of the garage. She went to the spot alongside the car where she'd seen them. Nothing was sitting there now. But when she crouched, she could see scars in the concrete floor. She set down the take-out bag and ran her hand over them. The floor had been eaten away, right through to soil underneath.

Evie remembered her chemistry. Acid dissolved concrete. She looked closely at the shape of the deterioration. Four rectangular outlines. Each could have been the footprint of a car battery.

Chapter
Forty-eight

Mina slept fitfully in her chair, dimly aware of workers tramping up and down the stairs, going in and out of the house. When she finally came fully awake, it was dusk. She couldn't see the time on either of the watches on her wrist. Ivory was curled up in her lap. From overhead, there were heavy footsteps, thumps, and scrapes. But no more debris was clattering down the chute.

She felt groggy and dry mouthed, and she groped for her glasses for a few moments before she remembered she'd lost them at the hospital. Annabelle had lost her teeth at the nursing home. She didn't know which was worse.

When she heard the doorbell ring, she wondered if that was what had woken her. "Brian!" Mina called. "It's the door." But she knew her voice was not making it up the stairs, and she certainly couldn't be heard over the workers' ruckus.

She cleared her throat and tried again. "Brian? The door!" The only response was the whine of what sounded like a drill.

Knock, knock, knock. "Mrs. Yetner? It's Evie. Are you there?"

Mina got her feet untangled from the afghan, pulled the walker closer to her, and stood.

"Wait. I'm coming," she said, though not with enough force for the girl to actually hear her.

She started toward the door, slowly, haltingly. Walkers weren't made for speed. By the time she got to the kitchen, she was sure Evie would have given up. But there was one more knock.

"I'm here," Mina called out as she pushed the walker ahead of her and shuffled into the entry hall, her voice stronger but probably not strong enough.

The light came on at the top of the stairwell. "Aunt Mina," Brian called down to her. "What are you doing up? I told you to call me if you need anything."

Well, what was the good of her calling him if he was going to be making such a racket that he couldn't hear her? And besides, the doctor had said she should get up and move around as much as she was comfortable. "I can get it," she called back.

Mina moved the walker forward and set it down, moved the walker and set it down, trying to get close enough to reach the door. She was almost there when she heard the hinged brass mail panel open and clack shut. Another step and the door was within reach. When she set the walker down and leaned forward to pull the door open, she heard something crack under one of the walker's front prongs.

Ignoring it, she turned the doorknob and opened the door a few inches. It ran into the walker and she had to back up before she could open it more. It was so frustrating—such a simple act and the walker made it so cumbersome, she thought as she jockeyed back and forth until finally she had the door open enough to see out. And then, of course, she couldn't see.

"Evie?" she called out. "Are you out there?" She groped for the wall switch and turned on the outside light.

Chapter
Forty-nine

Evie was halfway back to her mother's house when the light in front of Mrs. Yetner's came on and the front door opened. There stood Mrs. Yetner leaning against a metal walker and squinting out. Her hair had come loose and, backlit, it looked like a spidery halo around her face.

"Mrs. Yetner?" Evie said, hurrying back. "I'm sorry to bother you. You weren't in the hospital, and I saw the lights on, and I thought . . ." The metallic scent of overheated power tools wafted out at her. "I found your glasses and I wanted to return them to you."

"I'm afraid to ask." Mrs. Yetner backed up and pointed to the floor. "Are those my glasses?"

Evie came up the steps and through the door. She picked up the envelope she'd pushed through the mail slot and shook out Mrs. Yetner's glasses. With the lenses cracked and the frame bent, they reminded her of a mangled bird skeleton. "They were," she said. "I'm sorry. I knew you'd want them back right away, but I guess I should have waited until I could hand them to you."

Mrs. Yetner took the broken glasses from her. When she tried to put them on, one of the lenses fell out in pieces. "Well, no use crying over spilled milk." She set the broken glasses on the hall table. "Where on earth did you find them?"

Evie picked up the broken lens from the floor and set the pieces next to the frames. "In a potted plant by the hospital elevator. I came up to see how you were doing—"

"You did?" Mrs. Yetner put her hand to her heart.

"Of course I did." Evie found herself choked up. They'd barely reconnected, and yet there was something about her relationship with this woman, a simple pleasure in shared company, that she'd never experienced with her own mother or grandmother.

"Imagine that," Mrs. Yetner said. "There they were, in a potted plant by the hospital elevator. I wonder how they got there?" Evie followed her gaze halfway up the stairs to where Brian was standing looking down at them. "Whatever made you look there?"

Evie said, "I'd been helping the nurse look for them in your room. Then I was waiting for the elevator and there they were." In retrospect, it was amazing that she'd noticed them.

"It's a good thing my nephew has already ordered me another pair. Haven't you, Brian?"

Evie looked up the stairs again. Brian was still there.

"Is that chicken soup I smell?" Mrs. Yetner said.

"It is." As Evie showed Mina the take-out bag, she realized it had begun to leak. "Uh-oh." She hurried into the kitchen and set it in the sink. Mina shuffled in after her with her walker. Brian came in after.

"I know you mean well," Brian said to Evie, "but my aunt is exhausted." His shirtsleeves were rolled up and his pant legs and boat shoes were covered with dust. "She's been resting all day. She's still recovering from her injuries. The accident. The operation."

"The construction," Mrs. Yetner added. "Which somehow I managed to sleep through. My nephew is building me a new bathroom upstairs. Handicap accessible." Mrs. Yetner spit out those final words as if they had a bad taste. "Isn't that lovely?"

"That's wonderful. I saw the truck outside," Evie said. She hoped no one was planning to "renovate" the downstairs. But Evie suspected that if Mrs. Yetner's nephew inherited the house, the only way the period-perfect rooms could be preserved would be in photographs, and Evie would have to take them.

"Apparently I need grab bars." Mrs. Yetner turned to Brian, her face softening. "I don't mean to sound ungrateful. Really, Brian, it's very thoughtful of you." She turned back to Evie. "My nephew is making the changes so I can live here instead of going into a nursing home." She sniffed the air and shuffled to the sink where Evie had left the soup.

"And you'll have someone staying with you?" Evie asked.

Brian answered. "Dora will be here soon. She's making supper and staying overnight."

"My nurse, apparently," Mrs. Yetner said. "Evie, dear, why don't you get down some dishes and silverware and we can talk."

"Talk?" Brian said. "About what?"

"Nothing that concerns you," Mrs. Yetner said, winking at Evie.

Evie felt a little bad for Brian. "Would you like some, too?" she offered. "I've got soup, sweet plantains, black beans, and rice." She opened one of the take-out boxes to show him the black beans, releasing the smell of garlic and cilantro. Evie's mouth watered.

"No, thank you," Brian said. "Maybe later." He opened a closet, pulled out a vacuum cleaner, and clomped up the stairs with it.

Once he'd disappeared, Mrs. Yetner sat at the table. Evie pulled two bowls and salad plates from the cabinet. She found forks and soup spoons in a drawer.

"*Now* he's vacuuming," Mrs. Yetner said, under her breath. "When he was little, he'd never lift a finger to clean up after himself unless he got paid. In advance. We used to joke and call him the COD kid." She gazed up at the ceiling, which was creaking.

Evie took a cautious look to make sure Brian wasn't within earshot. "Has he given up on getting you to sign away the house?" she asked quietly.

Mrs. Yetner stared at her. "How do you know about that? Finn must have told you."

"I overheard your nephew asking about it. Then I found the agreement papers under your couch where Ivory was hiding."

"Hiding? But Ivory likes you."

"Apparently Ivory doesn't like Brian. He was here late last night trying to get her out from under the couch so he could take care of her."

"Take care of her?" Mrs. Yetner cocked an eyebrow. "He said that?"

"Pretty much word for word. He didn't know I'd be here."

"Imagine that. And you say the papers were *under* the couch?"

Evie nodded. "After he left and I looked underneath for Ivory, I found them. You know what else was there? The little whistle that goes on the spout of your kettle."

Mrs. Yetner beamed. "I knew it. I knew I couldn't have lost that, too. And Brian was here for the cat? If you believe that"—Mrs. Yetner lowered her voice—"I've got a bridge to sell you. My silver safety net? *Pfff.*"

"Safety net?" Evie said.

"Another of my nephew's cockamamie schemes."

"Maybe it's a coincidence, but that's the same term my mother used when I asked her about some cash I found in her house. And I'm wondering if Brian got my mother to sign an agreement like the one he wanted you to sign."

"Oh, dear. Your mother signed away her house?"

"I don't know." Evie set the take-out boxes on the table. "Monthly cash payments were part of the agreement your nephew left for you to sign. Maybe he offered my mother the same deal, only she didn't have the good sense to turn him down." She ladled soup into bowls and set them on the table along with plates and glasses of water.

Mrs. Yetner pursed her lips and gave her head a shake. "My Brian and your mother?" She considered that for a few moments. "No. Oh my, no. I'd be very surprised at that." She sounded so sure of herself.

Evie said, "The outfit behind it might be the same one that tore down a house a few blocks up."

Mrs. Yetner looked stricken. "I thought Finn was going to put a stop to that."

"He wanted to, but they moved the equipment over there while he was having one of his neighborhood meetings."

Mrs. Yetner groped on the table for a little plastic container with compartments for each day of the week and handed it to Evie. "Would you? I need to take one of these. What day is it? Tuesday, right? Please tell me it's Tuesday."

"You haven't lost track." Evie gave Mrs. Yetner the pill behind the little door marked TU.

Mrs. Yetner took the pill with a swallow of water and set down her glass. Then she lifted a spoonful of soup and blew on it. Took a sip. She closed her eyes. "This is as delicious as it smells. Where did you get it?"

Evie told her about the little bodega not far away. "They tucked a take-out menu into the bag. I'll leave it on your counter for when you've got your eyes back."

Mrs. Yetner laughed. Then she turned serious. "So how is your mother doing?"

Evie hadn't wanted to get into all the gory details, but it all came tumbling out. The hepatic coma. The acetaminophen poisoning. The rotted gas tank, and how the man at the gas station suggested that it had been vandalized.

Mrs. Yetner lowered her spoon. "Evie, dear, did it occur to you that someone might have been trying to do your mother a favor? I know you love her. But neither you nor your sister has been around." Mrs. Yetner reached across the table and patted the back of Evie's hand. "Perhaps it was a friend, someone who felt there was no other way to keep her off the road?"

Evie hadn't considered that, but it was certainly possible, and it made her wonder if Brian hadn't deliberately hidden his aunt's glasses to protect her as well. After all, they hadn't been under the bed or on the bathroom sink. They'd been nearly buried in fake moss. Putting the most positive spin on it that Evie could, maybe he thought it was the only way to slow Mrs. Yetner down enough to allow her hip to heal.

"But who?" Evie said. "Does my mother still even have any friends? Frank Cutler's the only one who's come to the hospital to see her."

"He was at the hospital?" Mrs. Yetner's eyes turned bright. "When?"

"Yesterday. I ran into him in the café. I told him she was in intensive care. He didn't know that they only allow family to visit."

"I don't think that man even knows how to be a friend, not unless there's something in it for him." The comment didn't surprise Evie. Frank Cutler could have pushed Mrs. Yetner from in front of a speeding truck and she'd have found a reason why it was self-serving.

Later, over cups of tea and Nilla Wafers from Mrs. Yetner's cupboard, Evie said, "That's a wonderful old map you have upstairs on the bedroom wall."

Mrs. Yetner smiled. "It was my father's, of course."

"This neighborhood used to be Snakapins Point, and it looks as if it was once part of Snakapins Park. Did you ever go there?"

"I was very little when we moved into the house," Mrs. Yetner said, blowing into her tea. "By then the amusement park had closed. It's been Higgs Point ever since I can remember."

"Your father must have known Finn's great-grandfather. He built the park, and your father developed all of this land that was once part of it."

"Of course they knew each other." Abruptly Mrs. Yetner set down her cup and pushed herself to her feet. "So, are you ready to hear about the day the plane crashed into the Empire State Building? Because I think I'd like to tell you about it."

Chapter
Fifty

Mrs. Yetner picked up the Empire State Building souvenir from the mantel. She looked at it for a moment, then set it on the coffee table. With the walker, she shuffled a few steps over to her chair, backed up, and sat. Evie tucked the crocheted throw over her legs, then ran into the kitchen to get her purse. She brought it back and pulled out a cassette recorder that, thank God, she always carried. She sat on the couch, opposite Mrs. Yetner, and turned it on.

"Tuesday, May 21, 2013. Evie Ferrante talking to Wilhelmina Higgs Yetner." Evie spelled the name, looking to Mrs. Yetner to make sure she got it right. At Mrs. Yetner's nod, she continued, "We're at Mrs. Yetner's home at 105 Neck Road, the Bronx, New York."

She played that much back. Then she pushed Record again and set the machine on the coffee table, the microphone facing Mrs. Yetner.

"You know, those Catholics saved my life," Mrs. Yetner began.

Evie smiled. She knew Mrs. Yetner was making a joke, but also knew she was probably referring to the Catholic War Relief Services, whose offices had been on the north-facing side of the seventy-ninth floor of the Empire State Building. One of the secretaries who worked there had told a reporter that from her desk she could see the pilot's Clark Gable mustache right through the cockpit window as the plane struck the building. That pilot and both of his passengers had been killed.

But Evie didn't interrupt to clarify. Oral histories took time to tell, and they were richest when the interviewer kept quiet and let them bubble up of their own accord. Not only that, people were surprisingly suggestible and obligingly conjured imagined details just to satisfy their audience.

"I had applied for a job there, but they turned me down," Mrs. Yetner went on. "They thought I needed experience to be a twenty-five-dollar-a-week stock-and-file clerk."

The sound of the vacuum cleaner started again upstairs. Evie could hear it being pushed across wood floor.

"Some of the people in that office were burned to death sitting at their desks," Mrs. Yetner said. "I remember looking through the names of the dead in the newspaper and wondering if one of them was the girl who got my job."

Evie sat quietly as Mrs. Yetner talked. The day before the crash, Mrs. Yetner and her friend Betty, an elevator operator whose station was on the eightieth floor, had gone up to the observation deck as they often did on their lunch hour to watch troop ships streaming into New York harbor and past the Statue of Liberty. The war in Europe was over.

"It was hot and windy up there, and my hat blew right off my head. Betty thought her husband might be on one of those ships. She'd already tendered her notice. I remember she took her compact out and was using the mirror to reflect the sun. She was trying to signal to soldiers on the ships. I was looking through binoculars to see if any of them noticed and waved back at us. We were so silly. Giddy as school-girls, really. But then, we were so very young."

Mrs. Yetner paused, gazing off into space. Then she shook herself slightly and continued.

"The next day. Saturday. I was supposed to work because we were taking inventory. I remember it was one of those soupy mornings when you look out the window here and the water is gray and the sky is gray, and there doesn't seem to be a horizon. From our office windows I could barely see the Chrysler Building.

"I had just gotten to work. I was coming out of the stockroom when I heard this roar. And I remember thinking it sounded like an airplane. I was heading for the window when someone shouted to get back. Then there was an enormous explosion. I was thrown across one of the desks. We all thought it was a German buzz bomb. Everyone was screaming. The Germans had tricked us, the Germans had tricked us! They hadn't surrendered after all.

"Flames were shooting up the sides of the building. One of the windows was scorched black. The office filled with smoke, and everyone was rushing around, trying to get out. I remember wanting to get my purse from my locker in the cloakroom, but Mr. Salamino yelled at me. Said to leave it. Save myself."

Evie picked up the cassette recorder and leaned forward with it to be sure it caught every word.

"I remember I had this miniature"—Mrs. Yetner pointed to the souvenir—"on my desk. I took it with me for good luck. I'd bought it in the souvenir shop on the day Mr. Salamino interviewed me for the job. My first job.

"We ran out of the office, but when we got to the elevators, smoke was already starting to fill the landing. Fire alarms were going off. People were running for the stairs. A woman was on the floor, screaming. People standing around her. I didn't realize who it was at first." Mrs. Yetner's face pinched at the memory, spots of color on her cheeks. "It was Betty. She'd been blown right out of her post. One side of her uniform was just ashes. Her legs were horribly bent, and she was in so much pain. There were ambulances on the street. We could hear the sirens. We needed to get her down there, but there was no way. Down eighty flights?"

The doorbell rang. Mrs. Yetner ignored it. So did Evie.

"Some people ran for the stairs. They just left her there. But I couldn't. The elevator was still sitting there, empty. Everyone kept saying, Don't take the elevator. It's too dangerous. But there was no choice. It was the only way for her to get down.

"Mr. Salamino and another man from the office carried Betty into the elevator. I didn't volunteer to ride down with her, it just happened. The elevator needed someone to operate it and of course she couldn't, and she was holding on to me, so I stayed. I got the doors closed. Got the elevator started. I remember praying that we'd make it. Praying that we'd get to the lobby in one piece. Praying that everything would be all right.

"And at first it was. One floor, three floors, ten floors down. Then I heard what sounded like a gunshot. The elevator jumped and lurched. The lights went out. And we began to fall. I remember screaming and not being able to hear my own voice."

The doorbell rang again. The vacuum cleaner stopped, and Evie could hear footsteps on the stairs. The front door opened and closed. Evie heard Brian talking to someone in a hushed voice. Mrs. Yetner seemed oblivious.

"You know how they say *time slowed down*? Well, that's not what happened at all. I felt sick, like I was going to throw up. And we were moving so fast that I had to hang on to the railing of the elevator to keep from floating. I knew Betty was thinking about her husband. I was sure it was the end."

"Aunt Mina?" Brian said.

Evie kept her focus on Mrs. Yetner, but out of the corner of her eye she could see Brian looking in from the dining room. There was a woman with him.

"Aunt Mina, this is Dora Fleischer, the woman—"

Mrs. Yetner sent him an icy look. "I'll talk to her later," she said. Brian hung in the doorway for a moment, then he turned around and went into the kitchen with the woman.

Turning back to Evie, Mrs. Yetner lowered her voice. "After that, my memories are jumbled. There was a funny smell. That must have been all that burning fuel. And a light overhead. Like a flashlight. I have no idea how long we were down there. The next thing I remember is being outside, lying on a stretcher. Astonished that I was still alive. This priest—he had a pale face, and his glasses were streaked with soot—was standing over me and reading me last rites. I told him to please stop. I wasn't Catholic, and I'd already forgiven them for not giving me that job."

She leaned forward and picked up the Empire State souvenir from the table. "I must have been holding this when I got into that elevator, because one of the rescue workers brought it to me later in the hospital. He said he'd been flabbergasted that either of us had a pulse. I'd broken my back, and the bones in my legs had to be pinned back together. He said the floor of the elevator had cracked like the shell of an egg." She shook her head. "Like the shell of an egg."

Mrs. Yetner leaned back and exhaled, her face relaxed. "I've never told that story to anyone but Annabelle and Henry. I was afraid people would think I was a hero. But there was nothing heroic about it. What happened just happened."

Evie turned off the recorder. "What an amazing, fascinating story. Thank you so much. This is just incredible."

Mrs. Yetner held the miniature out to Evie. "Here. Do you think the Historical Society would want this? I don't need any more good luck."

"I'm sure they'd love to have it. Thank you." Evie reached out and took it. The metal felt soft in her hand. Its blurred surface was a testimony to the destructive force of a fire that, against all odds, had spared at least two of its victims. Tomorrow she'd take it to the Historical Society. Already she knew exactly the spot for it in the exhibit. Too bad they hadn't gotten it in time to be featured in the poster.

"You know," Evie said, "you could have headed for the stairs and saved yourself, just like everyone else. But you didn't. You stayed to help your friend."

"See? There you go. That's what I mean. The truth is, I didn't do anything. It just happened, and I was in the wrong place at the right time."

Evie didn't argue. She saw her point. "Would you mind writing a note, saying that you're donating the souvenir and giving the Five-Boroughs Historical Society permission to use your oral history?"

"Oral history? Is that what they call long, old stories these days?"

Evie laughed.

Mrs. Yetner reached over, opened a drawer in the coffee table, and pulled out a pad and pen. In a careful slanting hand, like what Evie had seen in old penmanship books, Mrs. Yetner began to write.

"Just one more thing," Evie said, getting out her cell phone. "Would you let me take a picture of you signing the bequest?"

Mrs. Yetner put her hand up and smoothed her hair. "I suppose," she said, touching the pearls she wore around her neck. Then she put the notebook in her lap and held the pen to the page. Evie set the little statue beside her so it would be in the picture, too. As Mrs. Yetner signed and dated the note, Evie snapped a picture, then another. After that she took a picture of the old photo on Mrs. Yetner's mantel—Mrs. Yetner with her sister when they were girls. Then she carefully tore the page from the notebook and tucked it into her bag along with her cassette recorder and cell phone.

"So you weren't burned in that fire, were you?" Evie said, taking a seat on the couch opposite Mrs. Yetner.

"No."

"But how—?" Evie touched the spot on her own cheek where Mrs. Yetner had a scar on hers.

Mrs. Yetner tilted her head. "You really don't know, do you?"

"I . . ." Evie was baffled. "Should I?"

"No. But I thought you might."

"Why? Was I there? When?"

"A very long time ago. We'll talk about it. Another time." Mrs. Yetner leaned back in the chair. She looked very tired.

Evie couldn't push her, not after the story she'd just heard. "I'll come back and tell you all about what everyone says when they hear your story. I'll bring you a picture showing your little Empire State Building mounted in the exhibit hall. In fact, I hope you'll let me escort you to the gala opening. You'll come, won't you?"

Mrs. Yetner flushed. "Oh, good heavens. You can't be serious."

"You have to come. It won't be right without you. People will be dying to meet you."

"Really?"

"Really."

"And you won't make a heroine out of me, will you?"

"Promise."

Mrs. Yetner smiled. "Good. Then I wouldn't miss it for the world." Under her breath she added, "Go out in a blaze of glory, that's what I say." Then she called out, "Brian! We're done here."

Brian came in from the kitchen. Following him was the woman who'd arrived earlier. From the neck down she looked like a visiting nurse: loose but ironed pastel hospital scrubs and a man's watch on her wrist. But from the neck up she could have been on her way to a ladies' lunch at Olive Garden: not a strand of her dark hair was out of place, her pink lipstick thick and carefully applied.

But she seemed to know what she was about. She went over to Mrs. Yetner and crouched in front of her, trailing a wake of gingery scent. She took one of her hands. "My name is Dora. I'll be staying with you—"

Brian picked up Evie's purse from the floor and handed it to her, clearly her cue to leave. Evie stood and followed him to the door.

"I think it's great what you're doing. Arranging it so your aunt can live where she wants to." Evie looked up the stairs. The door at the top was closed. "Sounds like you're doing quite a bit of work up there. My mother always wanted a second bath."

"I am sorry about your mother," Brian said, holding the door open for her.

"You were friends?"

"Friends?" Brian looked aghast.

"No, of course not," Evie said. "Never mind. I'll try to get back soon to see your aunt."

"Dora will be here. She'll let you know whether Aunt Mina is up to company."

Evie wondered if there was something about Mrs. Yetner's health that she didn't know. She started to ask. Then thought better of it. Selfish of her, really, but she couldn't take any more bad news.

Outside, the panel truck was gone. In the dark, Evie could see that pieces of lumber and building debris were not so much stacked as tossed, willy-nilly, in Mrs. Yetner's driveway. It was just as well that Mrs. Yetner couldn't see it. She'd have pitched a fit.

Chapter
Fifty-one

"I had no idea that you liked Ivory," Mina said to Brian after Evie left. "Evie said you came over in the middle of the night to look after her."

"Is that what she told you?" Brian eyed her warily.

"And after you left, she found the whistle to my teakettle and those papers you brought over for me to sign. Know where they were? Under the couch where Ivory was hiding."

He gave her a cool look. "You need to be more careful about where you put your things."

"Me? Why would I put the whistle to the teakettle under the couch? And why would I stuff my eyeglasses into the base of a potted plant?"

Brian folded his arms across his chest. "I'm sure it made sense at the time."

She wanted to strangle him.

He shook his head. "Aunt Mina, I didn't take your teapot whistle, and I certainly didn't hide your glasses. But I'm not sorry those things happened, especially if it helps convince you that it's time to get some help."

That took some of the wind out of Mina's sails. She lowered her eyes and said, more into her lap than to Brian, "I don't know why I need someone sleeping in the house with me." The walker seemed like an unnecessary nuisance as well. She was sore, but not incapacitated.

"Let's try it this way for a few nights," Brian said, "and if you can get along without the help, we'll let her go. In the meanwhile, try to relax and enjoy having someone wait on you."

Mina was glad when he left a short time later, leaving her in the hands of the capable Dora. There was no point telling Brian that at her stage of life she got a lot more pleasure from taking care of herself. So she bit her tongue and let Dora take her blood pressure and listen to her heartbeat, turn down her covers, help her into her nightgown, and settle her into bed. By then, Mina's hip was throbbing like a bad headache. She took another pain pill with the glass of warm milk Dora brought her.

Dora positioned the walker alongside the bed and set Mina's bedroom slippers inside its perimeter. "If you have to get up in the middle of the night, it'll be right here for you," she said. "I know you'd rather take care of yourself, but if you need help, I'll be right out in the living room, sleeping on the couch. I'm a light sleeper, so just call out. That's what I'm here for."

Dora wished her a good night and left the bedroom door ajar. Mina hadn't even seen the day's headlines, and she'd missed two days' worth of obituaries. If she'd had her glasses, she'd have sat up in bed for a while, reading the paper. Instead, she lay there letting her mind wander.

What a relief it had been to talk about the day that the plane had crashed, practically right into her office widow. Evie had been a wonderful listener. She hadn't treated Mina like a sideshow freak the way reporters had treated Betty, trailing around behind her in the months after she was pulled from the wreckage. Other than to thank her rescuers, Mina had refused to speak with the press. But now she didn't want her story vanishing into obscurity along with the rest of her memories.

And what about the troubling news the girl had brought her? It never occurred to Mina that other homeowners were being offered the same deal with the devil that Brian had wanted her to sign, property in exchange for short-term ease. She wondered if Finn had figured out who was behind the demolition of Angela Quintanilla's house. And what about the demolished house a few doors up from Angela's? Were the same folks poised to bulldoze Sandra's house?

Bulldozed houses. A battery-less fire alarm. A whistle-less teapot. A golf ball that came out of nowhere. The more Mina tried to make sense, the more the pieces slipped around. She needed to make a list. But she couldn't rouse herself to get out of bed, never mind call Dora to get her paper and pencil. Finally she gave up and let her thoughts swirl as she stared up at the ceiling, whose cracks she knew like the back of her hand but could not see.

She could hear Dora padding around in the kitchen. An occasional thump from overhead. Could the men still be working up there? From outside came the sounds of the night. The high whistle of what might have been a nighthawk. The *burr-up* of a bullfrog. She'd seen one, so camouflaged he was nearly invisible, in her garden just the other day, and she'd been careful not to disturb him. Nighthawks ate what frogs ate. Insects. She was happy to share her marsh with all three.

Ivory settled and resettled beside Mina's pillow, resting her paw possessively on Mina's cheek. The cat had been doing that ever since she was a kitten, and it never failed to make Mina smile. She rubbed Ivory on the forehead, then turned over onto her good side. Soon she'd drifted off, only dimly aware some time later of quiet footsteps. Dora was in her bedroom. Closing the windows. Drawing the shades.

Mina tried to rouse herself, to tell Dora to stop. She liked to sleep with the window open and the shades drawn halfway. That way, when she woke up she could tell if it was morning without having to put her glasses on to check the clock.

But Mina could barely open her eyes, never mind say anything. Sleep was overtaking her like a thick fog. Was she dreaming, or could she hear a man and woman laughing together? Was that the smell of cigarette smoke? Maybe Sandra Ferrante was back. She often sat outside late at night, smoking on her back porch, laughing with a gentleman caller, the smoke drifting in through Mina's window.

Later—how much later Mina had no idea—she came awake to the sounds of a door shutting, thumps and scrapes like furniture being moved around. She strained to listen but heard nothing but silence until sleep pulled her back into unconsciousness.

A jiggle on the mattress awakened her again. A shift of weight. Had Ivory gotten up? Then a low *grrrowwRRRR* and a bounce, as if the cat had jumped down off the bed. The growl turned to a prolonged hiss and whine. *Wrowww.*

Mina knew the stance that went with that sound—back humped, head down, tail bushed out like a squirrel's, mouth open and teeth bared. Was she imagining shapes on the floor? Ivory and her doppelgänger facing off? Or were there three of them—like the Sorcerer's Apprentice, one splitting into two, two into four. As Mina drifted off to sleep yet again, she felt a breeze from an open window and warm bodies settling in around her.

Chapter
Fifty-two

Evie left for work the next day at dawn, energized and determined to put in as many hours as she could before she had to travel to the Bronx to spell Ginger at the hospital. She was halfway to Sparkles when she realized that everyone had their garbage at the curb, waiting for pickup. She'd have to remember to ask Finn what the schedule was.

Except for a security guard at reception, the Historical Society offices were dark and empty when she arrived at seven A.M. She waved her arms to coax the automatic lighting into flickering on as she walked from the elevator to her office.

First, she set about trying to confirm Mrs. Yetner's amazing survival story. Newspapers from the time were full of her friend Betty. Betty Lou Oliver, a twenty-year-old elevator operator, became New York's sweetheart in the wake of her miraculous survival. Her husband was a navy torpedo man, and he had been on his way home after a year and a half in the Pacific.

Evie found a *Daily News* photograph of Betty Lou, a slender woman with auburn curls, walking with crutches at Bellevue Hospital, months after the crash. According to the caption, the nurses had nicknamed her "Miss Sunshine." Evie smiled. She could not imagine Mrs. Yetner ever having been anyone's Miss Sunshine.

There was nothing in any of the news articles about a second survivor. But Evie did find traces of Mrs. Yetner in the records. A day after the crash, the *New York Herald-Tribune* listed "Wilhelmina Higgs" among seventeen dead or missing. In later accounts, the official death toll was fourteen and her name was no longer among them.

Still, Evie wondered how on earth anyone could have survived what must have been at least an eight-hundred-foot fall. She found article after article in which "experts" tried to explain what everyone agreed was a miracle.

The most convincing explanation came from a spokesman for Otis Elevator, interviewed soon after the accident. He started by saying that an elevator "free fall" was as unlikely to happen "as finding life on other planets." In fact, the elevator in the Empire State Building was the one and only instance he'd ever encountered. There were too many fail-safes, ancillary cables whose sole purpose was simply to prevent a disaster if the main cables broke.

The Otis Elevator inspectors found that in this case, however, all the elevator's cables did fail—including the automatic braking cable. They'd been damaged when the jet engine and burning fuel fell down the adjacent shaft, and so they'd all snapped while the elevator was being lowered. Ironically, it had been those severed cables that probably saved Mrs. Yetner and her friend Betty. The cables had piled up in a tangled coil in the subbasement under the falling elevator. That, combined with compressed air trapped in the shaft by the rapid descent, cushioned the final impact. Betty Lou and Mrs. Yetner had been pulled to safety moments before flames engulfed the elevator pit.

Evie pulled the metal miniature of the Empire State Building from her purse. It was made of pot metal and there was no question that it had gotten so hot that it had begun to melt—another piece of evidence supporting Mrs. Yetner's story.

She slipped Mrs. Yetner's bequest, donating her story and the miniature, into a Mylar sleeve. Then she photographed the figure and logged it into the archives along with the audiotape and photographs of Mrs. Yetner. She added a lengthy research note summarizing Mrs. Yetner's story. Under Provenance, she put: "Gift of Wilhelmina Higgs Yetner."

As she typed into the system, the name *Higgs* lit up. That meant another Higgs had made a donation to the Historical Society. Intrigued, Evie scanned through the system. A collection of ceramic pottery shards, attributed to the Siwanoy Indians, had been donated in 1940 by a Mr. Thomas Higgs. That had to be Mrs. Yetner's father. A research note said they'd been excavated in 1923. That must have been during the development of Snakapins Point.

"I didn't expect you to be here." Evie looked up, startled by the voice. Connor was hovering in her office doorway. "How's your mother doing?"

"Still the same. Thanks for asking. I'll go back to the hospital this afternoon. Ginger and I are taking turns, though I don't think my mother realizes we're even there."

"It's important to be there anyway. If not for her, for you. I told you, take the time you need."

Evie felt a rush of gratitude. "I will. I am."

"So what are you working on now that can't wait?"

"You're not going to believe what I've got." She handed him the miniature of the Empire State Building. He turned it over, looking puzzled. "I found a second person who was in that elevator that fell eighty floors after the plane crash."

"But that's . . ." His mouth dropped open as he stared down at the little statue, then up at Evie. "She can't still be alive?"

"She most certainly can. And is. Over ninety and completely coherent. I've got her on tape, talking publicly for the first time about what happened. And she's donating that miniature. She had it with her when she fell."

"Wow," Connor said. "I mean, well, wow! This is fantastic. It's got to be part of the exhibit and—" He stopped. "You know, it seems pretty fantastic that no one knew there was a second survivor and all of a sudden she pops up out of nowhere."

"I know. I've been researching some of the details, but as far as I can tell, it all checks out."

"Are you going to have Nick integrate her story with the audio we have?"

"Nick?" Evie knew exactly how she wanted Mrs. Yetner's story merged with what they already had. She practically had it written in her head. "I'm here. I have time to do it myself."

"It's your call." He gave her a long, hard look. "But here's some advice from a friend. You need to learn to let go. Not just because of your mother. Because it's part of being in charge. You don't get to do everything yourself. You have an excellent staff. You should be thinking strategically, not tactically. Giving them opportunities to be creative and giving them credit for it. And meanwhile, coming up with the next great exhibit we're going to mount and figuring out how to find donors to pay for it."

In other words, not logging acquisitions and editing copy. Evie knew he was right. There was no reason for her to do what her staff could do. Still, she felt a pang of regret later after she handed the tape over to Maia to digitize and transcribe.

Suddenly, Evie had time on her hands. She paid a brief visit to the

Great Hall. *Seared in Memory* was nearly complete. Some of the pictures she'd taken in the bowels of the Empire State Building had been blown up and mounted. She used her shirtsleeve to wipe a smudge off the Plexiglas over one of them. Then she returned to her office. She checked through her e-mail. Proofread their latest press release, even though it didn't need proofing. Sent an e-mail asking Maia to add Mrs. Yetner to the list of people invited to the opening and to make sure a VIP ribbon got affixed to her name tag. Then she tucked one of the engraved invitations into her bag. Even if Mrs. Yetner turned out to be too weak to attend, she'd have it as a keepsake.

Finally she sat down to work on a half-finished strategic plan. But her attention kept wandering. Higgs Point. Known to the Siwanoy as Snakapins, *land between two waters.* It had passed from Finn's great-grandfather to Mrs. Yetner's father, who'd chopped it into narrow lots where he'd built modest houses and sold them off. Now, one by one, houses were being leveled.

Evie logged on to the website that gave the Historical Society direct access to the city's property rolls. She typed in her mother's address first. A little hourglass blinked a few times, then was replaced by a three-digit BBL number—borough, block, and lot. She entered that number in the Search Deeds box and waited while the system worked.

A list of deeds for the lot came up, the oldest one dated 1925. Evie held her breath as she scrolled through the list. The house had changed hands nine times since then but—Evie exhaled with relief— her mother, at least according to the City of New York, still owned it. The current deed was dated 1980. It had last been updated in 2002, the year her father died.

But what about Soundview Management? Had they succeeded in taking over other properties? Evie changed the search criteria and typed in "Soundview" as well as her mother's zip code. Up came a list of about a dozen properties. She selected them all and clicked Map.

A map of Higgs Point flashed up on her screen with a dozen virtual pushpins highlighting those addresses. As she sent a copy to the printer, she realized how late it was. She was due at the hospital soon. She grabbed the printout and took a quick glance as she rode down in the elevator. As she'd suspected, Soundview Management owned both properties where houses had been demolished up the street from her mother's. They owned more lots along Neck Road as well, most of them on the water. Evie stuffed the printout into her bag to examine more closely later.

Chapter
Fifty-three

Evie spent the afternoon at the hospital, sitting at her mother's bedside and quietly free-associating. Talking. Singing. Though she had no idea whether her mother registered a single sound she was making, she rattled on about the new exhibit, about Mrs. Yetner's incredible story of survival. For some reason that made her think of Disney World. The Haunted Mansion. From there, to the hotel they'd stayed in on a family trip. The only family trip they'd ever taken, though Evie didn't say that.

"Remember the slide at the pool?" Evie gently pressed the back of her mother's hand. The skin was mottled, covered with angry purple blotches and as cool as bedsheets. "You slid down on a dare, and when you hit the water, you nearly lost your bathing suit top. And remember how Ginger freaked out when Chip and Dale tried to sit down with us at breakfast in the restaurant? And you'd paid extra for that?" In a squeaky voice, she sang softly, "I'm Chip, I'm Dale. We're just a couple of cwazy wascals."

Minutes ticked by as Evie shared more random memories. She

sang the lullabies and nursery rhymes she'd learned from her mother before everything at home went sour and boozy. She laughed. She cried. She surprised herself with how many good memories there still were to savor. It was time—past time, really—for her to let go of her anger and give herself permission to be her mother's daughter without being afraid that she was going to turn into her.

"I love you, Ma," she said.

But her mother just lay there, mouth open, each breath rattling in her throat. The numbers monitoring her vital signs didn't go up and they didn't go down. They just stayed stuck in place, and Evie felt the same way.

She was thoroughly drained by the time she caught the bus to Higgs Point. It was nearly dark, and Evie leaned her head against the bus window, feeling caught in a kind of limbo as familiar landmarks floated past. How many more times would she have to make this trip past that street corner, sit at this red light? When her mother died and the estate was settled, there'd be no reason to return.

As she walked from the bus stop, she realized she'd actually miss the neighborhood. Not so much sleeping on a mattress in the middle of her mother's still rank-smelling living room, but there was something special about Higgs Point. Where else in New York City was there both a saltwater marsh and a view of the Empire State Building?

Sparkles already had its outside lights on when Evie got there. She paused at the window to catch a glimpse of Finn, standing at the register and talking on the phone. She didn't go in. She wanted to get to Mrs. Yetner's before dark and tell her how excited everyone was about making her story part of the exhibit. Plus Finn had promised her dinner—she didn't want to keep showing up and make him think she was overeager.

Brian's Mercedes was parked on the street in front of Mrs. Yetner's house. The pile of lumber in the driveway had grown. Evie rang the bell. Almost immediately Brian opened the door. Before Evie could say anything, he said, "She's not feeling up to visitors."

"Is she all right? Can I do anything?"

"Let her rest. I'm afraid she's weaker than we expected her to be."

Evie heard a cat meowing. "I brought her an invitation to a gala where she'd be the featured guest. I could just pop in and deliver—"

"I can take that for her."

Brian reached for the card, but Evie held it back. "Thanks. I'd like to deliver it personally. It might even cheer her up."

"Well, now is not a good time. I said she's resting."

"I'll come back."

"You do that." Brian was closing the door when Ivory squirmed out through the opening and streaked across the lawn and around to the back of the house. Without thinking, Evie dropped her bag and took off after her, arriving just in time to see the cat slip under her mother's back porch.

Evie turned around, expecting to see Brian chasing the cat, too. But it seemed Evie was on her own with this particular rescue mission. She crouched and peered under the porch. It was so dark she couldn't see anything.

"Here, kitty," she said. She made some kissing sounds. "Come out now." *Kiss kiss kiss.*

After a few minutes of that, it was clear that Ivory was determined to stay hidden. So much for Mrs. Yetner's claim that Ivory wouldn't know what to do with herself outside. What Evie needed was something nice and smelly to lure her—like one of those empty cans of cat food she'd collected from her mother's kitchen. Plenty of them had what a cat might consider tasty bits still stuck to them. She'd thrown those cans into one of the already full garbage bags, so she could probably retrieve a few without too much digging around.

But which one were they in? she wondered as she stood contemplating the five bags of garbage she'd forgotten to put out at the curb for garbage pickup. Even closed they exuded a nasty smell.

Eenie, meenie, miney . . . She took a breath, held it, and opened *Mo*. It was a lucky guess. There, on top, were some of those cans. Most of them were surprisingly clean, and she had to pick through to find one with a few crusty clumps stuck to the bottom. She carried it over to the edge of the porch and set it on the ground. As she stood waiting for Ivory to come investigate, the last glow of amber and pink sunset disappeared from the sky. It really was beautiful out here. Why had Evie never appreciated it when she was growing up?

At last the cat poked her nose out from under the porch and slunk forward. Evie crouched. Nudged the can a little closer to the cat. Waited until the cat had sniffed, sniffed again, and finally settled, licking at the inside of the can before Evie grabbed her.

Ivory squirmed and tried to wriggle free as Evie carried her around to the front of Mrs. Yetner's house. At Evie's knock, Brian opened the door again. He took the cat from her arms with a grudging thank-you and closed the door.

Evie went to throw away the can and close up the garbage bag. This time, she'd drag all five of them to the curb. But as she was tossing the can into the open bag, she noticed a familiar-looking jar with a green-and-white label right on top. She lifted it out. NaturaPharm. Vitamin C. She shook the container. Pills rattled inside.

Trying not to inhale, Evie dug around until she found a second NaturaPharm container. Vitamin B_1. The rest of her mother's cache of vitamin pills that had disappeared from her medicine cabinet after the break-in were probably in the bag, too, but Evie wasn't about to scrounge around for them. But what were they doing in there? Who had taken them from the medicine cabinet, and why take them and then throw them away?

Evie took the two containers inside and set them on the kitchen counter. She opened the vitamin C. Shook out a large white oval tablet into the palm of her hand. One side was scored for easy breaking. Imprinted on the other side was the code L484.

She opened the container of B_1 vitamins. The pills inside were the same size. Same shape. Same L484.

It took Evie just a moment to Google the number on her phone. L484 was the pharmaceutical industry's code for acetaminophen.

Moments later, Evie had dug from her purse the card from the police officer investigating the earlier break-in. Sergeant Bruce Corday. He'd said to call if she discovered anything else, and now she most definitely had.

When he called her back an hour later, he listened. Said he'd come to the house first thing in the morning, and that he'd be bringing a detective with him.

Chapter
Fifty-four

When Mina finally woke up, it was dark in her bedroom, but bright strips of sunlight bled from between the window shades and sills. Her clock ticked quietly, but she couldn't see the time. She put her hand out, feeling for Ivory. But the spot where the cat liked to sleep was cool and empty.

She had no idea how long she'd been out. She struggled to turn over, but it was as if her muscles didn't want to respond, and to make matters worse, the sheets were twisted around her legs. She reached down to free her legs and realized she wasn't caught up in sheets but rather a long nightgown. Light cotton. She felt the neck. A lace collar. It had to be Annabelle's. While she'd been asleep, Dora must have gotten her up and changed her clothes. Her face burned with shame at the very idea of it.

She had to get out of bed. *Now.* She couldn't let herself fade the way Annabelle had, so rapidly once she was installed in that nursing home and no longer had to do for herself. All that lying in bed— meals being brought to her, a bedpan if she wanted and diapers if she didn't—had quickly atrophied Annabelle's muscles until her arms and legs were nothing more than twigs, and she couldn't even stand on her own. Just a few weeks later, ghastly raw areas formed on her backside, bedsores that eventually oozed and wept infection. She'd been too weak to even cough, so when she'd gotten a cold, it had quickly turned into pneumonia, the illness that doctors called "the old person's friend" because at least it pulled the plug. Now there was an expression Mina detested.

Even after all that, Mina hadn't been ready for Annabelle to go. And she was tortured by the likelihood that Annabelle's slide would have been more gradual had she been able to keep her at home. Kept her active. But there'd been no choice.

Mina pushed back the covers and sat up. She was stiff and achy, and her mouth tasted like old rubber tires. Her head felt like a big empty metal drum that was being hammered at from the inside. And she had to go to the bathroom.

She edged herself to the side of the bed, expecting the walker to be there waiting for her. But it wasn't. She stretched out her toes and felt around for her slippers but she couldn't find those, either. Never mind that. She pushed herself to her feet. Leaning against the wall, she felt her way to the door to the downstairs hall. The minute she opened it, Ivory slipped in, meowing and rubbing against her.

"Shoo," Mina said. The last thing she needed was to trip over the cat.

She paused, listening. The house was quiet. No more construction going on upstairs. The hall was dark, and she shouldn't have had any trouble navigating the few steps to the bathroom, but soon after she started inching her way along, she hit a roadblock. Stacks of bundled papers and bulging garbage bags lined the hallway.

What in heaven's name was going on? "Brian!" she called. No answer. Was Brian even there? And what about Dora?

Mina squeezed past the debris. At least the bathroom door wasn't blocked. It wasn't until she was sitting that she noticed the smell. She gagged. Her bathroom had never smelled this bad before. Had Ivory's litter box had been moved in here? Why hadn't Dora taken care of it? Wasn't that part of what Brian was paying her to do?

That's when Mina heard *scritch-scratch* from behind the shower curtain. Sounded as if the litter box was not only there, but in use. How had Ivory managed to slip past her? She'd have to tell Dora that the bathtub was no place for the cat box. It didn't take much cat litter to clog a drain. It solidified in there like cement.

She washed her hands, then pushed back the shower curtain. Sure enough, the litter box was a dark rectangle against the white of the tub. Ivory's white fur looked like quicksilver as she did a figure eight and then settled. But—Mina squinted, not sure if she was imagining things without her glasses—was that another Ivory perched motionless in the corner? And could that quick movement be another alongside the litter box in the tub?

A knock on the bathroom door startled her. "Wilhelmina?" Mina actually felt relieved to hear Dora's voice. "Are you in there? Are you all right? You were supposed to ring the bell I left for you."

Bell? Mina opened the door. "Why are there so many cats?"

"Cats?"

"There are at least three of them in here." Mina pointed to the tub.

"Of course there are." Dora tugged the shower curtain closed before taking Mina's arm and leading her from the bathroom. "And they're all white just like Ivory, aren't they?"

Mina knew all about that strategy—she'd seen it used plenty with Annabelle. Her caretakers called it entering into the delusion. "I suppose you're going to tell me that I'm seeing double. And that all this junk stacked out here"—she jabbed a finger toward the piles as they sidled past—"is a figment of my imagination, too."

"Certainly not. It's just part of the construction work." Mina was about to ask how stacks of newspapers constituted construction, but Dora was too quick for her. "They'll have them out of there in a day or two, and you'll be able to move upstairs to the new room. You'll see. It's so much nicer. And the new bathroom is lovely."

Distraction, Mina recalled, was another strategy for dealing with a demented old woman.

"Upstairs," Dora went on. "With plenty of space to move around in a wheelchair."

"But I don't have a—"

"You know, you slept right through lunch." *Lunch?* How had it gotten to be lunchtime already? "I'm not surprised you're feeling peckish. Come on. Back to bed and I'll bring you a nice tray. There's butterscotch pudding. You like butterscotch pudding, don't you?"

Mina did like butterscotch pudding, but she'd be damned if she'd say so. "I want to go outside."

"Come on now. Back to bed. I've made a lovely lunch for you."

Mina was hungry. Very hungry, in fact. She let Dora shepherd her from the dark hall and back to the equally dark bedroom.

"Why are the shades drawn?"

"My, my. We do have a lot of issues today, don't we?"

"And when will my glasses be here? I hate not being able to see."

All she got for that were a few tut-tuts. Mina caught a whiff of ginger and tangerine as Dora bent over and tucked her firmly into bed and plumped pillows behind her. The familiar smell conjured an image of plastic forsythia. Now she remembered—the woman who'd showed her around Pelham Manor had been wearing that scent. But her name hadn't been Dora, and she wasn't a brunette, Mina thought when Dora returned with a bed tray. Tomato soup. Mina could tell by the smell.

"Mustn't forget to take your pill," Dora said. She handed Mina a pill and a glass. "Careful. The glass is full."

Mina could feel the pill between her fingers. "What's this?" she asked. Did Dora think she wouldn't notice that the pill was twice the size of the ones she'd been taking for years?

"The doctor prescribed a new compound, Lipitor and Fosamax. To keep your bones strong."

"Why didn't he tell me about the change?"

"Don't you remember? You saw him this morning."

This morning? Mina thought it still was this morning.

"Poor dear. You don't remember, do you? No wonder. You're exhausted. You slept all day yesterday, too."

Thoroughly rattled, Mina put the pill in her mouth and choked it down with a swallow of water. She was afraid to ask, but she did. "What day is it?"

"Why, it's Friday, of course."

But how could that be? Could she have lost two entire days?

Chapter
Fifty-five

By the next morning, Evie could barely hold up her head. Tense and jittery, unable to sleep, she'd spent most of the night up and cleaning the house. Sergeant Corday showed up, as promised, at eight. The younger of the two cops who'd come to investigate the earlier break-in, he had another officer with him this time. A slender African American woman with straight black hair framing her wide-set eyes, she introduced herself as Detective Leslie Johnson. Evie poured them both coffee and sat across the kitchen table from them. The kitchen was still the only room in the house that was back to normal.

"So these are what you found outside in the trash?" Johnson asked, indicating the pill bottles that Evie had left on the table. "Why don't you start at the beginning. Tell us about your mother's illness."

The beginning. What was the beginning? Evie took a breath. "My mother is an alcoholic. Has been for years, so we weren't surprised when she was rushed to the hospital last Friday."

"We?" Corday asked.

"My sister, Ginger, and I. We've been through this so many times before. My mother falls. Or she collapses. Or she acts like a crazy person. She dries out, goes in for treatment. Says she'll stop drinking but she never does. But this time it was different. Turns out that on top of excessive drinking, she'd taken an overdose of acetaminophen. I thought it was accidental, because it wouldn't have taken much with her liver already so compromised. Then I found these." She pointed to the NaturaPharm containers.

"Vitamins?" Corday said.

"Only they're not. Both containers have the same pills. Acetaminophen. When you asked me if something more was missing after the break-in, I'd only checked for valuables. But someone took these bottles and more like them from the bathroom and threw them in the trash."

"How many more?" Detective Johnson asked.

"There was a whole row of them in her medicine cabinet." Evie tried to visualize it. "Six or seven."

Detective Johnson picked up a paper napkin and used it to turn over one of the containers. "No price sticker, but there's a bar code. We may be able to find out what store they came from." She unscrewed the top and shook a tablet into her palm. "So you're saying someone was trying to kill her."

"She was doing a fine job of that all by herself. I think someone was trying to speed up the process. And sabotage her car. And make it look like she's one of those crazy cat ladies. I've thrown out dozens of empty cans of cat food. My mother doesn't even like cats, and she's certainly never owned one." Evie went on, telling them about the money her mother was getting, and that she suspected someone had gotten her to sign away her house.

"Did you find this agreement that you think she signed?" Johnson asked.

Evie admitted she hadn't. "But Mrs. Yetner—she lives next

door—her nephew has been trying to get her to sign away her house, too. I have that agreement." Then she remembered she'd given the life estate deed to Finn. "I mean, I know where it is. I gave it to someone to look into."

"But you have the cash?" Corday asked. "There might be prints."

"I'm sorry, no. I deposited it all in the bank yesterday. That much cash made me very nervous, especially after the break-in."

"What about the envelopes that the money came in?" Johnson asked.

Evie sank lower in her chair. "I threw them away as I was leaving the bank. There was nothing written on them. Just twenty brand-new one-hundred-dollar bills in each one."

"Seems like it would have to be someone she knew and trusted," Johnson said. "Any idea who?"

"My mother's burned through most of her friends. But the man across the street, Frank Cutler, he's been spending time with her. He tried to visit her in the hospital, only she'd already been moved to intensive care." Johnson and Corday exchanged a look, and Evie felt her face flush. "Sounds crazy, I know."

"These"—Johnson pointed a long, manicured nail at the vitamin containers—"are not figments of your imagination."

"You said you found these in the garbage bag outside?" Corday asked. "I'll go see if there's more out there." He pushed himself up from the table and went out, closing the front door quietly behind him.

"Why don't you show me the medicine cabinet these were in," Johnson said. Evie led her to the bathroom and pointed out the empty bottom shelf. Johnson looked around, speculatively. "We're investigating another case. Another house—"

"The one that was bulldozed a few days ago?"

"It's been bulldozed?"

"We're probably not talking about the same house." Evie took

Johnson back to the kitchen. She took out the map that she'd printed at work and unfolded it on the table. "There," she said, pointing to the lot where the little house with bright red trim had once stood. "That house is gone."

"That's not the one we're investigating."

Evie pointed a few doors up. "The house on this lot has been leveled, too."

"That's the one," Johnson said. "An older woman lived there. A widow. Alone. She had emphysema." She looked up at Evie, as if she was deciding whether to say more. "But that's not what killed her."

"Don't tell me. Acetaminophen overdose," Evie said as she started to put away the map.

"I can't say," Johnson said, "but it's urgent that we talk to your mother."

"I'm afraid you can't. No one can. She's in a coma at Bronx Metropolitan Hospital."

Johnson frowned. "Can I see that map again?" Evie pushed it across the table at her.

"Why are those other properties flagged?" Johnson asked.

"They're all owned by the same company. Soundview Management." Evie watched as Johnson traced her long finger from one flagged property to the next. Most of them were on the water, including the lot next to Mrs. Yetner on the side opposite Evie's mother's house. Frank Cutler's house was flagged, too. He was young and healthy enough that a life estate deed at least made some financial sense.

"You mind if I take a picture of this map?" Johnson asked. Evie shook her head and Johnson snapped two quick shots with her cell phone.

Corday came back in. He had more vitamin containers, each sealed in its own baggie. He and Johnson exchanged a look.

"Thank you," Johnson said to Evie, offering her a card. "We'll be in touch. What's the best way to reach you?"

Evie gave them her cell-phone number.

She felt dazed as she let them out. Her mother really had been poisoned, and whoever had done it was trying to cover his tracks. She watched from the kitchen window as Detective Johnson and Officer Corday stood in front of the house, their heads bent, talking. The pair split up. Johnson walked up to Mrs. Yetner's door, Corday to Frank Cutler's.

Chapter
Fifty-six

A sharp, sweet smell drew Mina into the present. That, and a woman's voice. "Wilhelmina?"

Mina opened her eyes, feeling as if she were fighting her way up out of a dark chasm.

"Good morning." Now she recognized the voice. It was Dora, bending over her and helping her to sit, plumping pillows behind her. "So how do you like your new master suite?"

Mina struggled to see into the blur around her. She reached her hand up and hit a sloping ceiling. Felt behind her—an iron headboard. She was in the upstairs bedroom. How on earth had they finished the renovations so quickly? She didn't even smell paint or wood, just a whiff of plaster dust and citrus. Intense citrus. Mina recognized that as Dora's scent.

Mina groped on the bed covers for Ivory, recognizing the feel of the soft quilts she and Annabelle had pieced together years ago. She'd made one for her own bed, but this felt like Annabelle's. Annabelle's stitches were uniform and tiny. Her mother had called Mina's stitches "slapdash" and had made her pick them out and do them over and over again until they passed muster. *Passed muster.* That had been one of her father's expressions. She used to think it was "passed mustard."

Where was her cat? "Ivory?" She could barely get the word out.

"Ivory is fine. She's downstairs. I'll bring her up for a visit in a little bit."

"What day is it?"

"Monday," Dora said.

Monday? Mina bit her lip. Typically she woke up three or four times in the night; now she was sleeping so soundly that she was losing days at a time. Mina wanted her calendar. Needed her calendar, so she could keep track. Needed her glasses so she could read what she'd written on it, and read the newspaper, and stay anchored by the sights and smells and sounds of the present. Speaking of sounds—

"What is that hum?" Mina asked.

"Climate control. It's in the ceiling. Wonderful, isn't it? Keeps the room perfectly comfortable."

What was wonderful was fresh air. But before Mina could point that out, Dora pulled back the covers and helped her out of bed. Mina needed Dora's support to stand, but after that she managed on her own. The new bathroom did indeed turn out to be nice, and best of all it smelled clean. It had a walk-in shower with a chair, grab bars in the shower and by the toilet, all in a sea of pale-green tile.

When Mina was back in bed, Dora brought her a tray. Chicken noodle soup, sliced cheese and crackers, and applesauce. Food for sick people.

"Don't forget to take your pill," Dora said.

Mina couldn't actually see the pill Dora handed her, but just holding it in her hand made her gag. She set it on the tray and slid it under the edge of the plate. Ate a cracker with a slice of cheese. A spoonful of applesauce.

"Your friend from next door came by with something for you to sign," Dora said. Mina heard Dora rustle some papers.

"Why couldn't she come up and ask me herself?"

"You were sleeping."

"I can't sign something if I can't even see where to sign."

"I'll show you where."

Mina put another cheese cracker in her mouth and chewed slowly. Washed it down with a sip of apple juice. "I'm not signing anything until I can see what I'm signing."

As if on cue, there was a knocking downstairs, and Dora said, "That's probably her now. What shall I tell her?"

"Send her up to talk to me." Mina would gladly sign whatever it was if she could just be sure that it was a document Evie wanted her to sign and not one of Brian's harebrained schemes.

The knock came again. Dora wasn't making a move to leave.

"Answer the door and bring her up here. Please."

"Of course," Dora said. But it was just the kind of *of course* that Mina had learned not to trust. "Tell you what, you take your pill. Then I'll get the door and bring her up."

Mina put the pill in her mouth and took a sip of apple juice. The pill tasted bitter on her tongue.

Dora sat on the end of the bed. "Need another sip to get it down?"

Mina took another drink and choked down the pill. That seemed to get Dora out of the room at last.

With Dora gone, Mina sat forward, listening. The hum from the air conditioner made it hard to hear. She set aside her tray and pushed back the covers. Then inched her way to the edge of the bed, held on to the windowsill—its sawtooth cutouts reassuringly familiar—and stood. She felt around for her cane, but it wasn't there. Nor was the walker. She knew the door to the stairway was only a few feet past the end of the bed. Surely she could make it that far on her own.

Steadying herself against the sloping ceiling, Mina shuffled forward to the foot of the bed. She held on to the iron bedstead for a moment before continuing on. She was out of breath and her legs were shaking by the time she got to the door. She pulled it open and clung to the jamb.

"I'm sorry." That was Dora. Something garbled, then " . . . not here."

A low voice answered.

" . . . out at the moment." Dora again. " . . . have no idea. Of course I'll relay the message."

"I'm up here!" Mina's voice quavered. She edged toward the top step. What was it the physical therapist had told her about stairs? *Up with the good leg, down with the bad.* But just as she was groping for the banister railing, she heard the front door close and felt a little puff of air come up the stairs, like the wind shifting in a subway tunnel.

Mina slumped against the door frame. She heard Dora's footsteps downstairs, and a wave of dizziness came over her. She turned to make her way back to bed and ran smack into the sloping ceiling. A moment later she found herself sitting on the floor, dazed and disoriented.

She needed a few minutes on the floor to catch her breath before she could crawl over to the bed, but luckily she managed to pull herself up and into it. She was under the covers, trying to stay awake, when Dora finally returned.

"Why didn't you"—Mina's tongue felt thick—"bring her up?"

"It wasn't her," Dora said.

"Whowuzit?" Mina's words slurred together. She felt suddenly warm. Sweat trickled down the back of her neck.

"Who?" Dora said, as if Mina might forget what she had asked.

Mina gathered her strength. "Who was at the door?" she demanded, carefully squeezing out each word.

"Jehovah's Witnesses," Dora said breezily. "Did you want me to bring them up?"

Jehovah's Witnesses? Why would Dora promise to pass along their "message"? Wasn't that what she'd said? Or—Mina tried to remember.

"What's the matter?" Dora said.

Mina closed her eyes. She felt a light touch on her wrist. Dora was feeling her pulse. Mina knew it was racing, but Dora didn't say anything, simply lifted the tray from the bed with a slight rattle. A few moments later, the door shut and Mina was alone.

Mina's eyelids felt like they were being pushed closed. She needed to stay awake. She rubbed her temple and found a tender, swollen lump. When had she bumped her head? Her tailbone ached, too. But the hip wasn't nearly as bad as it had been. She needed to work her muscles. She flexed and unflexed her ankle—*one, two, three*—in one of the lying-down exercises she'd learned after hip replacement.

But her attention wandered and she lost count. As soon as she had her strength back, she promised herself, she'd do more. She'd sooner drop dead of a heart attack than wither away. That was her final thought before the room faded to black around her.

Chapter
Fifty-seven

Evie had caught up on sleep and managed to slip back into what already felt like a routine—morning at work in Manhattan, a late lunch with Ginger in the hospital café, and afternoon at her mother's bedside. Now, once again, she was on the bus back to Higgs Point.

Just like the all too familiar landmarks that flew by, one day was blurring into the next. Her mother hung in limbo, her hands growing clawed and so cold that no amount of holding warmed them. Evie had pictured her mother's death. She and Ginger had certainly had plenty of rehearsals. But she never dreamed it would be this soon or happen this fast.

It seemed much longer than a week since Evie had slept in her own apartment, since she'd spent time with her friends, since she'd had a life. She was sick to death of chicken potpies. As she walked from the bus back to the house, she found herself looking forward to dinner at Finn's. He'd texted her that afternoon. *Dinner tonight? Basement tour? See you at 8.* The basement alone, packed with material from an old amusement park, would have gotten her there.

The weather had turned unseasonably warm, up over eighty

degrees, and a stiff breeze gusted off the water. The black plastic garbage bags she'd finally dragged out to the street were gone. Even the soiled mattress had been collected.

She paused outside for a moment, taking in Mrs. Yetner's house. The Mercedes was still parked out front. Maybe Brian had decided to move in. The pile of building debris between Mrs. Yetner's and her neighbor's on the other side—the house that Evie now knew belonged to Soundview Management—had grown. Bundles of newspaper had been added to the lumber and construction materials.

The wind kicked up, and pieces of newspaper blew into the grass. Sheets stuck to the side of Mrs. Yetner's house and more blew toward the water. Evie ran after them. She snatched up a few. More that she couldn't reach blew into the marsh.

Returning to Mrs. Yetner's, Evie stuck the loose papers under a piece of wood with lath still nailed to it. She was still carrying around Mrs. Yetner's invitation to the gala, but she didn't have the energy to try talking her way past Brian again. So she just slid the invitation through Mrs. Yetner's mail slot and went home. She rested for a while, then took a shower.

At eight, she walked the three blocks over to Sparkles. Finn met her at the door, a big grin on his face. "Smell that?" he said.

What Evie smelled was aftershave, but she was pretty sure that wasn't what he meant.

"That's my all-day chili. It's been cooking—"

"Let me guess. All day," Evie said.

Finn squeezed her hand. "I'm glad you're here. And not just because it gave me an excuse to cook."

"I'm glad, too. It's been a long week."

"So how about we start off with a tour of all the crap that I've got stored in the basement of the store. Somehow I think you'll enjoy that more than a pile of guacamole."

"You made guacamole, too?"

"Later." Finn led her around to the back of the store and unlocked a metal bulkhead door. With a grimace he pulled the door open, then started down a flight of wide stairs. He turned and gave her his hand as she stepped over the threshold. "Watch your step. Hope you don't mind a few spiders." At the foot of the stairs he pulled the cord from a dangling overhead bulb and waved his arms to clear away cobwebs. "They're fascinating creatures, really. And the web builders are safe to be around. It's the jumping spiders you've got to watch out for."

"Oh, great. That's a useful—" Evie's voice caught in her throat at the sight of a giant face, at least eight feet tall, leering at her from the shadows. The wild, bugged-out eyes, flat cheeks, and forehead still had the remnants of war paint. The mouth, which took up most of the face, gaped open. Despite the rust and faded colors, it looked ferocious.

"Wow," Evie said. It was the only word that quite did it justice.

"This was the main gate to Snakapins Park. They weren't too politically correct in those days. They had a guy who sat behind a screen beating a war drum where you got your ticket, and then you could step through the mouth to enter the park. Would have scared the daylights out of me, especially at night when they had it lit up."

Evie noticed the metal feathers of the Indian headdress were studded light sockets. Her heart was practically dancing in her chest with excitement. She took out her cell phone. "Okay if I take pictures?"

"Be my guest."

Evie took one shot. Then another. She could almost hear the drumbeat now as she bent over and stepped through the mouth. On the other side she came face-to-face with a glass case containing the upper half of a bead-laden woman dressed in red brocade—a fortune-telling machine. Evie took a picture of it, too, and of the old wooden roulette wheel leaned up against it.

Nearby, leaning against a post, was a mustard-colored merry-go-round horse with a black saddle. Big teeth, bulging eyes, a real horsehair tail—Evie had seen the same style on carousel horses from Coney Island. Gingerly she touched one of the carved cabbage roses that adorned its side. It was clearly the work of a master craftsman. She took more photos.

"Come on back here," Finn said, his voice coming from deep in the recesses of the basement. Evie's mind raced as she followed along a narrow track between piles. Finn pulled one light switch, then another and another as they zigzagged past a decaying life-size papier-mâché clown and a pair of pedal boats, between crates and piles of cardboard boxes and tarp-covered mounds of heaven only knew what. Through one of the high narrow windows just above ground level, the beam from a headlight filled the darkness farther in and then vanished.

It was tantalizing, overwhelming, and Evie wondered if this was anything like what Howard Carter felt when he discovered Tutankhamun's treasures hidden under the ancient remains of workmen's huts in the Valley of the Kings. *Lost Amusement Parks*—she could envision an exhibit featuring these forgotten treasures that had somehow managed to survive. The final piece in the installation would be the Indian gate, its paint loss stabilized, all lit up. The ironwork was far too fragile to allow people to step through it, but she'd find appropriate sound effects, and some old photographs showing the entrance in its glory days. Some of those boxes might even contain photographs and advertising materials.

Finn pulled another switch, lighting the back corner. There lay what looked like a mass of twisted scrap metal about the size of a VW bug. It took Evie a moment to sort out what she was looking at: an upside-down passenger car from a Ferris wheel. Benign neglect could account for the paint that had long since rusted away, but the twisting and wrenching had taken a much more violent and powerful force. The bar that held passengers in was nearly bent double. Just looking at it made Evie smell hot metal. "What happened?" she asked.

"A freak wind squall. Might even have been a tornado. Blew over the entire Ferris wheel in 1916. Killed twenty-four people."

The smell grew stronger as Evie ran her hand lightly across a once flat piece of metal with a scalloped edge that had been the floor of the car.

"Kind of beautiful, isn't it, in an eerie way?" Finn said.

It was, almost like a piece of sculpture. It reminded Evie of one of the enduring images from the Triangle Shirtwaist fire: the horrifying beauty of a fire escape, pulled and twisted like strings of taffy from the fire's heat. It wouldn't be hard to research the accident that had taken down this Ferris wheel, to get a blow-up facsimile of the head-line and article that would have run at the time.

"The park closed just a few years later," Finn said.

"Prohibition," Evie said. "That's what did in so many parks and casinos."

"Maybe so. But that wasn't what did in my great-grandfather. He was swindled by a smooth-talking businessman, a guy who had all the makings of a two-bit robber baron."

"Thomas Higgs," Evie said, remembering her research.

"He and my great-grandfather were friends. Then business part-ners." Evie jumped, startled when Finn stamped his foot hard on the floor. "Sorry. Water bug."

"Higgs was a swindler?"

Finn looked toward the open bulkhead door and back at Evie. "You really want to hear about it?"

"Are you kidding? Of course I do."

"It was pretty simple, really. Thomas Higgs forged my great-grandfather's signature, transferring all the property except this building to himself. Then he subdivided, built the houses on the lots, and you know the rest."

"How could he have done that without your great-grandfather's permission? I mean, what's the difference between that and stealing?"

"That's what it was. Robbery, pure and simple. But that makes no difference when you have political connections and justice can be bought. That's one of the reasons I went to law school. To see if there was a way that we could get the property back."

"We?"

"Me and my cousin. We're the only ones left. We'd own it all if it hadn't been stolen."

Evie just stood there, trying to absorb what he'd just said. Finn and his cousin were still trying to reclaim their great-grandfather's estate—all of Higgs Point. At least that explained what a guy with a degree from Columbia Law School was doing in this remote corner of the Bronx. She wondered if it didn't explain much more than that. What if . . . ? But before she could connect the dots, she realized that the hot metal smell she thought she had conjured up with the twisted Ferris wheel car had grown so strong that her eyes watered.

"You okay?" Finn asked.

"What's that smell?" Evie started for the bulkhead. Walking, then running.

"Evie?" Finn called after her, but she was already halfway out, past the leering clown, the carousel horse, the fortune-teller, the smell growing with every step.

She ran up the stairs and out. Her eyes stung, blurring her vision, but she could see smoke was blowing in from the direction of the water. From the direction of her mother's house. It couldn't be happening. Not again.

Evie broke into a run and kept on running, pounding forward. One block. Another. Now she could see an orange glow. Hear the snap of sparks. Smell the acrid scent she remembered from when she was six.

She fully expected to find her mother's house ablaze. But it wasn't. The pile of lumber in the driveway between Mrs. Yetner's house and the house on the other side from Evie's mother had caught fire. Flames licked up the sides of both houses.

Evie stopped, frozen in horror. Was Mrs. Yetner inside?

With a loud crack, sparks exploded. Burning cinders rose on an updraft and landed on the roof of the house next door to Mrs. Yetner's.

"Evie!" Finn ran up behind her.

"Call 911!" she yelled to him as she ran up the front steps of Mrs. Yetner's house and banged on the door with her fists. "Fire! Fire! Mrs. Yetner! Brian! You've got to get out of there." She tried the knob. Kicked at the door.

"Wait!" Finn grabbed her arm and tried to pull her away. "Listen— fire trucks are on the way."

Not soon enough. Evie remembered how quickly fire had engulfed her parents' house. There'd been a stiff wind that day, just as there was one now. "There's no time," Evie said. "Go! Make sure there isn't anyone in that house." She pointed to the house next door.

"But—"

Without a backward glance, Evie ran around to the back, praying that Mrs. Yetner's keys were still under the whitewashed rock where she'd left them. They were. In a few moments, she had the back door open.

Smoke was starting to fill the house. Evie found the light switch and flipped it, but nothing happened. She felt her way through the dark to the couch, grabbed Mrs. Yetner's crocheted comforter, and held it over her face as she ran through the living room. She was almost at the downstairs bedroom when she tripped and fell heavily to the floor. As she pushed herself up she got a good look at what had gotten in her way. A broken lawn chair, just like the broken lawn chair that had been in her mother's house.

Evie looked at the chair more closely, then around at Mrs. Yetner's living room. The entire room was filled with the same kind of debris she'd had to clear from her mother's house. Not the same *kind* of debris, she realized, catching sight of a mattress that stood propped against the wing chair. This was the same debris exactly. It hadn't been picked up at the curb by a garbage truck. It had been dumped in Mrs. Yetner's house.

Evie threaded her way to the downstairs bedroom. The walls of the tiny room glowed orange. Burning lumber was right outside the window. The bed had been left rumpled and unmade, like Mrs. Yetner had just gotten out of it.

The door to the closet was closed. As Evie smelled the smoke and heard the fire roar, in her mind's eye she saw the closet door opening. Only instead of Blackie and her puppies, she was the one inside the closet, under her parents' hanging clothes, watching the closet door pull open. The memory was so vivid, it made Evie gasp.

In three steps, Evie was there. Opening the closet door. But this closet was empty. Completely empty. Not a single item of clothing, not even a shoe. Just a few empty clothes hangers.

Mrs. Yetner had probably been moved upstairs. Evie started for the hall when the bedroom window exploded, showering the bed with glass. Evie ducked as she ran out, slamming the door, hoping to contain the fire. She had to squeeze past piles of newspaper stacked outside the bathroom. She flew up the stairs and into the bedroom. And just stood, staring, not believing what she saw.

The beds and bureaus, white curtains, and hooked rugs were gone. Not only was there no new bathroom in the room that stretched from the front of the house to the back of the house, the interior had been completely gutted. The baseboards were gone. The sumptuous

Eastlake-style window trim had been ripped from around the doors and windows. Even the doors had been removed. No map hung on the wall.

A single item was left on the floor of the room, and it was the one thing Evie knew Mrs. Yetner would have taken with her. Her cane.

Evie heard sirens outside, each second growing louder. She returned to the doorway to the stairs. The stairwell had filled with dense smoke. It was too dangerous to try to go back down. She ran to the window. A hook and ladder was parked outside. An ambulance with its siren wailing pulled up behind it, and behind the ambulance, a police cruiser.

Firefighters were already hooking up a hose. People were gathering from up and down the street to see what was happening. Two police officers pushed spectators back. "Stay back!" one of them yelled through a bullhorn.

In the crowd, she spotted Finn. He waved at her. Shouted something she couldn't hear. Then he ran over and grabbed one of the police officers. Pointed to Evie.

Moments later, firefighters had a ladder off the truck. Evie tried to open the window, but it was stuck. She swung Mrs. Yetner's cane, using the handle like the business end of a bat, and broke the glass. Immediately she felt heat build behind her from the updraft she'd created. The smoke in the room thickened.

With a thud, the ladder hit the side of the house. Ratcheted up to the window.

Evie was about to climb out when she looked across the street. There, in the second-floor window of Mr. Cutler's house, stood a pale figure. At first Evie thought it was a child, standing there staring out, her hands up against the glass, pale hair haloed around her face.

Then she realized. It was no child. It was Mrs. Yetner.

Chapter
Fifty-eight

Twice in a row Mina had fooled Dora, using a trick she'd learned from Annabelle, and transferred that horse pill from one hand to the other and then only pretended to put it in her mouth. Sure enough, her head had started to clear. Otherwise she'd have slept right through the sirens.

She'd gotten out of bed and felt her way past the familiar pieces of furniture. When she pushed aside the window shade, she'd seen a beacon of rotating red light and more lights flashing blue and white in the street below.

Now she stood at the window in Annabelle's nightgown, her feet bare, her hands pressed to the glass. Fire was blazing across the street. It looked like someone had set a bonfire in Frank Cutler's driveway. Dark figures—probably firefighters—were swarming the street.

Mina heard more shouting, but this time it sounded as if it was coming from right downstairs. The windowsill shook as what sounded like the front door slammed.

"Stop!" Dora's voice. "You can't go up there."

"Get out of my house this instant!" It was a man. Not Brian.

Footsteps pounded up the stairs. Mina shrank into a corner of the room as the door slammed opened. A figure stepped into the room.

"Mrs. Yetner?" Mina recognized Evie's tentative voice. "Mrs. Yetner! You're here! Thank God, you're all right. I thought . . . I thought . . ." The girl wrapped her arms around Mina, sobbing.

Mina hugged her back. The poor thing was trembling, and she smelled of smoke.

"What on earth are you doing *here*?" Evie asked.

"Where else would I be?"

"In your own house. That's where I was afraid you were."

"Isn't that where I am?" But even as Mina said the words, she knew she was not. Ever since she'd run into the wall, trying to get back to bed from the top of the stairs, she'd felt as if she'd fallen down the rabbit hole and landed somewhere else—a place that was almost the same as her upstairs bedroom but not quite, a parallel universe the mirror image of her own.

"You're across the street in Mr. Cutler's house," Evie said.

"But isn't that my bed? And all my things? "

After a pause, Evie said slowly, "It is. It looks like they moved everything—the furniture, the rugs, the bedding, plus everything you had in the closet. They even moved the woodwork. Except for the new bath of course, this is a perfect replica of your upstairs. And then they must have moved you."

Mina shuddered at the thought that she'd been picked up, carried out of her own house and across the street, and installed there without being any the wiser.

"As long as you stayed in this room," Evie went on, "as long as you didn't have your glasses, you'd think you never left home. They left only one thing behind."

Mina took the cane that Evie handed her. "I guess they didn't think I'd need it any longer."

"You almost didn't."

"Then—" Mina turned and pointed out the window where emergency lights flared and flames shot toward the sky. She felt as if she were about to collapse. But she pushed Evie away and steadied herself with her cane. "The fire. That's not Mr. Cutler's house burning. That must be my house."

"I'm sorry," Evie said. "I'm so sorry. By the time I got there, the paper and lumber alongside your house had caught fire."

"What lumber?"

"From the construction. I thought they were building you a bathroom. But that lumber is probably the old woodwork from this room."

Mina remembered the sound of band saws and drills she'd heard coming from Mr. Cutler's second floor. He hadn't been putting in a roof deck or a Jacuzzi. He'd been preparing the room for her. Those workmen hadn't been putting a bathroom upstairs in her house. They'd been removing all the woodwork so they could install it across the street.

"Smoke and mirrors," Mina said, the taste of the words bitter in her mouth. "Tell me, how many days ago did we talk about the Empire State Building fire?"

"Day before yesterday."

The news went through Mina like a shot of adrenaline. She hadn't lost an entire week, after all.

"Come on," Mina said, exhaling and standing up straight. "Let's get out of here."

Chapter
Fifty-nine

Mrs. Yetner refused Evie's help as she held on to the banister railing and used her cane to feel her way down the steps, resting on each tread before taking the next. Evie couldn't tell if she was even aware of Frank Cutler and Mrs. Yetner's nurse, who were watching from the kitchen. Ivory was meowing at the foot of the stairs. Evie picked up the cat and followed Mrs. Yetner out.

On the sidewalk Mrs. Yetner held her head high and leaned on her cane, staring into the middle distance. Water hissed and steam billowed as firefighters turned hoses on the smoldering embers. There was no way to tell if Mrs. Yetner's house was salvageable, and it broke Evie's heart to think of that perfectly lovely interior in ruins.

The wind blew a particularly sharp scent of fire over them, and Evie gagged.

Mrs. Yetner held her hand over her own nose and mouth. "Brings it all back, doesn't it?"

It certainly did. Evie remembered standing in just this spot, watching her parents' house burn. That house now stood unscathed on the other side of Mrs. Yetner's.

"It was such a hot day, remember?" Mrs. Yetner said. "Windy, too."

"Like today," Evie said, burying her face in Ivory's soft fur. She'd been wearing a sleeveless top and shorts and her feet were bare. The crowd then, just like the crowd now, had been mostly strangers who'd looked on with disappointment as firefighters doused the last vestiges of fire. "Ginger was there, and so was my mother. And all I could think was that Blackie and her puppies were inside and there was nothing I could do."

"We all felt helpless."

Evie turned to face Mrs. Yetner. "The weirdest thing happened. When I was in your bedroom, I opened the bedroom closet door and I had the sensation that I'd been there before, only I was inside the closet looking out."

Mrs. Yetner pursed her lips and nodded. "You and Ginger had gone into your parents' closet with the dogs to hide."

"We did?"

"I was the one who found you there and got you out."

"You? But I thought my mother—"

"I was sitting out on my back porch when I smelled smoke. I banged on the door but no one answered. I ran down the street to pull the alarm, and when I got back, your mother's car was there. She was frantic. The house was burning, and she couldn't find you or your sister anywhere. The fire trucks hadn't gotten there yet. Some-one had to go inside, so I went." Mrs. Yetner's eyes went wide as she remembered. "I found you and Ginger in the closet in the downstairs bedroom. You'd been playing dress-up and trying to smoke your mother's cigarettes. You were still wearing her high heels."

"Trying to smoke? Me and Ginger?" It took a moment for the

realization to hit Evie. "You mean my mother didn't start the fire?"

"That's what she let everyone think. She didn't want you girls labeled as fire starters. I think she especially didn't want your father to know, him being a firefighter and all. But really, you were just children, and much too young to have been left alone. It's a lucky thing I was there." Mrs. Yetner touched the scar on her face.

Evie remembered after the fire had been mostly put out, watching in agony, worrying about the dogs. Finally, one of the firemen had gone inside. What felt like hours later, he'd come out carrying Blackie and her pups. They were alive, but barely. She'd watched as a medic held an oxygen mask over Blackie's snout. She'd promised God that she'd be good, really she would, if only Blackie didn't die.

It had been quiet then, just as it was quiet now. Evie realized the fire hoses had been turned off. A moment later there was a crash as the roof of the house next door to Mrs. Yetner's caved.

Firefighters in dark turnout gear broke down the front door and went into Mrs. Yetner's house. When one of them came out later, carrying three inert bundles, Evie was grateful that Mrs. Yetner couldn't see that they were cats. White cats. They must have been hiding when Evie had gone in, looking for Mrs. Yetner.

"Another crazy cat lady," the firefighter said to one of his buddies as he lay a tarp over the three little bodies. "And no batteries in the smoke alarm. That house is a hoarder's nightmare."

Of course, that was how it was supposed to look. Evie was about to go over and set them straight when she saw Finn emerge from the crowd of bystanders, vault the police barrier, and race toward her. Evie had to hold on to keep Ivory from leaping out of her arms as Finn flew past and up the steps of Frank Cutler's house.

Cutler was standing behind the screen door. Finn yanked open the door, grabbed him by the shirt, pulled him down his front steps. Mrs. Yetner's nurse came running out and tried to pull Finn off. Finn pushed her away. She staggered back a few steps and went down hard on her tailbone, stunned.

"This your idea of a business deal?" Finn yelled at Cutler. "You promised. You said no one would get hurt."

"You said do what it takes," Cutler spat back.

"You moron. I didn't expect you to try to kill people. You and your goddamned shortcuts." Finn turned to one of the policemen. "I'm getting myself an attorney. And then I want to talk to a police detective. My cousin here does, too. He just doesn't know it. Not yet."

Evie felt as if the air had been knocked out of her. Frank Cutler was the cousin Finn had been talking about? The one who was helping him right the wrongs done to their great-grandfather?

Finn turned to Mrs. Yetner and gave her a pleading look. "I wouldn't blame you if you don't believe me, but I am sorry. I never meant for any of this"—his gaze slid over to Evie—"to happen."

Evie couldn't bear to even look at Finn. The deception had been there from the very moment she'd set foot in Sparkles Variety. It was there when he'd stood on her mother's front steps like a goofy overgrown puppy, wooing her with a six-pack from Bronx Brewery. Just weeks before, his cousin Frank had seduced her mother with gifts and the promise of a steady stream of cash and then accelerated her death with "vitamins."

She heard Finn's voice as he went on explaining, as if there could be an explanation, but she tuned out. Instead, she focused on the minivan that had pulled up at the corner, which Ginger had just gotten out of. Her arms were folded tight across her chest, and as she got closer Evie saw that her face was puffy and her eyes red.

Evie handed Ivory over to Mrs. Yetner and ran over to Ginger. She didn't need to ask. She knew their mother had died.

Chapter
Sixty

A week later, Mina was getting used to living in the trailer that the city let her park in her driveway. She was sitting in its dining nook, savoring a final sip of tea and scratching Ivory behind the ears. Every day she was walking farther and feeling stronger.

It would be months before she could move back into the house. Fire had gutted her downstairs bedroom; smoke and water had had their way with the rest of the house. The marble mantel had survived, and of course the entire interior of the upstairs bedroom could be brought back from across the street once the house was scrubbed clean and painted. She was lucky: the house next door was a total loss, boarded up and waiting to be demolished.

So far, Frank Cutler had been charged with fraud, arson, kidnapping, and murder. Mina wanted him charged with hit-and-run, too. She was sure he'd been at the wheel of the black pickup truck, probably borrowed from Finn, that had tried to back over her. When she replayed that moment in her mind, she thought she could see his beady little eyes taking aim in his side mirror.

Newspapers detailed the exploits of Frank and his firm, Soundview Management; how they preyed on the elderly, getting them to deed their homes in return for a lifetime income and then speeding their demise. Mina still couldn't believe that Frank and Finn were cousins, and she didn't want to believe that Finn had had any part in the scheme.

Dora turned out to be Celeste Hall, the woman who'd taken Mina and Brian on their tour of Pelham Manor. Silver haired under a brunette wig, she was being held, too, though Mina wasn't sure on what charges.

Brian insisted that he'd known nothing about what the rest of them were up to. According to him, "Dora" told him that Mina had had a stroke after she returned from the hospital, and that it would be an *act of mercy* (Dora's words, according to him) to move her into Frank's house, where she could get round-the-clock care and wouldn't even realize she'd left home.

Brian admitted that the papers Dora had tried to get Mina to sign would have deeded the house to Soundview Management. But setting her house on fire and removing her smoke alarm batteries—he'd had nothing at all to do with that, or so he said. Mina was pretty sure he was responsible for putting her purse in the refrigerator, hiding her teapot whistle, and maybe even burning her chicken.

When Mina was feeling generous, she could convince herself that Brian believed he'd had her best interests at heart. And if it hadn't been for those poor cats, she might have been able to get past the betrayal. But standing by as the house burned with those poor creatures trapped inside? That was a bridge too far. Not that it was entirely his fault. He'd inherited all of Mina's father's ruthless avarice and sadly none of his common sense.

Since the fire, Mina had thought long and hard about her father. She came to the conclusion that for too long she'd basked in his name and swept his transgressions under the rug. It was time for her to make what restitution she could. But how? All she had to show for her father's thievery was the house. She'd spoken to a lawyer and changed her will so that the property went to benefit efforts to preserve Soundview Lagoons. On top of that, she was determined to air the truth about her father and his sins.

So, when Evie was helping her move into the trailer and asked her again about her father's dealings with Finn's great-grandfather, Mina gave her a straight answer. "I was very little at the time," she'd said, "but I do remember there was this man—a very angry man—who walked back and forth in front of our house with a sign. Yelling whenever he caught sight of my father. That was Finn's great-grandfather. My father told us he was crazy. And by the end, I imagine he was."

"Your father did swindle him out of his land, didn't he?"

"He did. My father was a visionary and a brilliant businessman. He was also a narcissist, a rogue, and a scoundrel. He could convince himself that whatever he wanted was right and fair, and that he'd earned it. Anyone who stood in his way was a fool. Sadly, Finn's great-grandfather owned what my father coveted. Snakapins Point."

Mina carried her teacup all of two steps to the sink. She looked out the trailer window at the boarded-up windows of the house next door. It was a myth that the Jamesons were ever coming back from Florida, a myth kept alive so that Mrs. Yetner and her other neighbors wouldn't start asking questions.

Evie seemed far more distressed than Mina at the damage to Mina's house and her possessions. The girl was crouched outside at that very moment, combing through the remnants of Mina's smoke-damaged kitchen, separating what was salvageable from the trash that had been dumped in the house to make the interior look for all the world like something out of a horror movie. The "vintage" kitchen utensils and appliances were all going to the Historical Society. A truck had already come and hauled off Mina's old stove.

As for Mina, she was looking forward to a brand-new kitchen. Secretly she hoped Evie would move into the sad house next door. But Mina hadn't dared say so, afraid Evie would take it as a plea for help. In no way did Mina want to become a burden to anyone but herself.

The one piece of furniture Mina had kept was her mother's mahogany coffee table. Its top was warped and the drawer stuck, but she preferred it to the ticky-tacky table that had come with the trailer. The spiral notebook she'd kept in its drawer survived unscathed, too, though Mina had lost her taste for listing the dead. On fresh pages she'd started writing down information about places to call about hiring a real health aide and calculating just how much help she could afford.

Sitting on that table now was an engraved invitation to the gala opening of Five-Boroughs Historical Society's *Seared in Memory*. Her story, her picture, her souvenir would be featured. *Cocktail attire,* it said at the bottom. Mina was having a black beaded dress of Annabelle's altered for the occasion. She couldn't remember the last time she'd had a cocktail, but she was planning to have a whiskey sour—after she'd been introduced and said a few words, of course. She hoped it would come with a maraschino cherry, or maybe two.

The phone rang, interrupting her thoughts. She let the call go to the answering machine that Evie had set up for her.

"Hello?" A man's voice came through the speaker on the machine. "I'm calling about the car?"

It was the eighth person who'd called in response to the ad Evie had posted for Mina on something called Craigslist. Mina picked up the phone. "Hello? Hello?"

"Hello?"

"You're interested in the car?"

"1975 Ford Mustang, V8 engine? Ad says fifty-six thousand miles on it. Not a hundred or two hundred fifty-six thou?"

Pffff. That was what they all asked.

"I hope you don't mind my asking, why are you selling it?"

"Because it's time." Brian might have been self-serving, but she did need to face facts. It was time to stop driving.

"Any problems with the car?"

"No problems. It runs fine. Not much rust. But you know, old is old. A certain amount of wear and tear is inevitable."

That brought a chuckle. "What are you asking?"

The current high bid, $2,550, was from Chet in Westchester. That was more than she'd ever imagined getting, and more than she'd paid for it brand-new.

"High bid so far is three thou," she said. *Thou.* Mina liked the sound of the slang she'd heard every caller use.

He whistled. "That's a lot. I'd take very good care of it."

"I don't care one way or another how you take care of it. It's not a house pet." As if on cue, Ivory rubbed up against her, demanding attention. "I'm selling to the highest bidder."

"But three thou?"

Mina smiled to herself. "You go over to the Sunoco station and sit in it for sixty seconds. The interior's leather. Steering wheel, too. You think you can find another one like it, go right ahead. Then you can call me and if it's still available—"

"Wait, wait . . ."

Soon, Mina had herself a new high bidder.

Chapter
Sixty-one

Evie stood for a moment in the arched doorway of the Great Hall at Five-Boroughs Historical Society. Waiters and waitresses glided among the guests, carrying silver trays of champagne and canapés. Evie took a moment to, as her father would have put it, "take a victory lap," greeting guests as she threaded her way past the eighteenth-century steam-powered pumper that could have been used to fight the Great Fire of 1776, through the displays for the Civil War Draft Riots and the Triangle Shirtwaist Factory fire, and finally to the Empire State Building plane crash. Evie was wearing a killer outfit, a white silk shirt with the collar turned up and billowing sleeves, with a black taffeta circle skirt from the '50s that rustled when she moved. At the waist, she wore a cinch belt she'd made using a vintage brass buckle in the shape of an eagle's head and wings.

Mrs. Yetner was there, too, seated on a little platform alongside the jet engine whose plummet down the elevator shaft had almost killed her. She had on an elegant black beaded dress that Evie guessed was from the 1940s. Her face glowed as cameras snapped her picture and she answered questions from a reporter.

Evie stepped closer and picked up snippets of what she was saying, "Her name was Betty Lou Oliver . . . ," "Eightieth floor . . . ," and " . . . terrifying. I thought I was going to die."

Across the room, Connor was talking to another journalist. Evie caught his eye, and he flashed her a covert thumbs-up. She smiled. This was the kind of publicity they'd only dreamed of getting for the exhibit opening.

Next week, Evie was returning to a regular work schedule and moving back to her apartment. There was still plenty of work to be done, preparing her mother's house to go on the market. Finn had gotten Frank Cutler to officially nullify the life estate deed that her mother had indeed signed. Finn had left the canceled document at the house for her along with a handwritten letter. He was truly sorry, Finn had written. He only wanted to preserve Higgs Point and save it from further development. He had no idea that Cousin Frank had gone off on his own and made a deal with developers whose vision was a gated community of high-rise apartments with fabulous views and an exclusive water shuttle to Wall Street.

Above all, Finn wrote, he'd never meant for Evie's mother or Mrs. Yetner or anyone else to get hurt. He went on to say that he stood by his offer to donate the remains of Snakapins Park to the Historical Society, or as much of it as Evie felt was worth saving.

He'd ended the letter with, "I can't tell you how deeply I regret what happened. I only hope you can forgive my naive stupidity, and I'll keep hoping that you might one day be willing to consider me your friend. At least keep this letter and think about it."

Evie had kept it.

Ginger came up behind her and linked her arm in Evie's. "I'm so proud of you," she said. "Daddy would have loved this so much. Mom, too. Here." She slipped Evie the sapphire earrings that their dad had given their mother on their twentieth wedding anniversary. "Put these on."

Evie clipped the earrings on, and she and Ginger hugged.

"I just wish I could have told her that I loved her," Evie said. She tried not to tear up and run her eye makeup.

"You didn't have to. She knew."

"Do you think so? Because I've been so angry with her for so long. And all these years I blamed her for starting that fire when it was us. We nearly got ourselves killed, and the dogs, too."

The room quieted. Connor was up on the dais. He stepped to the microphone, tapped on it, then cleared his throat. "Welcome, everyone, to the gala opening of *Seared in Memory*. First of all, I'd like to thank our generous donors. Without your support, none of this would have been possible." Applause rippled through the room.

"We are especially delighted," he went on, "to have Wilhelmina Yetner here today, who was on the eightieth floor in the Empire State Building when a B-25 bomber crashed into it on a foggy day at the end of World War Two. She survived the fire. She survived a fall . . ."

As Connor went on, Evie watched Mrs. Yetner. She sat in her chair, her hand to her mouth, her head nodding ever so slightly as she listened. This, Evie thought, was what healing looked like. She understood now that this exhibit, her idea from start to finish, was her way of taking her anger and fear and putting them in a safe place, the way Mrs. Yetner had set her melted souvenir of the Empire State Building on the marble mantel and gotten on with her life.

"And now I'd like to introduce you to Evie Ferrante, who conceived this installation and assembled this compelling story." Connor gestured to Evie to join him.

Evie squeezed Ginger's hand and started up to the dais, the crowd parting for her. She walked past Connor to the microphone. She looked out at the crowd. "Fire," she began, "has shaped this city and changed the lives of so many people in it. When I was a little girl, it changed mine."